THE ADVENTURES OF SPACE GIRL RED

VS. THE EVIL GOD KING BRUNO

R. A. DAVIS

REACTUATE
Publishing

Cover by Steve Huntriss.
ISBN: 978-1-957764-02-3

Visit https://www.SpaceGirlAdventures.com/ for more information.

I wish the places and characters in this book were in any way real. I'd love to meet Rainbow Capricorn, Queen Natalie, or the Flying Monkeys. Probably prefer not to meet the ruler of Xerces or Planet X, though, so it is a good thing this is a work of fiction.

Names, characters, business, events and incidents are the products of the author's imagination. Any resemblance to actual persons, living or dead, or actual events is purely coincidental. Or the result of the multiverse taking the authors thoughts and manifesting them in another reality.

Published by Reactuate Publishing, https://www.reactuatepublishing.com/.

To my very own Space Girl,
Suanna Davis.

May the adventures never end.

CHAPTER 1
THE CHASE

"DOES anyone have eyes on the target?" asked Space Cadet Red. She was standing on an overpass scanning the downtown Capital streets with binoculars. She wore a red jumpsuit with a utility belt of items that might be useful in the capture and a silver jet bike idled behind her.

"Yes, girls, does anyone have eyes on me?" came the voice of Space Woman Black over the comm in her right ear, which was the standard Space Girl comm. "I've been avoiding you for so long I'm starting to wonder if I overestimated Rainbow Capricorn. Maybe I should just take the day off and do a little shopping."

Red ground her teeth, but didn't rise to the bait. They had to find her and soon. Red's Rainbow mates were spread all over the city and had been for an hour.

"I've got her," came her Rainbow mate Orange's voice in Red's left ear. That comm was a special one Yellow modded to a frequency only the searchers could hear. "She just exited Madame Lefoux's Boutique."

"That's on Spectrum," said Blue. "I'm at the north end of Spectrum. ETA, 1 minute."

Red had already stowed the binoculars and jumped on her bike. "I'm at the South end, ETA, 30 seconds."

"Coming in from the east," said Yellow.

"Hey, girls," said Purple, "I just found her saucer parked in the stadium at Rainbow School. That's less than 5K from Lefoux's."

Leaning her bike into the curve onto Spectrum, Red said, "She'll be heading that way as soon as she sees us. Purple, you have to find a way to keep her from that ship."

"On it," said Purple.

Red was now less than a block from Madame Lefoux's Boutique and slowed, looking for a woman dressed in black. Madame Lefoux's was one of the most stylish stores in Capital, but also housed a secret workshop for devices only Warriors and Space Girls might need. Black was dangerous all on her own, no telling what she'd picked up in the boutique. Saturday morning was slower than the afternoon, but there were lots of civilians on the street.

"Red, you just passed us," said Orange as Red saw their quarry. Dark skinned and in a form fitting dress that ended at the top of her thighs, Space Woman Black was casually walking down the busy sidewalk. She wore knee high boots and a black raygun on her belt.

"There you are, finally," said their target.

Red slid her bike to a stop in the middle of the street and triggered its siren. The loud squalling mimicked the air raid alarm every girl of Home learned and people scrambled off the street. A lorry screeched to a halt next to the bike as Red jumped off.

Space Woman Black dropped one of her shopping bags and ran from Red. She'd only moved a couple of meters when Orange stepped out of an alley almost in front of her and threw a net toward her. Black slid under the net, plucked her raygun off her belt, shot a stun ray at Orange, and rolled back to her feet.

The beam missed Orange by three or four millimeters, but the stun effect still made her movements wonky and she fell to the ground. Black turned down the alley and ran.

As Red got even with the shopping bag Black had dropped, it exploded, slamming her against a stone storefront. It also sprayed confetti and smoke into the street.

"Ahh, you have your own comm channel," said Black. "I should have known when I didn't hear Red and Blue bickering."

As Red and Orange were getting to their feet, a jet bike blasted through the smoke with Blue on it. She stopped so hard she was launched over the handle bars and into the alley entrance. "We didn't have to bicker," said Blue over the main channel. "Red had her chance, now it's mine."

With some abrasions and undoubtedly bruises Red got up and moved as quickly as she could to follow Blue. "Right behind you, Blue."

As she rounded the corner into the alley, she saw Black at the dead end 20 meters away. Black was facing the opening empty handed with her knees slightly bent. Blue was running full tilt down the alley, pulling a bolo off her belt and swinging it. "Blue, watch out!" shouted Red as she noticed the other shopping bag in the middle of the alley.

"I've got thi..." Blue started to say when the grav wave bomb went off as she leaped over the bag. It threw her up in the air at least three stories, and she was lucky to get a hand hold on a balcony.

The Space Woman had known it was coming and rode the wave up the wall at the end of the alley. The buildings on either side were five stories tall and while the end didn't have balconies, it did have enough outcroppings any Space Girl could free climb with ease. Which is exactly what Black did, disappearing again.

"She's on the roof of the buildings heading West," said Red, as she ran down the alley and began to climb the wall.

"That's toward the school," said Yellow.

"Think of it as a training exercise, Educator Woman Violet," said Purple to someone off comm at the school. There was a lot of shrill little girl screaming in the background and a siren. "I've set off the school defense alarm, and the shield is up. No one is getting on or off campus for awhile."

Red and Blue had both gotten to the roof and were sprinting West after Black. The Space Woman did something at her belt and dropped out of sight off the edge of the building. "She just dropped onto Field Street," said Blue.

Blue reached the edge a few seconds before Red, snapped a line to a pipe and repelled over the side. Red stopped at the edge just as Yellow came around the corner on her jet bike. Black didn't miss a step as she clotheslined the Space Cadet off the bike. Yellow, by some feat of instinct, wrapped her arms around Black's and tried for a hold. But Black had taught them those moves and Yellow was tossed one way as Black moved the other at top speed.

"Those boots must be augmented," said Red from her vantage point on the roof. "She's moving fast down Field toward Monroe." Monroe ended at Rainbow School. Red could see the school's multicolored force field shimmering at the end of the street as she borrowed Blue's line and repelled down the building.

Blue had picked up Yellow and the two of them were jumping on Yellow's jet bike. Yellow looked at something on her wrist. By the time Red was on the street, Black was missing again. "Where'd she go?"

"I've got a tracker on her," said Yellow. "She's angling back toward Spectrum and weaving through the alleys toward the school."

Red started to run after Blue and Yellow raced off. With a whine of jets Orange appeared on Red's jet bike. "Need a ride?" asked Orange.

"Don't mind if I do." She jumped on the back of the bike. "Can't let Blue and Yellow have all the fun."

"Hey, girls," said Green over the comms, "Isn't there a really tall oak at Monroe and Klien? If Black climbed the building across the street, she could throw a line onto that tree and slide across. Over the shield."

"Gloom," cursed Purple. "I'm moving toward it."

"And so is Black," said Yellow. "But we are almost..." she cut off.

"Ease into that intersection," said Red into Orange's ear. The bike slowed as it came around the corner. They found Yellow and Blue splayed on the ground and their bike caught on a line strung across the opening. Orange leaned the bike over and slid under it. But they lost the bike and rolled away.

In the center of the street about 10 meters away stood Green. The petite green haired girl had thrown a bolo at Black which wrapped around the Space Woman's legs and forced her to her knees in the middle of the alley. The Cadets thrown from their bikes were getting to their feet when Space Woman Black pulled her raygun and shot Green in the chest.

"Green!" Four voices cried and the whole Rainbow converged on the black clad woman.

What ensued was an exchange of blows too fast to follow ending with the Space Woman standing and a group of panting bruised Space Cadets surrounding her. During the exchange Black had lost her raygun, but freed her legs.

Red glanced at the school shield and saw Purple standing on the other side pressed against the barrier. Purple stepped back and said, "Yellow, will your gadget work through this shield?"

Without taking her eyes off the Space Woman, Yellow thought for a moment and said, "Yeah, I think it will, but we need Green."

Red looked at Green laying on the pavement, then at Blue, who said, "Do it."

They dove toward Green while pointing their left arms at the Space Woman. Yellow pointed at the target and pressed a button on a chunky bracelet on her left wrist. A yellow cord of light shot out and found the nearest companion, Purple's. Purple's bracelet lit up and a purple beam shot to where Red knelt next to Green. With her right hand she grabbed Green's left and pulled. On the other side Blue held Green up. Red connected to Green, then Green to Blue. Blue to Orange and back to Yellow.

When the cord of light was a full circle it detached from the bracelets and shrunk toward the woman in the middle. Like a giant rainbow-colored python, the light wrapped itself around the Space Woman and constricted. Her arms and legs were trapped and she fell over – captured.

The alley was quiet.

A groggy voice said, "Did we win?"

Red laughed and said, "Yes, Green, I think we did."

Blue and Red helped the stunned girl to her feet and led her to the captured woman. "What say you, Space Woman Black? Did we win?"

The older woman laughed. "Yes, Rainbow Capricorn, you have passed your Space Girl Final Exam." After another strained attempt to free herself, she said, "OK, Yellow, let me out of here."

———

A 100 PARSECS away the Battle Saucer *Angel* exited the galactic Spaceways and moved toward Planet X. On board Warriors stood ready at the guns, and infantry teams loaded gear onto landing craft.

A few seconds behind, the five remaining Space Girl flying saucers of Rainbow Aries, hulls set to black, exited as well. They fanned out and made their way faster, but less obviously, toward the planet.

————

AS SOON AS Space Woman Black was free of the light coils, her comm erupted. "None of you move. I have orders for you."

All the members of Rainbow Capricorn glanced at each other. Red was looking through Green's medkit for a hypo of something called Monofilla. Green was the healer of the group, but still too wonky to treat herself, so she'd just mumbled the name to Red.

Tapping a control on her wrist, Space Woman Black said, "This is Space Woman Black. What do you need Head Woman Crimson?"

Black held her hand near her ear and grimaced, though Red couldn't hear anything. "No, Head Woman, I didn't order a drill, but Capricorn was involved in their final exam... Yes, I did leave my saucer on your sports field. I'll come get it in a minute as soon as you lower your shield... Of course, you can lower it whenever you feel like it..." She scowled at Purple who shrugged. "Wouldn't think of it...Yes, of course."

Then there was a pause and the leader of the Space Girls of Home smiled. "As a matter of fact they did. I'll make sure you get a notification for their graduation."

She looked up in a way that indicated the Head Woman of Rainbow School had cut off. Red found the hypo and pressed it to Green's thigh. The smaller girl shuddered and her eyes went wide. She stood more easily on her feet and looked around like she was seeing the place for the first time. "That's more like it."

"Capricorn," said Space Woman Black, "let me add my congratulations to those of the Head Woman of Rainbow School. You are officially certified as Space Girls for the protection of Home."

There was a ripple of excited movement around the circle.

"Which is good, because I'm going to need a full Rainbow of Space Girls in a couple of days for Color Guard duty." All of the new Space Girls froze. "Therefore, you are graduating tomorrow."

"Tomorrow?" said Space Girl Blue.

"Color Guard?" said Space Girl Purple.

"To answer Blue first. Yes, tomorrow you will receive the High's confirmation, your rayguns, and flying saucers. Messages went out to your families this morning, telling them to prepare for a ceremony tomorrow, assuming you passed your exam."

While Red and her mother were very different people, she was sure Diplomat Woman Pink was moving as quickly as she could to get back to Home before high sun tomorrow.

"A color guard is only assembled for a Space Girl funeral," said Purple.

"There are other occasions, but in this case you are right. Space Girl Blue Aries was captured and killed by the leadership of Planet X. Battle Saucer *Angel* has been dispatched to retrieve the body, and should be back before the end of the week. You, Capricorn, will bring her home to HQ."

"They sent a battle saucer to rescue a Space Girl?" asked Red. "I thought we didn't do that."

"Where is her Rainbow? Wouldn't they want to stand Color for her?" asked Orange.

"You are right, Red. We don't rescue Space Girls. This is not a rescue, but a recovery and a show of force. The High and the council feel she was captured and killed primarily to threaten Home itself. To send us a message. The *Angel* will send a message back.

"As for Rainbow Aries, at this moment they are on Planet X expressing their displeasure in ways they feel will bring the change needed."

Capricorn was uncharacteristically still until Space Woman Black clapped her hands. "Space Girl Purple, Head Woman Crimson would like to speak with you." Purple's shoulders slumped but nodded. "Yellow, you will bring your gadget to HQ in the next hour and show it to Tech Woman Quartz. The rest of you are to go back to the barracks and prepare for tomorrow. Dismissed."

CHAPTER 2
GRADUATION

IN THE CENTER of the capital city of the planet Home stands the Loop, a large four story circular building. At the north point of that circle is the Spire. It reaches 400 meters in the air, and, like the rest of the building, is made predominately of crystal. The Spire's bottom two floors are called the meditation garden, but Space Girl Red and her Rainbow mates were having a very difficult time meditating.

Designed to be peaceful, it was a mix of plant life, water features, and marble. Quite beautiful and impressive to most, but on graduation day all of that was lost on her. Red looked around at the rest of her bow-mates. Trained to be statue still when the occasion dictated it, today there was a not-so-subtle flutter of skirts as they moved nervously around.

All were dressed in Space Cadet dress dresses. Dress dresses were worn only on ceremonial occasions and harkened back to a different era and different style. Made of a smooth, slightly shiny fabric that was currently grey with accents in the color of the wearer. It had an angular hour glass shape, with a wide shouldered bodice on the top, connected to a wide belt in the middle. The skirt angled away from the waist and had a hoop that held it wide away from the body just above the knee. Red's belt had an empty magnetic holster on one side in her color. Matching transformer heels completed the uniform. These shoes adjusted intelligently in height based on gait. They could also be commanded to make a row of nervous cadets the same height, which they would do when they were finally allowed to stand on the graduation platform outside.

Trainer Woman Apricot called them to attention and they lined up in spectrum order, which put Red at the front. The double doors opened into the inner park and they marched forward. Inside the Loop was a park over a kilometer across, with the Founder's Monument in the center. At each of the cardinal points a path radiated from the monument to the Loop. A white terrazzo path led northward from the Spire to the Monument and shone brilliantly in the morning sun.

There were people lined up all along the left side of the path, dressed in the style of Capital. Each woman wore her color and had come out in their finery to see a Space Girl graduation. A rare enough occurrence they normally drew a crowd, but today's was larger than any Red could remember. Probably because the story of Space Girl Blue Aries was all over the news.

Along the other side of the walkway there were Space Cadets every few meters. The Cadets looked painfully young to Red. They stood at relaxed attention as Rainbow Capricorn walked forward.

The big surprise was what looked like an entire tribe of Wild Women sitting in the grass behind the Space Cadets. The Wild Women reject the color and rainbow oriented society of Home, and while they contributed members to the Warriors, they had never attended a Space Girl graduation. Among them there was a deeply held dislike of the Space Girls in general. Many of the Wild believed they spied on them. Every Wild Woman wore an outfit designed with every color of the rainbow on purpose. It took all her training to not look back at Yellow to see if her eyes were gleaming or her jaw was clenched. Probably both, Red decided.

There was a wide area around the monument and a low platform had been set up on it with a double row of chairs facing it. Rising from the chairs were the families of Rainbow Capricorn. Red looked for and found her mother's Pink and her father standing tall next to her.

Trainer Woman Apricot marched the Space Girls onto the platform and lined them up facing the audience. She stood in the center of their line, faced the crowd, and said, "I, Trainer Woman Apricot of Space Girl HQ, hereby certify that all the members of Rainbow Capricorn have completed the full course of training to be Space Girls."

There was light applause at the announcement. Apricot continued, "Of special note, Rainbow Capricorn has the highest score ever certified." There was a delighted murmur from the crowd, and Red stifled a smile. She was a little surprised her motley crew had done so well.

Trainer Woman Apricot about-faced smartly, brought her hands together in front of her, and said, "It has been an honor to travel with you on your journey. May the Light shine on you." Then she bowed her salute and marched away.

Everyone settled into their seats as silence descended over the park. Just as Red was starting to get self-conscious *she* appeared in front of them.

The High of the Light That Is All Colors was the epitome of the women of Home. Everything about her was white. She wore a form-fitting body suit in white. Her bob cut hair was the color of snow. The cape that waved in the breeze was white. Still there was always a hint of color. When the cape moved, all the colors rippled across it like water: red, orange, yellow, green, blue, and purple.

"I see you, Rainbow Capricorn," she said with a soft expression on her face. There was pride there but also sadness, not unlike the look on Red's mother's face. "It is quite possible you are the best of us. Home was founded by the physically, mentally, and morally best of the source world. Men and women who had dedicated themselves to the highest ideals of humankind, but who were forced to flee because of persecution."

She moved along the line of Space Girls and their families, telling them a story everyone knew. On occasions like today - or a Space Girl funeral - they needed to hear it again.

"They - like you - were willing to accept hardship. The journey into an unknown universe and the discovery of our beautiful planet. This very park was the first landing site of the people of Home." She motioned to the statues of the memorial: a family of women, men, and children, both girls and boys.

"Then chaos rose like a dragon from this garden. In a mirror of this path," she motioned to the white stone leading to the Spire, "is the dark one on the other side. Engraved on it are 176 names of the boys who died in that first year and those young men crippled by whatever darkness lives somewhere on this planet. A darkness that leaves us half of what we should be."

She paused and the traditional low moan went up from the crowd. Something on Home hated the Y chromosome, insuring no boys were even conceived on Home. History said any boy brought to the planet would sicken, and the Fathers were rendered unable to have male children if they lived on Home long.

"We could have left then. But the first High spoke to her sisters and it was decided we must stay. This is our Home. We will defend and tend it in hope of a day the curse will be lifted."

"May it be so," said the crowd.

"Just as the source world, the universe always seems to

produce those who do not want the Light to spread. It is for that reason every girl on Home must discover a Purpose and a Vocation. For you, Rainbow Capricorn, that Vocation is Space Girl."

She moved in front of Purple, lay a hand on her shoulder, and said, "By choosing the Purpose of Love, Space Girl Purple, you will confront hate." Under her fingers light flowed over the grey of the cadet's uniform and turned it white.

"Space Girl Blue, you've sworn to resist poverty with wealth." The two women locked eyes for a long moment while many unsaid words passed between mother and daughter.

"Space Girl Green, you will bring life in the face of death and destruction." Tears flowed from Green's eyes a quickly as the light from the High's hand.

"Space Girl Yellow, may you spread knowledge in the face of ignorance."

All of the Wild Women had risen to their feet and when the blessing was pronounced on Yellow, a shout of triumph went up. The cry of a clan name she had given up to become a Space Girl.

"Space Girl Orange," said the High after a moment's pause, "beauty to replace ugliness," Orange's eyes gleamed in response to the High's blessing of her purpose.

"And completing the circle in so many ways, Space Girl Red, please bring law and justice against crime and oppression," the High concluded, locking her silver eyes on Red for a moment.

She stepped back from the new Space Girls.

"It is for this purpose Home was made. For this reason the Warriors guard it. The scholars study and improve it. The scientists unlock it. The farmers grow and nurture it.

"Home is what it is so little girls of all kinds are protected, guided, and nurtured, allowing them to find their Purpose and Vocation. When they find it, they bring more light into the universe and drive out darkness."

"You Space Girls are agents of change in the universe at

large. You will take light to darkness. Give hope to the hopeless. Make other worlds and other lives better in the name of Home."

"Thank you. Congratulations. And may the blessings of the Light That Is All Colors go with you." From where she stood, a wave of white light burst away in all directions. It passed over the crowd leaving golden motes flitting around them.

Space Girl Red felt the light fill her. There was a tingle on her skin, an expansion of her mind. It was official. Years of dedication, training, and effort were complete. Now she could do important things, finally.

The High of the Light That Is All Colors gave each Space Girl one last look and smile. Then she disappeared.

Overhead there was a boom and everyone looked up. A bright contrail appeared in the sky, directly above the Loop. It resolved into a flying saucer. The dark saucer stopped hundreds of meters above the ground. A hatch opened on the bottom and a dark figure stepped out. She fell toward the place just vacated by the High. A few meters above the heads of the crowd her jet pack engaged and she slowed.

Space Woman Black landed in a crouch.

Where the High was the pinnacle of what it meant to be a woman on Home, Black was what every Space Girl dreamed.

Black saved the Prince of Caldonia from slavery just days after she'd stood where Red stood now, a brand new Space Girl. Within a year she'd thwarted the Trill invasion of Naxis 9, won the Warrior Games of Alanon Omega ending the patriarchy forever, and become Miss Universe on the fashion planet Par 7.

During training Black magically appeared every time you screwed up. She'd stare at you with those animated pupils of hers for a long second. Then show you, with grace and ease, exactly how it should have been done.

She wore a skin-tight pressure suit the color of Space. The

belt at her waist held a number of useful gadgets, and on her left hip was a scratched and scarred Space Girl raygun.

"The motto of the Space Girls is: Order to Chaos and Chaos to Order," boomed the Space Woman's voice. Where the High's voice flowed over you like a bubbling brook, Black's punched into you like your first boxing match. "The trick is knowing when to do which."

She stood in front of Capricorn and they all tightened into attention. "That ability to discern what is needed is what the Educators look for when forming a Space Girl rainbow. It is their gift to look at hundreds of daughters every year and know who belongs with whom."

Red thought how difficult it must be to take a group so different as her and her friends and see what they could be. Much more difficult than knowing when order needed chaos.

Pacing like a panther sizing up its prey, Black paused in front of Space Girl Purple. "Some of you want to do this by taking worlds in your arms and giving them a big hug."

She kept walking and talking. "Others want to water and nurture them. And some study or explore."

"But others of you want to do it by being better than everyone: faster, stronger, smarter." As she spoke she looked first at Blue and then Red pointedly.

"Watch yourselves." She started walking again. "There is not one way to bring light to the darkness." She stopped in front of Orange and said, "Sometimes that big ugly monster needs a hug to make it beautiful."

In front of Space Girl Green, "And sometimes that Tree-man deep in the forest of Epi Alpha needs a punch in the face to grow."

The commander of the Space Girls made a motion and Trainer Woman Apricot walked over with a large box. "There are two devices iconic to a Space Girl. The first is, of course, her flying saucer."

She snapped her fingers and there was a throbbing whine from all around them. Six Space Girl Flying Saucers rose from outside the Loop. Each was silver, tinted with one of the colors of the rainbow. Red searched out the red one as her heart pounded and her mouth watered.

"The other is your ray gun." Black and Apricot moved in front of Space Girl Yellow. "Each of you built your own raygun. We do this so you will throughly understand them and they will be truly yours." Black pulled out a yellow pistol, its plasma bubble glowing. "Not so you can modify it to make it twice as powerful and ten times as dangerous." She gave Yellow a long look and handed her the weapon. The new Space Girl had the grace to smile sheepishly and nod her head before putting the weapon in the holster at her belt.

Each of them took their rayguns in turn and attached them to their belts.

"You know I'm not one for long speeches, and you are all Space Girls, so I know you want to get at your saucers. One last piece of advice, say good-bye to your family and friends today. You may not see them for awhile or ever, as we have recently been dramatically reminded.

"Such is the life of a Space Girl."

She flipped her helmet effortlessly onto her head, then she crouched down and lept into the air. Her jet-pack cut in with a roar and she was a speck in seconds. The dark streak of her flying saucer appeared in the sky and intercepted her trajectory. Space Woman Black was back in her saucer and gone.

Black's departure completed the ceremony and the new Space Girls went looking for family.

A couple moved toward Space Girl Red. Her mother Diplomat Woman Pink had adopted the latest style of lightened hair, which was to use natural hair colors. This meant her shoulder length hair was strawberry blonde, a natural lightening of red. She wore a long flowing dress in a deep pink.

Red, like her mother, was a tall woman, and her father was of a height with both of them. His dark hair was starting to get the speckling of grey that made him look more distinguished. He wore a long grey and white coat, over a light shirt and dark trousers. Both her parents beamed at her.

"Mother," Space Girl Red said, embracing the woman. Then she hugged him and said, "Father."

"We are so proud of you, Red." Her mother's eyes glistened with tears.

Her father used her birth name, that only he used on Home once she got her color. Then he said, "The universe awaits you. I hope it is ready."

Red laughed, "I hope I am."

"Of course you are. How could you not be?"

Red just shrugged.

"Before you leave, I have a couple of things for you," said her father, producing a box from his coat. He handed it to her and she opened it. Inside was a simple bracelet of intertwined multi-colored wires.

"It's beautiful," she said.

"It is a Kantarian house signet. My house signet—and yours." He raised a hand to forestall any comment. "I know, Home women don't do that kind of thing. Think of it as a symbol of your color or Rainbow, if you happen to be on Kantar."

She smiled and put the bracelet in a pouch on her belt. "Thank you, Father."

"And this is a message for Queen Natalie of Kitch 10 if you end up in that part of the galaxy." He handed her a data coin. "I think you'd like Queen Natalie. She's got spark."

"Is it important? The Kitch system was not where I was planning to go first."

"No, more an update on my diplomatic status and an introduction for you."

Red made the coin disappear too. "Of course, Father."

"Goodbye," her Father said. "Be safe."

Space Girl Red almost laughed, but knew it was the way of the men of Kantar.

Her mother's statement was all Home.

"Go with Purpose and fulfill your Vocation."

Red turned on her heel, looking for her flying saucer and almost ran directly into Space Girl Green.

"Can you believe it! We're Space Girls!" Green was actually bouncing up and down. It made the curls of her forest green hair spring around her face. "Of course for you it was always a given. You're like the perfect Space Girl. No one doubted, least of all you, that you'd make it. Me though..." Green leaned around Red and waved. "Hello, Diplomat Woman Pink. Father Pink. Can you believe it?!"

"Space Girl Green," Red said, reaching out and putting her hands on the other woman's shoulders in an attempt to ground her. "Green, slow down a little. I know you are excited. So am I."

"Right, right." Her shoulders twitched under Red's hands. "Sorry, sorry. I'm sure you want to go. Saw Blue run right to her saucer - so like her - but I knew that meant you would want to go right away. But you were talking with your parents, so I thought I had a chance to get over here." She pointed to a man on the outskirts of the crowd moving away. "Went to talk with Father, but this a really hard time for him. What with Mom having been a Space Girl and me now, and what happened with Aries. Plus I'd just start blubbering and maybe never get to my saucer."

Red raised her voice to cut through Green's torrent of words. "Space Girl Green." Green froze like a deer caught in a light. Red smiled at her and asked, "Why did you want to talk to me? We've got a day or less to get our saucers broken in before we'll be back together for Color Guard. What couldn't wait?"

Green took a deep breath and seemed to settle into a landing. "Right. Right. I just wanted to congratulate you and, you know, tell you how much you've helped me over the years." She looked up at Red with an awkward expression. "And I wanted you to know - you know because we are Space Girls and all - and after what The High said - I hope we stay in touch. Maybe meet up later - I know you probably have really big plans to deliver justice and all. I'm already planning a trip to a couple of planets as well to do the environmental healing." Green realized she was rambling and took a deep breath. "Anyway. Thanks for everything and I hope we see each other again."

She jumped forward and grabbed Red in a tight embrace. "If you ever need me, all you have to do is call."

"Oh, Green," said Red, returning the embrace. "You are going to make a great Space Girl. We've always known it." Red broke the embrace and held the other woman at arm's length. "It is time for you to go off on your own and learn you are way better than you think you are."

Green wiped her eyes. "Sure, sure." She stepped back out of Red's grip and smiled. "Well, see you later."

Red smiled and reflected her mother's blessing onto Green. "Go with Purpose and fulfill your Vocation."

———

THE RAINBOW'S FLYING saucers had landed in the park quadrants north of the monument where there were no crowds. Red got to hers just as a blue-tinted saucer lifted off. Blue'd settled things - well as much as she ever was going to - with her mother before the ceremony was over.

"Oh what a beautiful boy you are," said Red as she stepped into the entry room at the top of the gangplank. The ship was exactly like all the flying saucers she'd trained on, but this one was hers. That made it the most beautiful thing in the world. And it smelled new.

"Ya ain't so bad yourself, toots," came a heavily accented voice.

"Oh, no. That won't do," said Red at the nickname.

"Personality adjustment in progress," came a mechanical acknowledgment and a pause.

"You are looking fabulous yourself. Way to rock those heels," said the ship.

"Why thank you, ship. What is your name?"

"I am Astroboy," and he played a little fanfare.

Red smiled as she continued into the central core of the flying saucer. A Space Girl flying saucer was a one-person home in space. Its circular shape meant there were no hallways, and all of the rooms on the main level were pie shaped. Even the entry room that contained the gang plank was pie shaped. Hanging on the walls were various gadgets and equipment for extravehicular work.

The core was a circular room at the very center of the ship. In the middle was a ladder that lead up into the glass-domed control room. Around the circular walls were openings to the other rooms of the ship. Directly across from the entry was her cabin, which she went to now while talking with Astroboy and taking off her dress dress.

"Tell me about yourself, Astroboy," she said and tossed her utility belt on the bed that took up much of the cabin. Everything in the room was standard issue white. *That will have to change.* "Are you a standard issue flying saucer, or did engineering give me some surprises?"

"Let me tell you, sister, there is nothing standard about me," the voice, said a little hurt. "While I have the same specs as all the other pretty boys sitting in this park, I've got 110% more style."

"Style, huh?" She was now standing in front of the closet. Inside hung a number of white outfits. "Astroboy, we need to red up this...ok everything."

"Red? You sure about that?"

She arched an eyebrow high and looked at the ceiling. "Do you know who I am?"

"Of course, you are Space Girl Red of Rainbow Capricorn. Your mother is Diplomat Woman Pink and your father is..."

"Enough. The point is I'm Space Girl *Red*," she said, emphasizing the last word. "I expect all of my clothes and gear to reflect that. You can start with the pressure suit."

Red could have sworn the ship's voice sighed. "Whatever," said Astroboy.

In the closet, the pressure suit turned red.

"Astroboy, is my pressure suit sparkling?"

"Of course, girl. Glitter makes everything better. I'm thinking about adding glitter to the hull."

She closed her eyes and counted to 10. "I do not find that idea appealing."

The mechanical voice said, "Personality reset."

"Something a little more proper this time, if you don't mind."

"Do you have a particular shade of Red you prefer, Ma'am?" said a new voice. There was just a hint of the mechanical in it, like a British butler chewing on ball bearings.

"I'm partial to the darker shade of red. More burgundy than tomato."

In the closet all of the clothes changed to a dark red, almost the color of wine or blood—depending on how you looked at it.

"And with no glitter whatsoever," said Astroboy.

She reached in and pulled the lightweight pressure suit off

its hanger. It was just like the one Space Woman Black had been wearing. One piece with an opening on the back. There was a ring at the top where the helmet attached, right above where atmosphere bottles would connect.

"That is much better," she said. "Sparkle should be limited to jewelry and jewelry-like gear." She slid her legs into the bottom of the suit, then found the arm holes with her hands. Before sliding them all the way down, she grabbed the top ring and stuck her head through it. Extending her arms straight out brought the suit all the way on and exposed her hands. When the ring settled on her neck, the opening in the back sealed and the whole suit shrunk to the contours of her body. She took a pair of gloves out of the closet and tossed them toward her belt on the bed. Then she grabbed the boots and sat down on the bed to put them on.

"Of course, Ma'am," said Astroboy, with just a slight shudder at the idea of glitter anywhere. "Would you like me to close the gangplank and start warming up the engines? I assume we are preparing to leave Home."

Boots sealed to the rest of the suit, utility belt around her waist with gloves secured to it, and bubble helmet under one arm, Space Girl Red stood and said, "Yes, I would. Thank you, Astroboy."

"As you will, Ma'am."

She moved purposefully out of her quarters and toward the ladder to the control room. Behind her, invisible hands picked up her discarded clothing and put it where it belonged. Every surface, piece of clothing, and furniture faded to shades of red.

Red climbed the ladder to the control room. From the outside a flying saucer could be divided into roughly four parts. The bottom part curved down toward the ground, with the lowest point being in the center. Out of this part came three legs that looked too thin to hold the craft. When down, the gangplank exited between two of these legs. The central part of the body of the saucer was a ring with sides perpendicular to the ground. When the drive engaged, lights would chase each other around this ring. Above this ring was another curved surface, mirroring the one on the bottom. At its apex was a glass bubble that held the control room. Projecting out the back end of the top surface were two fins. At the top of each was a rocket shaped pod that was the source of the repeller drive.

Inside the control room Red sat down in the seat at the center of the space. With a twist of a control on the arm the seat rotated a full 360 degrees. There was a ledge all the way around with various controls and indicators. This ledge was broken a few degrees to the left of the main flight controls. There a globe came out of the ship. Inside was a swirling mass of colors, bubbles, and streaks of light. Those colors changed when Astroboy spoke.

"The gangplank is up. Impellers are warmed up. Repulsor power rising," said Astroboy.

Red looked at the control panel in front of her. The surface was red and the meters changed from dark to light to indicate their value. Repulsor power was at 75% and rising quickly. Her chair spin had shown her most of the flying saucers were still sitting in the park. The audience had collected their younglings and left. That meant she was clear to take off just, like Blue had.

"Let's go," Red said and gradually pulled the impeller lever back. There was an increase in pitch of the engine whine. Outside the lights that had started to move around the ship's center increased in speed and the ship lifted off the ground. As soon as it was clear, the landing legs flowed back into the ship. She let the impellers carry the ship a few hundred meters into the air, then tilted his nose up and engaged the repulsors.

"Main engines are at 100%. Here is a plot for orbit."

On top of the console in front of her were two silver tubes

with three flat disks of gradually increasing size floating around them. The small silver spheres at the top glowed slightly and a screen materialized between the tubes. A drawing of the planet with a dotted line coming from its surface appeared. A little flat red silhouette of her ship followed the line from the surface to orbit. Tiny numbers orbited the ship like little electrons giving her the vectors for orbit.

She maneuvered the ship to put it on the pictured trajectory. Once on course she said, "Astroboy, zoom out and show me everything inside lunar orbit."

The drawing changed. Now the planet was much smaller with her ship just a red dot. A number of other dotted lines, appeared showing other orbits for other craft. There was a blue dot just a little higher than the orbit she was moving into, and two large round ships further out. The larger craft were the Home protection satellites. Shaped much like her saucer, they were crewed by over a 1000 Warrior girls and women. Their armaments were more than enough to protect the homeworld and they housed hundreds of attack saucers.

"INCOMING MESSAGE FROM SPACE GIRL BLUE," said Astroboy.

"On screen."

The front screen replaced the system view with a visual of Blue in her saucer's control room. "Took you long enough," she said.

"Had family to say good-bye to. How's your new saucer?"

"He'll do. We'll see how he breaks in. We've only got a couple of days before we have to be back for Color Guard. But he's faster than yours getting to orbit."

The bubble to her left changed to an roiling color. "Oh Blue, you are fast off the line, but slow on the road. Just because you took off fast, doesn't mean you have accomplished anything. Still in orbit I see."

Red could see Blue's jaw muscles clinch. "Maybe I'm just waiting for the Warriors to clear me for maneuvers."

"All talk, Blue," Red said pressing the mute button and turning toward the ball. "Astroboy, plot a course to Mother," referring to the fifth planet in the system. "Also ask for clearance from the Warriors."

"Space Girls don't require clearance to navigate in system," replied Astroboy, as a new dotted line appeared on screen. It stretched between the two giant space destroyers and out of the lunar system. Red smiled and grabbed the repulser control.

Before she could pull it and launch, Blue's saucer took off out of orbit. Red yanked back on the control. The engine bulbs mounted to the top of Astroboy's fins glowed, and a pulsing light lit the control room. The red light coalesced down the guide cones, hit the thrust discs encircling them, and turned into a ring of light. These rings exited the point of the cone growing in diameter as they moved away from the saucer. The birth of each new thrust generating ring was accompanied by a burbling ping from the ship's hull. At their current speed about three were visible at a time before fading away.

"Race you to Mother," said Red.

"You're on," replied Blue and they both took off, weaving between Warrior satellites.

CHAPTER 3
COLOR GUARD

THE FLYING saucers of Rainbow Capricorn flew in a line toward Home's main Spaceway portal. The Spaceways were a network of tunnels outside of normal space that allowed faster than light travel. Mapping them was one of the tasks of the Scout Girls. There were certain places in a system where a space drive equipped ship could enter or exit the Spaceways. If the Spaceways are extra dimensional highways, the Portals are the on and off ramps. The Home system had two such entries, but one of them was inside the corona of the star. Capricorn flew in formation toward the other one.

Advanced word said the *Angel* would be here any second. Space Girl Red stood in her cockpit wearing her space armor. It was a matte red with the sinuous lines of a jet bike.

Above her the enormous battle sauce appear out of an opening invisible to the naked eye.

"Align to *Angel's* main bay," she said over the command channel to the other members of her Rainbow. There was a slight change in the attitude of the line of saucers. The canopy in front of her was displaying the distance to the missive ship.

"Rainbow Capricorn, prepare to deploy color guard." Aside

she said, "Astroboy, turn yourself Red and follow Space Girl Blue's lead from here on out." Because they returning another Rainbow's dead Blue, Capricorn's Blue would be leading the ships and leaving a hole in their formation.

"Yes, Ma'am."

What came next was the hardest maneuver any Space Girl had to master. It required perfect timing from her flying saucer and a willingness to let the physics do its thing. Fighting it or trying to control it would cause a less than perfect deployment. "In 5," Astroboy said, counting down the seconds.

"4," She shook her limbs then held them against her side.

"3," Her saucer shifted and the main bay of the Angel was directly above her.

"2," A quick glance at the other saucers to her left and right showed the furthest one already deploying their Space Girls.

"1," The saucer canopy disappeared into her ship.

"Launch." Astroboy slowed in space and Red continued forward. From her perspective her saucer fell away under her feet and she was rocketing toward the other ship.

Below her the saucers changed configuration into the Missing Color formation, leaving a hole in there V where a Blue belonged.

Red was concentrating on *Angel's* bay doors meant to launch an armada filled her view. In the center of the door was the symbol of Home and she was moving toward a small personnel airlock at the bottom of it. Her Rainbow mates were close enough now to be in her peripheral vision. Red rotated her feet under her and landed beside the door. The rest of Capricorn landed around her in a circle.

"Well done," she said over the Rainbow channel. And it was. No falters. Everyone where they were supposed to be and no need of corrective measures. Exactly what they wanted to give their fallen comrade.

The outer door of the lock opened, revealing markings orienting them to the artificial gravity's down direction. Purple was at the top. She grabbed a handhold and somersaulted in. The others followed.

"*Angel* control, this is Space Girl Rainbow Capricorn. Color guard assembled in airlock."

There was no reply, but the outer door closed and a few seconds later her helmet auto-retracted.

"Guard formation," she said. Her Rainbow mates formed into two lines of three with Blue's place empty.

The airlock opened onto the cavernous carrier deck of the *Angel*. One of the largest ships in Home's fleet, it carried every other kind of craft used in warfare. Needle fighters were lined along the walls. Troop carriers squatted in rows ready to disgorge Warriors onto hostile fields. Saucers, medium and large, watched over all of them ready to command.

Normally a bright bustle of activity, the deck was empty and dark except for the pool of light Capricorn marched toward. The light illuminated a shiny blue metal coffin. A four squad formation of Warriors stood in dirty armor. They were clearly the troops sent down to retrieve the body of Blue Aries. Scrapped hands held rifles at parade rest as Capricorn walked into the light.

The Space Girls formed two lines, one on either side of their fallen comrade. They faced the coffin and brought their hands together in front of their chest in a Space Girl salute. Red gave a silent signal and Capricorn snapped about face to look at the soldiers who had rescued Aries's fallen.

They smacked a fist into a flat hand in front of their chests, a Warrior salute. Red and Green said in unison, "Honor to the Warriors, who rescued our fallen."

Somewhere among the Warrior Girls there was a guttural

sound and the two ranks snapped to attention. "Honor to the Light. May it guide the Space Girls."

Then the troops marched from the bay, leaving the Space Girl color guard alone.

———

ALL OF CAPRICORN turned back to the coffin and silently laid hands on it. Red felt a little sad for Blue Aries, but also proud. Being a Space Girl was dangerous. That was one of the reasons she'd wanted to be one. But often the dangers were...well, she thought of them as accidental. Getting lost in the Spaceways, or crashing on some unexplored moon. Maybe you'd get bitten by a strange insect on an unknown planet and your flying saucer found years later. Blue Aries had gotten a good death fighting evil.

"Was Aries the Rainbow we helped with that space station evac in year one?" said Yellow. Space Cadets were often called in to do grunt work on some of the Space Girl's bigger projects.

"No," said Green, "that was Gemini." There was sadness in her voice. Red knew evacuations were painful for Green.

"Some of Aries were our opponents in our saucer final," said Purple, "But I don't know if Blue was one of them."

What was a Space Girl doing getting crucified, thought Red, on some planet so backwards they didn't even have Space drives? How could they justify killing someone just to send a message? Muscles tensed across her chest and her hand momentarily made a fist on the coffin. It was a good thing Planet X was on the Girl-no-go list from HQ.

"We are half an hour from orbit," said Blue over their comms. "Are you ready for pick up?"

Red replied, "We are, Space Girl Blue."

She heard Blue request landing clearance from *Angel*. Then

a voice came over the loudspeakers in the bay. "Depressurizing of central bay commencing. All personnel should evacuate inside the illuminated lines."

Around the bay just in front of the parked space craft, a blue line appeared. This line marked where a shield was. The shield had a pressure bias, causing air movement from the inside to the outside. Protocol dictated a slow ramp up of this bias allowing anyone caught inside time to move.

Rainbow Capricorn raised their helmets and turned to face the bay doors which slowly opened. Saw first a star field, then a V of flying saucers, and finally the curve of the blue and white planet below.

A silver, white flying saucer entered the bay and flew near where the Rainbow stood. It rotated 180 degrees to face the opening and landed. The gangplank lowered, and the hull turned a bright blue.

"Color Guard, march," said Red.

They forward and the coffin automatically stayed between the two lines. When the last of them stepped on the gangplank and it rose to close.

"Color Guard Point, we are all inside," said Red, "Including Space Girl Blue Aries."

"Acknowledged," said Blue from the cockpit. "Correction, Space Girl Red. Our passenger is now Space Woman Blue Aries, by unanimous agreement of the Council of Womanhood, and Space Girl Headquarters."

"All honor to the Space Woman," said Red.

"We have clearance to leave," said Blue. Blue knew they would stand guard for the whole flight in the entry room and could not see out, so she gave them a run down as they descended. "*Angel* is taking a stationary orbit over the Loop.

"As an aside, news drones broadcast your Color Guard

maneuver to all of Home," said Blue, "so it is a good thing you didn't screw it up."

Red rolled her eyes at her Rainbow mate.

"They will also be following every move we make from here on out," said Blue.

Red knew the plan, Capricorn's saucers maintain the Missing Color formation until they reached the top of the Spire. Blue will land on the balcony of the Hall of Remembrance. They will march the coffin out, and Blue Aries lie in state for 48 hours. Capricorn will stand four hour watches in pairs that entire time.

The descent was slower than any Space Girl would normally use due to the solemn nature of the duty. Red looked around at Blue's entry room. A jet bike hung from the ceiling to one side. A selection of weapons and tools were displayed on the walls. In the center of the weapons was a very large something covered in a blue tarp. *I wonder what that is?* thought Red. As she was cataloging all the possible weapons of that mass in her head, Blue said, "Orienting to balcony."

There was a slight feeling of rotation and then a stop. The Rainbow rearranged themselves in reverse Spectrum order, giving the two Blues prominence.

"Buck, open gangplank," said Blue to her saucer.

"Yes, Ma'am."

The gangplank descended revealing the bright light of day reflected through and off of the Spire. The majestic funeral march of Home filled the room.

When the gang plank touched down, Blue said, "Color Guard, forward march."

They slow marched onto the balcony. Small news drones floated around to get proper angles of the ceremony. The balcony was empty but through the wide opening Red could see the funeral party. The High stood in the center of the Hall of

Remembrance. On either side of her were the members of the Privy Council of Home, including Space Woman Black.

The Hall of Remembrance was not large, being at the top of a spear shaped building. It could hold maybe fifty people if they were crammed in tight, but today there were few. The Council, Red knew, but the group of four to one side she did not. A tall woman with grey-green hair and tears running down her face. A bald older man had an arm around her and tears on his face as well. Next to them stood two girls, one in the uniform of the Capital Medical Center, and the other a Warrior Cadet.

They must be Blue Aries's family.

Capricorn marched the coffin to the center of the room, saluted it and the High, then Blue said, "Color Guard, begin first Watch."

Red said, "Space Girl Orange. Space Girl Green. You have first watch."

Leaving those two standing at the foot of the coffin, the rest of Rainbow Capricorn returned to the balcony to give the family and council privacy.

———

TWO DAYS LATER, Red was leaning on the balcony of the High's Tower looking at the stars. Watch was over and they were sticking around for the reception of honor. Blue came up and leaned next to her.

"Ready to go, Red?" said Blue.

"Yeah, you?"

"Of course. We graduated four days ago and have only gotten to spend like a second with our new saucers."

"Yeah, had to change mine's personality twice to get one that wasn't just offensive."

Blue laughed. "Took me five."

"You always were easily offended," smiled Red.

Blue snorted and said, "So how long you think it will take you to make Space Woman?"

"Sheeze, Blue, we just started a couple of days ago. And we are at a Space Girl funeral, for Light's sake."

"Don't tell me you weren't just staring at the stars and calculating what adventures would get you there the fastest."

Red didn't say anything for a long moment. "It took Space Woman Black a little over a year."

"You think you can do it in that time?"

"Of course not. I'm not as good as she is."

"Yeah, but she wasn't as good then as she is now. Took her years to go from Space Woman Yellow to being selected for Black."

"You think you're good enough to do it in under a year?"

"Nah," Blue said and looked back at the stars, "but it's also a matter of luck – or the Light shining on you - what adventures you find. I figure at least a couple of years. I've got some plans though."

"Yeah, me too."

There were footsteps behind them and Purple wedged herself between them. "Hey, primaries."

"Hey, half-red," said Red to her Rainbow Mate.

"Hey, half-blue," said Blue completing the gag.

"You two out here arguing about who is going to make Space Woman first?" asked Purple.

Red and Blue suddenly had an intent interest in the city scape below them.

"Thought so," said Purple. "Here's a question for you two crazy girls to argue. Which one of you is going to end up in a coffin first?" She thrust a thumb over her shoulder and added, "Blue Aires just made Space Woman. All you have to do is be an icon of Home on a diplomatic mission and get tortured to death."

The other girls scowled at her.

Purple huffed. "I had some very, very small hope this would make you realize this is real now. Blue Aries is the unusual that gets a Color Guard. Most Space Girls just disappear and get a star on HQ's wall."

Red and Blue shuffled their feet.

"Well, I tried," said Purple. She wrapped an arm around each them and hugged them to her. "Didn't have much hope. It is in your nature to take risks. Mine too, really."

"That's what makes us Space Girls," said Red.

"We bring chaos to order," said Blue.

"And order to chaos," reminded Purple.

Then they all went silent and stared up as space called to them.

CHAPTER 4
EVERY DAY ADVENTURES

"ASTROBOY, bring up the Space Girl Mission Queue," Red commanded, once the saucer was on course for the Portal. "I've been watching it for days planning my first win, but I want to see if anything new has come up."

"As you wish, Ma'am."

On the screen in front of her a list of missions appeared. Put out and maintained by Space Girl HQ, this was a list of the things Home wanted Space Girls and Women to investigate or work on.

"Filter out those limited to only Space Women." She said and the list shortened. Some tasks were known to be something only an experienced Space Woman could handle. While a Space Girl might take it upon herself to go ahead and investigate, they were generally too involved for a first mission. Even for Red.

"Also filter out claimed missions." Once a Space Girl said she would look into something, it was marked taken. You could go join in if you wanted, but that wasn't what Red wanted for her first mission.

What was left looked like this:

- Disruption of Scout Girl Cookie production on Keblr.
- Diplomat girl missing on Chapra.
- Medical rulers of Pandom may have reached unacceptable levels on the tyranny scale.
- Communication lost with artist of Kenix.
- Criminal syndicate on Ziabos.
- Climate change on Altar threatens native inhabitants.
- Trade route disruptions near Kitch system.
- Collectors rumored to seek Home artifacts.
- Confirm Unubtanium deposits and claim planet in Indigo System.
- Forest rainbow out of communication on Amypso.
- Possible new breakthrough in Spaceway communication announced on Obrov.
- Cultural tipping point in mating rituals may be happening on Grozeliv.
- Possible new definition of aesthetics on V'Shu.

There were also standing missions like the interdiction of slavers and destabilization of oppressive regimes, but to do those required finding them. She didn't have time to do that if she wanted to be first on the board.

"Astroboy, set a course for the Indigo System," she said as she marked the que item *In Progress*. "I think claiming a planet is a good start."

———

ONCE THROUGH THE portal and on the Spaceway, Red lay asleep on red silk sheets, her skin a pale contrast to the rich burgundy. She had star tattoos that started just above her right breast, wound over her shoulder diagonally downward across her back, snaked around front over her left hip, and trickled to an end just below her belly button. They were a cluster of various sizes and colors, dark against her skin.

One star glowed and blinked. Then another. And another, till the glowing cascaded across all the stars on her body.

Music came on in her cabin and got louder the longer she slept. The tattoos flashed brighter and brighter.

Then electricity traced a path from star to star and she shot up with a scream.

"What the Hell! Astroboy!"

"Ma'am," the ship said. "You told me to wake you when we arrived at Indigo Omega. We've arrived in the Indigo Omega's system."

"I didn't say to shock me," she said as she rubbed a star near her shoulder. "I didn't even know you could shock me."

"Your bio-embedded interface system has a number of abilities, allowing not only you to integrate with me, but me to integrate with you. Mild electric stimulation is just one of those abilities."

"I really should have read the manual closer." She rolled the bottom half of her body one direction and the top the other. Looking up at the mirrored ceiling she could see most of the stars on her belly, hip, and back. "Speaking of which, run diagnostic."

Each of her star tattoos blinked and flashed. As they did she felt something a little different inside. New sensory input.

"Interface working within optimal parameters, Ma'am."

"Looks and feels good," she said as the lights faded. "Give me your feelings about the system." She got out of bed and headed for the fresher. Her stars twinkled and she understood everything Astroboy had learned about the star system since exiting the portal.

She came out of the fresher latching the bubble helmet to her pressure suit.

"All scans checkout. Prodigious deposits of Unubtainium. No activity from any other species or claim beacons. We are free to claim it for Home and the Light That Is all Colors."

CHAPTER 5
THEFT OF THE PLANET HEART

SPACE GIRL RED brought her flying saucer in for a landing on Kenix's main landing field. The natives used a flat glade as their space port, not hectares of concrete. It was night and the field was empty and dark.

"Astroboy, something is up. There are no lights anywhere. Kenixans require light to move."

"Yes, Ma'am. As plant based life-forms they are dependent on the Sun for energy. But according to Home records, they have abundant energy and generally keep inhabited areas lit for the entire 15-hour planetary rotation."

Recorded images appeared on the view screen. They showed a breathtakingly beautiful city bathed in an ethereal light. There were glowing yellow points of light everywhere, some on poles, others hanging from trees and intricate sculptures. One of the images was clearly the same glade they were currently sitting in, but with a ring of lights on poles illuminating the whole area. Various Kenixans of all of their races moved around the area, greeting people of various planets.

"Can you scan for energy signatures?"

"Scanning," said Astroboy. Red's tattoos felt lifeless and dull —a reflection of the energy of the planet.

"That is not good." She got out of her seat and dropped down the ladder from control. In the main bay she stripped off the lightweight two piece red ship suit. She had expected a temperate paradise just a few degrees warmer than Home. "Do you detect any movement around the field?"

Again her stars gave only the lightest of touches. "No, Ma'am. Nothing bigger than insects are moving." She opened a special closet and pulled out her Space Girl armor. She thought while it wrapped itself around her and sealed.

"Okay, power-up the impellers to minimum levels. That will cause the ship's ring to light up. Maybe someone is out there and just can't move," She strapped a second raygun to her belt.

"Yes, Ma'am," replied Astroboy. A low hum rose in the ship.

Red walked to the exit room. "Lower the gangplank."

The floor of the room slanted to the ground and she strode down it. The light pulsed around the ship illuminating the ground for 20 meters. She couldn't see much from the gangplank and stepped away from the ship. As she left the glow of the ship, she pressed a button and two lights telescoped out of her shoulders. They came on with a cone of light that reached 100 meters and tracked her head movements.

As she approached the edge of the landing field she could see a series of poles surrounding it. Following a worn path to those poles she realized they were lightstands, but the globes at the top were dark. She followed the path a little further till she saw the first Kenixans.

The figures were humanoid in shape and appeared to be kneeling in the middle of the path heads down. When her lights hit them, nothing happened. As she got closer there was movement from the one on the right. The female figure had brown skin with a rough texture. Her hair was leaves, and they tilted toward the light. She wore no clothes, though there were leaves growing in various places on her body giving the impression of clothing.

The Kenixan on the left had green skin with dark and light lines running vertically. He had no leaves, though a few flowers dotted his body. Red thought at first he had short spiky hair, but realized they were literal spikes. Kenixans were a multi-race species and this person was obviously from the desert area of the planet, while the other looked native to the forest.

Red thought to her suit and each of her lights focused on one of the two figures. The beams narrowed to give more light to the focus of its attention. It took a few minutes, but the forest creature began to stir. The forest Kenixan head came slowly up revealing a triangular face with wide dark eyes. The nose started small above a green lipped mouth. Grooves and ridges fanned upwards between the eyes and defined the forehead. The beautiful creature stared at Red for a moment before inhaling deeply. "Thank you, stranger, for your light," her voice was high and mellow. "I am Quercus. Who, may I ask, are you?"

"I am Space Girl Red of the world Home."

Quercus slowly got to her feet. She did not move out of the light. "Welcome to Kenix, Space Girl Red. If you had arrived during the day we would have been better able to greet you. As it is, only your light allows me to move."

"My light will follow you if you desire to walk around. The one on my other shoulder has been on your companion just as long, but he is not yet moving."

Quercus looked at the other and said, "Caryophyllales is a native of our more sun drenched continents and will require more light to awaken, but it shouldn't take long now. Your light is quite bright."

"I was surprised when I landed to see no lights. I was given to understand that the Kenixan architecture provided light everywhere all night long."

Quercus looked down and shook her head slowly, "Once it was so, but no more. Not since we lost the World Heart."

The other figure suddenly jumped to his feet and screeched. By reflex the other two leaned away, with Red's hand moving close to her raygun. But the cactus man just started shaking himself. When he had settled down, he said, "Sorry about that. Always a bit surprised by a sudden sunrise."

Then he looked around and realized it was still night. "Oh, not sunrise yet." He glanced at his wrist, but the black ring there didn't tell him anything. "Ahhh, nothing works." He looked up at the light and saw Red for the first time. Then he noticed Quercus standing in another cone of light. "Oh goodness me. I believe I'm being rude. I'm not very good when I first wake up. One of the reasons I try to avoid sleep if I can."

Caryophyllales looked Red up and down. "You must be a Space Girl. I recognize the saucer and armor. And judging by your bark, I'm guessing you are Red."

Red smiled, "Indeed I am Space Girl Red. Have you encountered others before?"

"Yes, Yes, of course. Oh, but I'm doing it again. Still a bit fuzzy noggened. I am Caryophyllales, diplomatic liaison for this landing field. It is my job to greet visitors and guide them where they might want to go. Though I must warn you, there won't be much activity until sunrise. All we of Kenix are asleep until sunrise." He again glanced at the band on his wrist, then said, "I would tell you how long that is, but my watch no longer works either."

"The sun will rise at this longitude in 1 hour and 23 minutes," came Astroboy's voice from Red's suit.

Quercus started a little, but Caryophyllales took it in stride. "Also much of our industry has stopped with our artisans having to return to the use of only the most primitive tools. And only during the day. If you have come looking for art."

"The normal visitor quarters I would direct you to," Quercus said, "were damaged in the recent troubles. Repairs have been very slow." Both of them seemed embarrassed.

"It is disappointing to see the fabled Kenix so dark. My mother visited here and always told me it was the most beautiful city she had seen off Home. What happened?"

There was a long pause as the two plant people looked at each other. Red added, "I'm sorry. I don't mean to pry. Oh, and is this light sufficient for you both? The bulbs will track your location, so you don't have to stand still if you don't want to."

"No, no, the light is wonderfully bright," Caryophyllales said. "Thank you so much. As to the story of all this darkness. Well...."

Quercus took up from the pause, "It is still fresh in all our roots and we don't like to talk about it. Perhaps we could walk with you toward the city and show you as we go."

As they walked along the path she got the whole story. It had been a sneak attack, starting from that very landing field. One day a large dark ship had landed. As soon as it settled heavily on the grasses of the field it had begun to bellow smoke.

"We have no defenses. No soldiers," said Quercus. "We are a peaceful people and do not even have – what do they call those that stop evil doers in a country?"

"Police," offered Red.

"Yes, we don't even have those. So when they started polluting the landing area, we could do nothing but protest."

Then Zorans poured out of the ship. They knew exactly where they were going and destroyed everything in their path. They were mechanical beings, each with their own destructive purpose. Saws cut through trees. Drills and shovels dug up the ground. They showed Red the trench of dark earth, now left oily.

"And they stole the World Heart," said Quercus with tears of sap leaking slowly from her eyes.

"The World Heart?" Red asked.

Caryophyllales took up the tale explaining that millennia ago the Ancient Ones had given the Kenixans a powerful energy source. Everything on the planet ran off it. Wireless power available everywhere. "The curious thing was the Zorans knew exactly where the Heart was. Most Kenixans don't even know where it is buried. Only a few of our leaders and scientists. But the Zorans went straight from their ship to where it was and dug it up in minutes. Then they were back in their ships and off world before we knew what to do."

"And the lights went out as soon as they left the atmosphere."

Since that time the Kenixans were plunged back into primitive times. They could only work during the day and all must sleep at night. Nor could they communicate with the universe at large because their transmitter equipment was also powered by the World Heart.

Red stood on a mound of dirt left next to the hole the Zoran had dug. It was not in the center of the city, rather to the south. The sun was just beginning to rise. As she stood there with her two new friends, she became angry. The light reflected off a multitude of surfaces in the city proper. Even with no power you could feel the beauty of it.

"You are the first visitor we've had," said Caryophyllales. Both of the plant people were turned to face the rising sun, eager for its rays of light. "Perhaps you could take a message to others letting them know what has happen. I know there are many who value our art and would desire to help in our time of need."

"Of course. I know the women of Home will send help as soon as they get word. And there are others. Astroboy, my ship, is sending word as we speak. Help is on the way."

The other two's faces lit, not just with the rising sun, but with hope.

"Do you perhaps have an image of the World Heart? So I might know it if I see it."

"There are some in the council archives," said Quercus, "This way. I believe we have hard copy images, even if the computers are down." She started down the hill toward the center of the city and the Space Girl followed, visions of what she was going to do to the Zorans when she got to them filling her head.

———

"WHAT HAPPENED TO THEM?" Space Girl Red said looking at the Zoran battle cruiser. They had exited Black Space via the portal with shields up and weapons powered to be immediately confronted with a Zoran battle cruiser blotting out the stars in front of the portal. By reflex Red had fired her lasers, but there was no response. It didn't take long to realize the ship was floating dead in space.

"I don't know, Ma'am. Scans show some mechanical movement onboard but no large power source. You would normally expect a ship that size to have a large nuclear or Q-energy generator. But there is no indication of either."

Red let the flying saucer continue on its course toward the dead ship. As they got closer the ship rotated toward them revealing a hole all the way through the craft.

"I'll be a blinking light," she said.

The hole was shaped like a flying saucer.

"Astroboy, could we even do that?"

The bubble flashed through a series of colors and percolated black and blue bubbles for a moment. "I had never considered the possibility, but now... If you exited the Spaceway covered in counter Q-energy and pushed that out from the hull with full shields, going full speed...."

"Yes, ma'am. I think we could punch a hole like that. Quite clever to come up with it."

"Mmmm, but you'd have to know it was here before you exited the portal. Otherwise you would have purged the counter Q-energy."

"And you would not be going full speed for the same reason, you'd be afraid of running into something."

"Any indication who did it?" She asked, though she had a pretty good idea who would be that bold. Had Blue heard about Kenix and wanted to relieve their poverty?

"No, ma'am. Obvious a Space Girl or Woman, but there is no indication of which one. I am getting an energy signature on the other side."

"Space Dimension energy?"

"No, ma'am. It is not a Home energy source. This seems to be simple nuclear power."

They had gone past the derelict and a few thousand kilometers away the main power plant of the ship floated. Apparently it had been knocked out as the flying saucer broke through.

"It is still functioning?"

"The power plant itself seems to be in working order, though not up and running. Space based nuclear power plants tend to be tough because of the shielding needed to stop the radiation."

Red rotated her chair to another set of controls. After a few quick motions, a panel just outside the canopy opened and a miniature flying saucer rose out of it. She told the drone to attach to the power plant and claim it as salvage.

She rotated back to the ship controls, and put them back on course for the planet Zoran.

———

ZORAN WAS a black and blue ball in the sky. The blue came from vast oceans that covered 80% of the planet. The black was from the clouds and dark land masses. Astroboy's scanners plotted a few more derelict spacecraft in orbit and a lot of debris. As Space Girl Red sat in her armor, hands still poised over weapon control, she began to almost feel sorry for the Zoran. Once in orbit she could look down on the night side of the planet and see many crimson cities lit up for the night. They were connected with razor sharp lines of orange roads. Even as she floated there, waiting for Astroboy to make sense of the huge amount of radio traffic coming from the surface, entire cities would go dark. The after a moment the lines connecting them would go out like they were transmitting the darkness. The city would glow back to life and another would go dark.

"What is going on with the city lights?" asked Space Girl Red.

"It seems there is not enough energy to power all the beings on this planet. They war with each other over the power grid. Through some mechanism I can't quite figure out, one city will take control and pull all the power from another. Then another will attack them and the cycle continues."

"Any word on the Kenix World Heart?"

"There is an incredible amount of radio traffic, Ma'am. I'm starting to believe the beings that live here actually use it for all of their communication. It is how they talk to one another." Astroboy paused distractedly, "Needless to say, Ma'am, it is all very confusing."

Red left him to it and brought up the specifications for her own weapons systems. The Home flying saucers were deceptively powerful. They had a full complement of beamed weapons, laser, plasma fluid, disintegration rays, even death rays. Also non-beam weapons, bullet cannons, unobtainium missiles, photon cannons. Space Girls were not warriors, but they went into dangerous places on their own. Home was not going to leave them unprotected. She was trying to figure out what could have caused the levels of destruction she was seeing here. Nothing as big as the first ship next to the portal had been seen closer in. Astroboy had indicated there was only one portal in the system at the moment, but in a few months there would be a second and probably a third. So maybe the Zoran only needed one cruiser to guard the system. But that cruiser seemed to have more than enough weaponry to take down one flying saucer.

Unless they were taken by surprise.

The ramming maneuver just out of the portal would only work if planned in advance. Which meant whoever had done this had know the ship would be there. They probably also knew the rest of the system defenses and could cut through them just as easily. Sure enough, a quick scan of orbit, showed residual unobtainium and plasma fluid. A crude back trace on debris orbits indicated those weapons were the origin of the destruction.

Now the question was Who and Why. She could send a query to Blue but she didn't want that answer just yet. It could be any of a number of Space Girl Rainbows for a number of reasons. She herself might have unleashed the same level of destruction to get the World Heart back for the Kenixans.

"Ma'am, I think I have something," Astroboy said and brought up the main viewer. It showed a video of a flying saucer hovering over a dark city. "This appears to be a news report on something that happened a couple of days ago."

The buildings looked like a steampunk tinker's junk pile. There was no central theme or plan, but each building gave the impression of being exactly what the builder wanted. Some were mounds of pipes and wire, others spires of steel and nails. Swarming over them and pouring tracers into the air were all manner of mechanical beings. The flying saucer's bubble of protective shielding shrugged off all the fire being aimed at it. It hovered over one particular tower. That spike of metal was topped with a glowing ball of warm orange.

"I am unable to decipher the actual language of these beings," said Astroboy, as if personally affronted the mechanical folk spoke so strange a tongue. "It is too strange a combination of mechanical, digital, and acoustic symbols."

On the screen the saucer lowered itself next to the orange ball, its forcefield covering it. Then the gang plank lowered and Blue walked down it. She was in her armor, battle helmet attached. Over one shoulder she carried a heavy laser normally used for astroid mining. She swung it horizontal and fired it at the wall of the orange ball.

Red had to admit, with projectile fire bounding off the shield, smoke billowing all around, and a giant laser cutting a hole in the building, Blue looked pretty damn cool. She finished the hole, tossed the massive laser back into her ship, and jumped through the hole with the help of her jet pack. A few seconds later, she came jetting back out. Tucked under one arm was the World Heart. Her raygun was firing blue bolts back through the opening. Projectiles raised sparks off Blue's armor as whoever had been protecting the World Heart tried to stop her.

Just as Blue reached the top of the gangplank and it was starting to close, a rocket shot out of the orange ball and impacted the ramp. There was an explosion of fire, the whole saucer rocked from the impact and it wobbled for a moment in mid air. The shield bubble flickered, and sparks peppered off the hull as projectiles from below got through. The control canopy filled with black smoke.

Red held her breath, worried she might be seeing the end of one of her rainbow mates. She and Blue had never seen eye to eye, but she was still as close as a sister. Red longed to have been there to help, but could only watch helpless. She hated being helpless more than anything.

Then Space Girl Blue appeared in the canopy, her blue armor charred black, but moving quickly and with purpose. The ship steadied. The shield returned. Blue tilted the nose of the ship skyward and repulsor rings poured from the fin pods.

"I guess that tells the story."

"Indeed. Might I suggest, Ma'am, that we don't go down to the planet. I expect they won't take kindly to a flying saucer in their skies."

Red shook her head in wonder. "Yes, that does seem prudent. I guess I need to send Blue a message. Do you have any idea where she is?"

"No, Ma'am. Space Girl Blue has not been on your rainbow's private channel, nor the general Space Girl channel. I do have updates on the assistance mission from Home on Kenix, including a message from Space Girl Yellow about needing an alternative power source. But nothing from Blue."

"Plot a course back to that derelict by the portal. I might be able to help with the power. On the way I'll compose a message to Blue."

"As you will, Ma'am."

———

"YOU HAVE TO GIVE IT BACK," Red said.

"Pfft. No, I don't," said Blue.

"But it is theirs. The Zorans stole it from them. Without it they have no energy source on their planet." Red was incredibly frustrated with her Rainbow mate. She'd sent a message complimenting her on getting the World Heart back from the Zorans and asking when she would be returning it. Blue's reply had made this conversation necessary. She had jumped through the portal and fired up the Spaceway Radio. The only way to have a video conversation over the vast distance was to do it in the Spaceways to someone else in the Spaceways.

Blue was sprawled in her control chair. Much of the room was still covered in soot. Blue herself seemed clean, wearing a pair of blue shorts and a bandeau top. Behind her Red could see minibots working to clean the cabin.

"Justice is your thing, Red," said Blue. "I'm about relieving poverty. My understanding is the Kenixans are some sort of rich artists. People from all over the galaxy come to their world for art. They can just up their prices a little and buy a new power plant."

"Who are you going to help by stealing their World Heart?"

"I'm helping the Altarian slugs."

"Who?"

"The Altarian slugs. They are a race of gastropods on Altarv 3. They live in the forests and streams there. There is no industry or trade to speak of. No way of making money. The sad thing is the slugs are smart. Savants really at math and languages, but they have few schools. The leading cause of death is starvation. The money I'm going to make selling the World Heart will allow them to build a new system of schools and increase their agricultural output ten fold. It will put them on track to be self-sustaining and a part of galactic civilization in a generation."

Red was conflicted. Blue did find worthy causes, but this wasn't the way to go about it. Just like Home and the other Space Girls were mobilizing to help the Kenixans, they could come together and help the slugs. "Blue, there are alternatives. We can bring the rainbow together and figure out solutions, without having to plunge the plant people into darkness. Did you know they go to sleep when out of the light? So now everyone is unconscious for half their planet's day/night cycle."

"So let them sell some paintings or whatever and buy a flashlight." Blue sat up and leaned into the picture. "Did I tell you about the salt?"

"Salt?"

"Yes, salt. There has been a change in their climate recently and the salt water oceans are rising. Most of their cities, well, really just big settlements, are near rivers and often close to the coast. So this water, that is like acid to them, keeps getting closer and closer. It destroys farmland, making hunger a bigger problem. Once it reaches habitations it makes those places unlivable. What they need to do is a mass migration, but they don't have the resources. And they may be fast of mind, but they are still slugs, and slow of...well, feet isn't the right word."

"I feel for them Blue, I do. But you can't help them by stealing from someone else."

"What? You weren't going to steal from the Zorans?"

"No, no. That wouldn't have been stealing. It would have been reappropriating stolen property. And I would have tried to talk to them first."

"Yeah, the Zorans are hard to talk to. Was your ship able to decipher their language?"

"No. And his name is Astroboy. Was yours?"

"Buck couldn't either. Not that I planned to talk to them. My intelligence made it clear the Zorans are not talkers. That was why they had that big cruiser at the portal."

"How did you know about that?"

"I had my sources."

"And they are?"

"Look, Red, I'm not giving it back. I'm going to sell it and use the money to help the poor. Don't get in my way."

"It is unjust to steal, or take possession of stolen property. Did you know it was stolen before you blasted into the Zoran system?"

"Whoa there! You aren't putting me on trial."

"If I don't, someone else will."

Blue smiled. "Let them try. They have to catch me first."

"What about Home?"

"If the High or Space Woman Black, want me to stand trial, they can recall me." Blue was doing something with her controls off screen. "But as for you, Miss Goody Two Shoes, stay out of my way."

"You know I won't do that," Red said, but Blue had already cut the connection. "Crap, and there is no way to track where she is in the Spaceways."

"That is so, Ma'am, but we can tell when a ship exits a portal. And which portal they exit."

"Oh, really," Red said with admiration. "You are a smart boy, Astro."

The bubble next to her blushed pink. "She hasn't exited yet, but I will keep an eye out."

"Good. Let me know."

CHAPTER 6
RECOVERY OF THE PLANET HEART

SPACE GIRL RED lay at the top of a low hill looking through the scope of her long rifle. A flying saucer was parked in the center of a dry river bed. Clustered around the saucer were a group of big green men. They were over two meters tall, shiny green, muscled but thin with large tear drop shaped heads. Their eyes were so big she could see them plainly even without the scope's magnification. They were dressed in a minimum of clothing and carried only the crudest of weapons.

The flying saucer was Blue's with black marks on the underside near the gangplank. As if on call, the gangplank lowered and the Space Girl walked out. She wore a dark blue jumpsuit, dual pistols, and had the World Heart tucked under one arm. She yelled at the group of men and they moved slowly away from the saucer, forming a loose perimeter. These were the guards. They didn't look like the kind of people who could pay the billions Blue claimed she could get for the World Heart.

"Ma'am, I have detected another spaceship in bound to the planet."

Red nodded and said, "So this is a meeting to sell, not the actual buyers."

With a flick of a control on the side of the gun, Red lowered her aim to a spot on the ground behind where Blue paced. There was a soft hiss as she pressed the trigger, and a small puff of sand. Red set her rifle down and scooted backwards down the hill.

She grabbed the backpack she had left there and pulled out two grabboids. They were silver and shaped like fat worms, bigger in the center and tapering to a point in the back. She stroked each one and whispered to it. When she set the grabboids on the ground they burrowed into the sand and disappeared.

Then she crawled back and picked up her rifle. She changed a setting again and waited, centering Blue in the sight.

"The spacecraft has left orbit and is heading to this location," said Astroboy.

"Will they pass over you?"

"It does not appear so," he replied. "Unless they decide to circle the site before landing. The craft seems rather primitive, and I'm not sure it is capable of circling."

Blue was talking into her wrist communicator. This was a trick because she had to balance the World Heart in the same arm. Then she shrugged, pulled a grenade off her belt, spun a dial on it, and tossed it a dozen meters away from her. When it landed a plume of blue smoke started filling the air. The green men on that side moved away from the smoke.

A few seconds later Red heard a roar. Looking up she saw a contrail terminating in an orange dot. That dot moved closer and resolved into to a rocket ship. It was sliver, with a pointed top and four large fins on the bottom. It homed in on the blue smoke and settled expertly down on top of it before the engines cut off and there was silence.

Blue stood halfway between her saucer and the cooling rocket ship, tossing the World Heart between her hands like a football. Red said quietly, "Is that an actual Rocket Ship, Astroboy?"

"Indeed, a fusion steam engine to be precise. It will take them a moment to let the landing area cool before they will be able to exit."

True to his words, once the steam dissipated a door opened between two fins and a ladder extended to the ground. A human began climbing down the ladder. The bulbous suit in a multitude of colors told Red very loudly this was a Collector. The Collectors were a multi species group of beings that collected the technology of the Ancient Races. Which explained why she was here. She must be Blue's buyer.

If a Collector bought the World Heart, there was next to no chance of getting it back. They were a secretive lot. The location of only a few Collector Centers were known, and those were mostly for recruiting. Where they kept their acquisitions was a big unknown.

As the woman moved toward Blue, Red settled in behind her rifle. Blue was still, holding the World Heart under her arm. This kept her right arm, the one away from Red, free if she needed to grab her gun. The crosshairs in the scope moved down to the woman's calf.

Red pulled the trigger, and things happened very fast.

The rifle wasn't firing lasers or bullets; it fired targeting darts. As soon as the tiny silver dart hit Blue's calf, one of the silver grabboids rose half out of the sand. Its front end opened and tentacles slithered out and encircled Blue's leg and tried to pull her underground.

Red realigned her sites on the World Heart and pulled the trigger again. When the second dart hit the World Heart, the other grabboid launched out of the ground like a little silver missile. Its tentacles grabbed the World Heart and jerked it out of Blue's grasp. Then it sprouted spider-like legs and started racing up the hill toward Red.

She rose to one knee, and pressed a button on her rifle. Out the side slid a small missile. She aimed it at the open door of the Collector's ship and pulled the trigger. The red and white striped missile flared down from the hill and exploded in the airlock.

Blue had been pulled half underground by the grabboid. The other looked much less like a worm and more like an actual spider as it clambered up the hill and dropped its charge at Red's feet. Red tossed the rifle over her shoulder where it automatically attached itself the back of her armor. The grabboid climbed up her leg and found a place on her belt.

A quick look down the hill showed the Collector standing confused halfway to her rendezvous. Blue had pulled a raygun off her belt and was firing laser bolts into the ground at the thing holding her. The green men were the only ones actually moving toward the hill.

Red picked up the World Heart and started running toward Astroboy.

SPACE GIRL RED pounded up the gangway into the saucer yelling, "Astroboy!"

A couple of blue bolts of light zapped past her leaving glowing marks on the walls. There was also a thunk as something metal lodged in the wall. Out of the corner of her eye it looked like a the bolt of a crossbow. *Couldn't fault this planet for being boring.*

"You called, Ma'am?" Astroboy's voice rang out around her.

"Put up the shields. Close the gangway. Make ready to lift. It's time to vamoose, skedaddle, hit the road!" Sounds came alive around her: the swoosh of the gangway closing behind her, the weeehhhh of the engines starting to spin the saucer. *What's another way to say let's go?* she thought, swinging round the control room ladder in the circular center of the ship. She pressed a hand to a wall panel and it swished open. She tossed the object of all the fuss into a vault.

"¡Ándele!" she said as much to herself as Astroboy then climbed the ladder to the control room. The bubble showed a clear blue sky above with dry scrub all around her. Red dropped into the pilot's seat and spun the wheel on the chair. The whole control room twirled on the ship's axis so she could see behind her.

Her closest pursuers were the big green men armed with the crudest of weapons: clubs, long knives she wouldn't dignify with the name sword, and, sure enough, a few crossbows.

"Shields are up, ma'am. Engines at 80% and rising."

Red looked at the mob of big green men pressed up against an invisible wall 10 meters from the flying saucer. "Any of them make it inside the field before it went up?"

"No, ma'am."

There was blue flash on the shield. Then four more. She followed the rays back beyond the sea of locals. Space Girl Blue was a stick figure in black at this distance, with a shock of blue on top.

Red smiled.

A quick glance at the control panel showed the engines at 90%. "Close enough," she said and yanked the impellers lever all the way back. The ship squealed like he'd been kicked, but the ground disappeared below the saucer. In seconds the sky started to darken.

"The engines weren't ready to maneuver, Space Girl Red," Astroboy said.

"I can see the indicators, Astroboy." Indeed there were a

number of gauges turning from white to black in front of her. "I just used the impellers to lift. I'm not maneuvering yet."

The sky was starting to show stars, so she eased up on the impeller lever. She also tapped the seat control with her other hand and the control room reoriented to the front of the ship, leaving the fins behind her and out of view.

"As you will, Ma'am." *He's being a pouty*, she thought. "Main engines are at 100%. Here is a plot for orbit."

On the main screen in front of her a line drawing of the planet with a dotted line coming from its surface appeared. A little flat red silhouette of her ship followed the line from the surface to orbit. Tiny numbers orbited the ship like little electrons giving her the vectors for orbit.

"Forget orbit. Didn't you see Blue? She'll reach her ship and be after us in seconds." Red's hands ranged quickly over the control panel. "Give me a vector for the nearest star portal".

"The nearest portal is currently within the gravity field of one of the planet's moons."

Red rolled her eyes. She looked to her left at the bubble she thought of as where Astroboy lived. It was glowing an amicable yellow with bubbles of red and green.

"You know what I mean. The nearest gate I can use." A new diagram started drawing on the screen even as she castigated him. "Don't make me mod your personality."

"Wouldn't think of it, Ma'am. Plot is on screen."

Glancing at the vector numbers, she grabbed the control stick and pulled right to rotate the ship. Once the rotation numbers matched, Red's thumb came down on the thrust button. The pulsing light of the repulsors lit the control room from behind her.

On the screen the little red ship began moving toward a blinking white disk. A time appeared and started to count down the minutes and seconds until they reached the portal.

Red sat back smiling and said, "Looks like I have about half an hour before we reach the portal." She rose out of the control chair and pressed the control that started opening her armor. "I think I'll get a quick clean up."

Hoping to get a long warm moment in the cleaner, she was disrobing rapidly while heading below. She was filing the image of the graboid grabbing Blue's leg in her happy place. It had also been a very dirty planet and Red hated being foul a minute longer than needed. She was standing in front of her shower testing the water temp when Astroboy called to her.

"You need to see this, Ma'am. It's to the rear."

She muttered theories about Astroboy's birth and climbed back up the ladder. Stepping back into the control bubble, she turned to look out between the saucer's fins. At first it was hard to see anything through the thrust rings; then Astroboy did his magic with the display. There was a ripple and the rings disappeared though she could still hear the bubbling pings from the engine.

A blue oval was just visible, with rapidly blinking rings behind it.

"It's Blue," she said. "Told you she'd be after us."

The Space Girl swung around in a twirl of crimson hair. Each new engine ring bathed her white skin with light. Sliding back into the control chair, she saw the little red ship now had a little blue friend on the display. A number whizzed back and forth between the two ships. The time to intercept. A quick check of the other time on the screen told her Blue would catch her before they got to the jump point.

"She must really be pushing her saucer."

"Yes, Ma'am, it seems to be at max thrust."

Red began adjusting controls and said, "Her ship's one of your brothers, isn't it?"

"He's my brother as much as she is your sister."

Red laughed. "Well, they haven't made a faster Space Girl since Blue and me. Is there a faster flying saucer than Astroboy and company?"

"Not that I'm aware of, Red." Astro commented. "But Engineer Woman Black doesn't confide all her doings to me."

Red thought about that for a second and replied, "Nor me, so I guess we'd better punch it and hope she didn't confide in Blue either."

A thrust of her hand on a large silver lever fed power to the coils and the number of rings coming out the back of her ship increased. The new more powerful rings stayed visible longer before fading out.

On screen the time to intercept increased while the time to jump decreased. White gauges on the red control surface started darkening as she pushed her little flying saucer toward its limits.

Sitting in the pilot's chair, her legs pulled up under the seat, moisture began to condense on her forehead and chest. She was most definitely not sweating. Red knew she only sweated with physical exertion, not because she was being pursued. This wasn't even a glisten. There must be something wrong with environmental controls. Have to talk to Astroboy about that when this was all over. Maybe it was the engines. Maybe they were making the ship hot. Of course ring repulsors don't generate heat.

Then the two numbers on her screen flipped. Blue couldn't catch her before jump. The control room was suddenly a bit cooler. A second later the blue oval slowed. Blue knew she wasn't going to make it.

"Incoming message." Astro stated.

On the screen Blue words appeared. *Point to you, Red. But this isn't over.*

Red smiled and started moving controls to prepare for jump. "No, Blue, it isn't."

IT WAS afternoon when Space Girl Red landed on Kenix. Two other Home ships sat in the landing glade. A flying saucer like hers, and a larger Home ship she knew was from the Engineering group.

She wore her standard suit uniform, no need for armor or a pressure suit here. She sported red spandex pants, transformer heels that were 100mm in the ship, but lowered as she walked down the gangplank, and a bandeau top that allowed almost all of her stars to be visible. These glowed expressing both her and Astroboy's happiness to be returning the World Heart, which she held carefully in both hands in front of her.

At the bottom of the gangplank stood her two Kenixan friends, Quercus and Caryophyllales. With them were to other Kenixans, Engineer Woman Aquamarine, and Red's Rainbow mate Yellow. Aquamarine and Yellow had been working to bring power to the Kenix city while she was gone. The power from the Home ship was wired and the Kenix city wasn't set up for that, which meant very little of the city had light at night. But it was a bright day and Kenixans surrounded the landing field.

A Kenxian she hadn't met stepped forward with Caryophyllales. She was tall, with light colored, smooth bark. Her hair was yellow rose petals held together by thin flexible branches. She had chosen to grow a petal covering over her upper body that curved around her breasts and down her belly. At her waist thicker branches formed a network to support a skirt of petals that faded from yellow at the waist to crimson at her ankles. Caryophyllales spoke first, "Space Girl Red, it is good to see you again. Allow me to introduce Rosaceae, the Head of the Order of Keepers of the World Heart. She is the foremost expert on the World Heart and will be reinstalling it."

"While words may be able to express our gratitude for the

return of the World Heart," Rosaceae's voice was a rich contralto that filled the space around her, "it will take generations of musicians and poets to do so." She bowed with liquid grace, her petals flowing around her as her head almost reached her knees.

Quercus and Caryophyllales mirrored her bow with less grace, but no less fervor.

When Rosaceae again stood straight she stepped forward and took the World Heart from Red's hands. Then she turned and stepped a few steps toward the crowd at the edge of the landing field. "Our heart is returned to us," she said and raised the World Heart high. The whole time Red had held the World Heart it had been a grey football. But raised high in Rosaceae hands, it glowed a warm sun color.

Rosaceae began a slow walk away from Red.

Caryophyllales and Quercus touched Red gently, then bowed low, eyes shining.

"You have saved us," said Quercus. "Never again will we be found kneeling is weakness and defeat in the night."

"It would have been enough if you had just brought us the help from others of your world," Caryophyllales said gesturing to the Home women behind her. "But you did so much more. Fighting to bring back our World Heart. To make us independent again. If you ever need anything from us, know our whole world is in your debt."

Red bowed low to them. "It is my purpose to bring justice in the galaxy. This was that. You owe me nothing."

The two plant people bowed again and moved off after Rosaceae.

Yellow stepped forward and gave her a long hug. "Red, it is so good to see you back. And with the World Heart! I can't wait to learn how they install it."

Engineer Woman Aquamarine added, "I also hope we can

encourage them to have a backup in case something happens with the World Heart again."

"How were you able to get it back from the Zoran?" asked Yellow. "I understand they are a race of robots."

"They are that," Red said. "Their language was so alien even my saucer couldn't ever figure it out. But I didn't get the World Heart from them. By the time I got to Zoran, Space Girl Blue had already liberated it. I just liberated it from her."

Yellow laughed, "You two. I'm sure that didn't go over well."

"I did try to talk her into giving it back to the Kenixans first but she had another purpose for it."

"Do you think she will come here for it? The Kenixans still have no defenses," said Engineer Woman Aquamarine.

"No, I don't think so. She knows Home is now involved on Kenix. She didn't know the World Heart was stolen from the Kenixans at first. She was hired by a Collector to steal it from the Zoran. I tried to convince her it was justice to return it, but she felt the money she would earn would alleviate a great deal of poverty on Altar. I stole it from her right before she could deliver it to the Collector."

Yellow laughed again. "Red, you sure know how to make trouble. Blue's going to be out for blood. Have you gone too far this time? In training you two's rivalry was just a game. This is the real world."

Red shrugged. "Don't know. I did what I thought was right. We'll see how badly Blue takes it."

"Does the Collector know where the World Heart really came from? Or where you are taking it?"

"Don't know," Red smiled. "Didn't really talk to her after I disabled her rocket ship. I was too busy running from Blue."

"They had a rocket ship?!" both engineers exclaimed.

"Yep, with a big pointy cylinder and curved fins. The whole wavelength. It wasn't very maneuverable, but it got her to the surface. I launched a rocket into her airlock, which probably kept them from taking off for a while. I was afraid if I shot the fins, the whole thing would fall over and crush Blue."

Engineer Woman Aquamarine shook her head. "Your Rainbow is a piece of work."

"It is the nature of Space Girls to be... boisterous," said Yellow.

The other two women laughed.

"If you will excuse me, Red, I need to catch up with the Rose lady and see how they install that thing." Yellow gave Red another quick hug.

Then both the engineers left her. As she turned back toward her ship she remembered something. "Hey, Yellow, you might want to tell your saucer to watch space for the Collector ship."

"Conner's already on it," the other woman turning and walking backwards. "Hope the guy actually comes. I'd love to see a real life rocket ship."

CHAPTER 7
QUEEN NATALIE & THE FLYING MONKEYS

SPACE GIRL RED stepped out of the cleaner, her bare skin glistening. She walked over to her dresser and started brushing her hair while thinking about what to do next. Her hair was long. Many Space Girls, like Blue, kept theirs short. It made things easier in a helmet, and allegedly better in combat. But Red liked hers long.

On the dresser in front of her were a few personal basics: skin care and enhancement products. A jewelry box that held very little jewelry. Most of what was in it were actually Space Girl gadgets, like lock-pick rings, hologram necklaces, and laser watches. There were a few pieces of actual jewelry she'd been trained to wear on formal occasions in the wide universe.

The only truly personal thing in the open box was the bracelet her father had given her. It was quite beautiful in a simple way. Three wire circles connected in such a way they seemed to form three orbits around the wrist. There were two points where the orbits intersected. One was the clasp and the other was a diamond shaped piece of metal with three round stones in it. The center was bigger and a rich blue color. On either side of that were two smaller stones, one orange, the other red.

Looking at the bracelet reminded her of the the letter he had given her— an introduction to the Queen of the Kitch system. The queen of a world. Red wondered if that was like the High. She had studied various forms of government of course. Understanding the strange ways of other worlds was part of being a Space Girl. She knew Home was different in its combination of so many authorities from government, to science and religion. It might be interesting to meet a queen.

"Astroboy, how far away is Kitch 10?"

"Quite close, Ma'am. We could be there in a matter of hours. Shall I lay in a course?"

Red thought for a moment. There was no point system or leaderboard on Home that tallied what deeds would make a Space Girl into a Space Woman. Still it was hard for her, and she was sure Blue, to not keep score in their heads. She had claimed a new planet, one she knew had Unubtanium deposits, within hours of becoming a Space Girl. Then she had organized a rescue mission of Kenix and ultimately returned the World Heart. People on Home were sure to notice.

I'll bet a queen would have something for her to do that would be worthy of womanhood.

"Yes, Astroboy. Lay in a course."

———

"SO CYNWRIG MARRIED A WOMAN WORLD DIPLOMAT," said Queen Natalie using the term many outsiders used to refer to Home. Red guessed it must be difficult to refer to a planet as Home when it wasn't your home planet. The Queen sat on her throne with the data coin in her hand. She wore a long sheath dress in metallic silver. On her head was a dome-like helmet that V-ed down almost to her eyes. There was a large ruby right in the middle of her forehead. Draped around her and over the throne was a silver cape. Projected above the data coin was a scroll with a message on it Red couldn't read from where she stood. Queen Natalie was not what Red imagined a Queen looked like. "And you are his daughter."

Space Girl twinged a little inside at the discussion of her parentage. She wasn't ashamed of Father. Mother wouldn't have married him and brought him back to Home if he weren't a man of quality. She knew he had been a high ranking diplomat on his world. He had helped Mother negotiate the peace treaty of Onerous Gamma, that ended a centuries long war between the moon people and those of the sea of the planet. Still all this discussion of her father seemed a little weird.

"My mother was a diplomat bringing peace in the face of war when she met my father on Onerous Gamma. I understand their courtship was a bit whirlwind during the standoff of the two sides."

"I remember that conflict. My brother died trying to find peace a decade before Cynwrig and your mother..." the queen glanced back to the message. "Diplomat Woman Pink? Doesn't she have a name?"

"When a native of Home reaches a certain age, they receive a color. For the rest of their lives that is how they will be known. My mother, like me, was given Red as a child. When she ascended to lead the Diplomatic Corps she was lightened to Pink."

"Hrumph," said the Queen, uninterested in delving any deeper into such a foreign culture. "Your father helped negotiate the current *peace* we have with *God* King Bruno before he went off to Onerous Gamma." She looked off with a small smile for a moment. "Those were good times, during that negotiation. Well, except for the King. That man is an ass."

Red said nothing.

"Your father speaks very highly of you. How long will you be on Kitch?"

"I came primarily to give you that message, your majesty," Red replied. "But I thought to see the sights. I particularly wanted to meet some of the Flying Monkeys, if possible."

Queen Natalie smiled widely. "It is certainly possible. I expect it is unavoidable if you landed a Woman World flying saucer at the space port. They do love anything that flies. Did you not see any when you landed?"

"No, Ma'am, I was on a mission to deliver that message and didn't doddle."

"Well, return to the spaceport and look for a building that looks like a giant tree. It will be surrounded by all manor of flying machines. That is the home of local squadron of the Flying Monkeys."

"Thank you, Queen Natalie." Red began her bow to leave, but the Queen interrupted.

"We are having a state dinner tonight and I would like for you to come. There will be representatives from many planets in the region. It would be good for you to meet them. It is not often we get a Space Girl on our peaceful planet."

Red smiled, "I would be delighted to attend. What time should I come?"

"Eve Tide, I believe," said the Queen. "The steward can give you all the details. Time, dress, customs." She glanced back at the letter from Red's father again. "The ambassador of Xerces will be there. I'm sure he'd like to say something to Cynwrig's daughter."

Red raised an eyebrow, but the queen made no reply, engrossed in the letter. Red bowed and left.

———

FLYING monkeys were indeed easy to find when she got back to the space port. Her tattoos had been itching all the way there and now she knew why. There must have been a dozen monkeys swarming over Astroboy. He was sealed up, but his displeasure was coming to her through her connection to him.

"Hey, get the flame off my ship!" Red yelled when she got close enough for them to hear her. "Do I go climbing your glowing tree without permission?"

The shocked expressions on the monkeys' faces were priceless. They all froze in place at the sound of her yell, looking sheepish at having gotten caught. They weren't really monkeys per se, not like the monkeys back on Home. For one they were a lot bigger. But they weren't apes. They were much more like chimpanzees, but at least a meter and a half tall.

One of the monkeys high up next to the emitter pod on the starboard fin, screeched a command and they all started swarming off the saucer. When they reached the tarmac, they formed up into two lines. The last one off saucer was the one who issued the commands. As he walked toward her she noticed he wore a leather collar around his neck and on that collar were sergeant stripes. He walked directly up to her and said, "Pardon us, Ma'am. Ms. Space Girl Red, we just got over excited when we saw the flying saucer. None of us have ever seen one before. Delight got the better of our manners."

She smiled down at him, "How do you know my name, Sergeant?"

"I just figured it. You have a flying saucer; that makes you a Space Girl. Space Girls all have color names," he smiled back at her. "And you're wearing nothing but red."

She laughed, "Very good. Sergeant?"

"Sergeant Major Rudy James, Ma'am." He snapped a sharp salute.

"I do not know how to return that, Sergeant Major. Please assume I did the right thing."

He dropped his salute just as smartly.

"Astroboy, are you all right?" Red said knowing Astroboy would hear her and reply through the ship's external speakers.

"I am fine, Ma'am," though his tone sounded indignant. "I fear I may be covered in paw prints now."

The Sergeant went stone faced.

"Don't be petty, Astroboy. I'm sure the Flying Monkeys were just excited by your beauty," Red said sternly.

"You are right, Ma'am. Sergeant Major Rudy James, I do apologize for my outburst."

"No worries, Mr. Astroboy," the Sergeant Major replied. "Ms. Space Girl Red is right. We shouldn't have jumped on you without permission. If you will accept it, I'll have these imps shine you so bright Ms. Red here will be able to see her reflection in your chrome."

"Well, Sergeant Major, that sounds positively wonderful," purred Astroboy and Red laughed again.

"You apes go get cleaning supplies," barked Sergeant Major James. The troop broke formation and started running toward the giant metal tree in the distance. "I expect you'll be wanting to talk the to the Captain, Space Girl Red."

"Why do you think that, Sergeant Major?" She probably should talk to someone in charge since her troops were working on Astroboy, but his tone implied a problem.

"To report our jumping all over your ship, of course."

"I think we settled that between ourselves. Astroboy seems happy enough and I wasn't really that upset to start with," Red said with a smile. "I would though like to talk with some of your pilots."

"We ain't pilots. We just keep them flying. But the Captain can help you with that. I'll take you to him." He motioned for her to go first toward the shining tree-like structure across the tarmac. "If you don't mind me asking, are those repulsor pods on the top of the fins? How much do they output?"

They had a companionable walk talking ship tech.

———

"PLEASED TO MEET YOU, Space Girl Red," said the tall blue-skinned monkey, putting a hand out for her to shake. "I'm Captain Winchester Powell, lead pilot for the fourth wing of Her Majesty's Flying Monkeys."

The captain wore a blue uniform with a red floral pattern on the jacket. His hands and feet were bare. There was a helmet sitting on his desk of a smooth bluish metal with a fin on the top. He also wore a leather collar with Captain bars on one side and a flying monkey wing pin on the other. He held himself upright as an officer should, but continued to exude simian power.

"Nice to meet you Captain. I have heard so much about the Flying Monkeys' prowess I wanted to meet you."

"It is heartening to hear the fabled Space Girls think highly of us."

"I have a special insight because my father was a diplomat here during the negotiation of the peace treaty with Xerces. He told me the Flying Monkeys as a threat were key to getting the Xercians to agree to peace."

An expression passed over Winchester's face, but Red couldn't read it. "That negotiation was before my time. I wonder how much *God* King Bruno considers us a threat now." Red was starting to notice every Kitchian put a sarcastic emphasis on the 'god' part of Bruno's title. "The field is mostly empty of our craft because we must run constant patrols at the edge of the system. We seem to have a pirate problem, with ships that are very Xercian in design."

"How do you find them as pilots?"

"They are squirrels," Captain Powell said in obvious distain. "But even squirrels in great numbers are a menace. Or in lesser numbers but hidden in the empty, outer parts of the system. Do you know much about the Kitch system?"

"Only what I've read and the little my father has told me."

The Captain came over his desk and motioned to a wall display. "This is Kitch 10, which gives you an idea of just how different the system is from others. Kitch has more planetary bodies than any other known system." He brought up a drawing on the screen with the system's star in the center and a large number of dotted lines around it indicating orbits.

"Depending on how you count, there could be as many as 100. Only 3 are habitable." Four of the orbits about a third of the way out turned blue. "I say habitable, but I mean habitable by oxygen breathing mammals like you and me. The Snoozians inhabit a couple of the gas giants, but you don't see them much."

"And who are the pirates attacking?"

"There are outposts on many of the smaller planets, for mining, research, and what not. Even a prison on one. The pirates tend to raid these. We have a couple of military bases out there too, which is where most of the Monkeys are right now."

"Are the Flying Monkeys the only pilots?"

"There are a few human pilots. Mostly from the royal families. They require special ships as you humans are lacking in hands." He waved one of his lower limbs.

Her tattoos buzzed and she activated her communicator. "Yes, Astroboy?"

"Ma'am, you have to be at the Queen's Ball in 2 hours and you haven't even picked out your dress."

Red sighed and turned to Captain Powell. "I'm sorry, Captain. I need to go get ready for the Queen's ball tonight. Perhaps we can talk more about this later."

"Of course. I will see you there as I'm currently the highest ranking member of the Flying Monkeys on planet and must make an appearance at the Ball as well."

"See you then," she said and headed back to her saucer, her mind already thinking about the dress she was going to wear inspired by the volcanoes of Indigo Omega.

CHAPTER 8
THE DANCE CONTEST

"SPACE GIRL RED," the doorman's voice boomed over the ballroom. She stood at the top of the stairs leading down to the dance floor filled with the other guests. "Of the world Home. Daughter of Cynwrig Pembroke, high diplomat of Kantar and Friend of the Royal Family of Kitch 10, and Diplomat Woman Pink."

After that introduction she was glad she wore her father's gift. She always thought of her parents in terms of her mother's exploits to gain her womanhood. But on this planet it was Cynwrig who brought peace. The title Friend of the Royal Family was the highest honor a non-Kitchian could receive.

Looking out she noticed people tended to dress in black and white with a lot of metallic silvers in honor of their queen. Red of course had worn red. Astroboy had outdone himself fabricating this dress. It was red, orange, and black, made with thousands of small glass beads. They were patterned to look like lava flowing down and around her body. The flow began a few millimeters below her bare shoulders, across her chest, and slanting to one side winding under her right breast. The volcano pattern flowed all the way to the floor on the left. On the right the dress split at her right hip, revealing a stretch of hip and leg. The dress was backless with just wisps of volcanic embers rising suggestively up her spine.

Every person in the room stared as she slowly moved down the crystal stairs in 125mm platform heels.

As soon as both her feet were off the staircase, the doorman began to announce the next guests, a rotund couple in black and grey. Red moved forward looking for anyone she might recognize. Since she didn't know anyone but Captain Powell, she just kept moving across the room. She found a slightly raised area to one side and turned back toward the entry way. A waiter passed and she took a flute of champagne.

There was a pause in the procession of people at the top of the stairs. Then two figures appeared, Queen Natalie and a younger man on her right in escort. Gone was the dome helmet and sheath dress Red had seen earlier. It was replaced by a outfit made a shiny black material and silver metal. Three silver rings arched over platinum blonde hair piled high on the top of her head, and two thick braids that fell on either side of her face. A black and silver vertically striped collar fanned up from her shoulders behind her neck. Her neck was encircled by a metal collar with the royal ruby in the center. She wore an intricate metal corset with a double row of rubies down the middle. A black skirt with stars sparkling all over it trailed behind her. It opened in the front to reveal black leather thigh high boots, with platform heels. Metal swam up from her feet swirling around her calves, and matching silver braces on each forearm.

Red thought *this* looked like a queen.

"His Royal Highness, Prince Alfred Morgan the Third. Captain of the guard. Pilot of the Flying Monkeys, and heir to the throne of Kitch. Tonight escort of the queen."

The younger man nodded his head in acknowledgment of the announcement. He was slightly taller than the Queen even in 150mm heels and him in low black boots. His pants were midnight with sliver stripes up the side. He wore a white high collared shirt, and a uniform-style jacket that hung long on the sides, but stopped just below his belt in the front. There were medals Red couldn't read on his chest. Around his neck the same leather collar she had seen on the monkeys earlier, with the Flying Monkey wings on one side and captain bars on the other.

"Her Majesty Queen Natalie Armond Morgan of the Kitch system. High ruler of the inhabited planets. Foundation of the Snooze. Alpha of the Monkeys of Kitch 8. Commander in Chief of all the armed forces of Kitch. And accolades too numerous to recite tonight."

Like a wave everyone in the room went to one knee for their queen. The only ones not kneeling were Space Girl Red, and a group of four people dressed in bright orange and blue near the base of the stairs. *Those must be Bruno's ambassadors,* Red thought. They were the only others in the room not ruled by the queen.

Everyone stayed in position as the Queen and Prince came down the stairs. Queen Natalie's heels made the crystal staircase no easier than it had been for Red, but she made it look easy. The prince kept pace with her and half a step behind, having let her hand go at the top of the stairs. Once both of her feet were on the main floor, everyone rose from their bows.

The queen stood for a moment, eyes scanning the room. They passed over the nearby ambassadors indifferently and stopped when they found Red. She leaned over to the prince and said something. Then she walked across the room toward the area set aside for her, ignoring the ambassadors who had moved closer to get her attention.

The prince let his mother move off on her own and began to

negotiate the crowd. He nodded greetings to many, and shook hands quickly with one or two, before arriving in front of Red.

"You must be Space Girl Red," the Prince said with a slight bow.

"Kind of hard to miss in this crowd, aren't I?" she replied with a slight smile.

"Indeed," he said and looked her up and down. "I must say that is a most spectacular dress. I wouldn't have thought ball gowns – let alone ones so impressive they will be talking about them in the society papers for the next year – would be standard issue on a flying saucer."

"When it comes to clothing, Space Girls have significant tools at their disposal. I may not be on the same level as my rainbow mate Orange, whose calling is Beauty, but I can throw something together when the situation calls for it."

"You have a sister that is more be..." Prince Alfred cut himself off. "Sorry, I believe I was about to be impertinent. Forgive me."

Red tilted her head in puzzlement. "It would be impertinent to indicate you think I'm beautiful? Why would that be?"

"Ummm, well, you see..." He was clearly at a loss for words. "On your world do men just blurt that kind of thing out unasked?"

"On my world there are only the Fathers, all of whom are married. It would be fine for any of them tell me I'm beautiful. Why would it be otherwise?"

"But what about single men?"

"There are almost none on Home. Still I don't see why telling a woman she is beautiful is a problem. Is it bad form here? Can you explain why?"

Prince Alfred, Captain of the Guard, Pilot of the Flying Monkeys, blushed.

"Ummm... I guess because it might be taken as an indication of desire."

"Desire, mmmm," Red was still confused. On Home beauty was honored. It was something to strive for in everything, from engineering to cosmetics. Here it seemed personal beauty was regarded differently. "So on Kitch 10, beauty is only seen as an indicator of sexual value. Is that it? So it would be impertinent to express beauty because you would be expressing sexual desire, which might be unwanted to the recipient."

The Prince sighed, "I'm sure it is a little more complicated than that, but let's leave it there. Since I've been taught we must deal with other cultures in a sensitive and open way, let me assure you that you and that dress are very beautiful."

Red smiled and curtsied to the Prince. "Thank you, sir."

Prince Alfred bowed back, then said, "Mother sent me to do more than shower you with well deserved compliments. She desires me to introduce you to the Ambassadors from Xerces."

"Does she now? Why send you instead of coming herself?"

"Because she is avoiding a very unpleasant, difficult, and possibly undiplomatic conversation with the Ambassadors." He leaned closer to her and said in a quiet voice, "I think she hopes you will have better luck making them see reason. Perhaps because of your father."

Red moved forward, revealing more leg by the motion, touched one of his elbows, and put her mouth next to his ear. "I will tell you now, Prince Alfred, Space Girls are not diplomats. We have a very real tendency to break things if we want to see change. If she needs diplomacy she could send a message to Home and get my parents here to negotiate."

Alfred's head was spinning with the proximity and scent of this colorful woman. "Perhaps breaking things is what she thinks is needed. There are many who do. Myself and the monkeys for instance. We desire more direct action against God

King Bruno." He stepped away whispering, "Now we had best separate as tongues are already going to be wagging at our proximity."

Once they were separated and the Prince could think straight, he said, "I would like you to meet some special guests at this party Space Girl Red. They may even know your father."

———

SPACE GIRL RED strode toward the Xerces ambassadorial party next to Prince Alfred. He had offered her his arm, but she didn't know what the gesture meant and had simply stepped next to him. The Prince had shrugged and began to lead her across the room. She noted he was popular by the greetings he got as they moved through the crowd. No one approached or stayed in their way as they moved. A number of women took in her dress, exposed skin, and proximity to the Prince with expressions of distaste or jealousy. Men took in the same information with expressions of a different kind of jealousy.

The Xercian party consisted of four, two men with two women behind them. All had the matte black skin and white hair of Xerces. That skin color was as unnatural as the color of Green's hair. Not a dark brown pigmentation like Yellow's but a slate-like color. All four of them dressed in typical fashion of Xerces, bare torsos and long fur skirts in God King's colors of orange and blue.

Red noticed the women first. In a concession to the Kitchians, they wore sheer tops in a color that exactly matched their skin. Red was sure it was a statement showing they would follow only the letter of Kitchian expectations.

One was a tall thin woman with an athletic build. Her white hair was cropped so short it reminded Red a little of Caryophyllales's cactus spikes. Her fur skirt reached to mid-calf. Made of two rectangular pieces with 10 centimeters between the front and back connected by three straps across her hips. On her right arm was a white tattoo like the branches of a tree. They started at her wrist and spread up her forearm, stopping just below the elbow. She looked at Red with dark angry eyes.

The other woman looked vaguely out of place among the tall Xercians. Where the others were tall and built like distance runners, she was compact and muscular. Still lean, she had a full chest and broad shoulders. Her white hair was cut in a bob and the bottom few centimeters was died the royal orange. Her sheer top consisted of two vertical lines from shoulder to waist. She too sported a branching white tattoo, but hers started at the top of her sternum and spread across her chest. It looked more like lightning than a tree and crawled over her chest stopping short of her solar plexus. Her calm eyes took in the Prince and the Space Girl.

The men stood with one crowded slightly behind the other and they could not have been more different.

"May I introduce you to First Ambassador Alexandr Bohbmil Prazak of Xerces," said Prince Alfred motioning to the man in front. The First Ambassador looked old. In a galaxy full of regenerative technology, this was a statement. Humans had been able to control their appearance as they aged for at least a century and Red wondered why this man choose to be truly old in appearance. His skin was wrinkled and loose on his no longer muscular body. His white hair had gone grey, and there were pronounced crows feet around his eyes. "This is Space Girl Red, daughter of a Friend of the Queen."

The man smiled at her in a way she felt was honest. He bowed ever so slightly and said, "You are Cynwrig Pembroke's daughter, lady, are you not?"

By now Red was getting used to all this talk of her father and barely flinched. "I am."

The man next to First Ambassador Prazak coughed rather more pointedly than was polite. It earned him a quick disapproving eye dart from the shorter woman, Red noticed.

There was a pause long enough to be noticed, and then the Prince said, "And Second Ambassador Ctirad Drahoslav."

Red looked at him for a moment and he started to move around the Ambassador. Then she pointedly look to the First Ambassador and said, "Did you know my father, First Ambassador?"

The man smiled again, "I did. I was the Second Ambassador when the first treaty of peace was negotiated between the God King and Kitch. I spent much time with him writing up the terms that serve us today."

"Serve Kitch you mean," mumbled the Second Ambassador toward the woman with the spiky hair.

First Ambassador Prazak ignored the easily heard comment and said, "I was a brash and energetic Second Ambassador eager to make a name for myself. As all Second Ambassadors are, I suppose."

Ctirad's teeth clenched and knowing smiles went around the group. Before the conversation took a further turn against him, he said, "Do you dance, Space Girl Red?"

Somewhat surprised the Space Girl answered, "I do. Are you asking me to dance, Second Ambassador?"

"No, no. I have my own partners here." He motioned to the two still unnamed women behind him. "I was just wondering if you were going to compete in the dance off? Perhaps as the Prince's partner."

Red looked at the Prince.

He answered, "It is the fashion now to have a dance contest at balls like this. My mother enjoys them and the Second Ambassador here is quite the fiend for them." He turned to the Ambassadors and continued, "I will not be competing tonight because I am judge, along with the First Ambassador, I believe, in the interest of fairness."

Second Ambassador Drahoslav looked surprised, "I didn't know Alexandr was judging tonight. He didn't mention it to me."

"The Space Girl is our guest tonight and does not know our ways, we perhaps should not push her into a contest," said the Prince.

Red laughed. "A Space Girl turn down a competition? Never."

"But you don't have a partner," said Ctirad.

"I imagine I can find someone in this crowd willing to take you on," she said looking around the room. She smiled again when she saw Captain Powell slip into the room in full dress uniform. There was also a fanfare from the band at that moment.

"We will be starting with a non-competitive dance in just a moment," said Prince Alfred. "Perhaps I could have this dance as a warm up for you, Space Girl Red?" He offered her his hand.

"Sounds wonderful," she said and took it. "And I look forward to meeting you two after the contest, Ambassador Girls."

This managed to put shocked looks on the faces of every member of the Xercian contingent.

"They aren't Ambassador Girls!" said Second Ambassador Drahoslav. "They are my servants."

The First Ambassador recovered quickly. "They are servants of the embassy, Second Ambassador," he said patiently. "Space Girl Red's mother is a diplomat of much repute on their world. She would naturally assume the female members of our embassy to be part of the diplomatic core. She referred to them as girls, because that is what they call junior members of any profession. Like we might use the terms Second or Third. You should really read the briefing materials, Ctirad."

The First Ambassador turned back to Red and smiled. "I believe a meeting can be arranged, Space Girl Red. I would also like some of your time to catch up about your father and mother."

"It is a plan," she agreed and let the Prince lead her toward the dance floor.

———

THE YOUNGER AMBASSADOR was chagrined at the concepts professed by someone who was a servant of the God King. "I didn't have time to read. I was preparing to represent the God King tonight in the contest."

"Of course, Second Ambassador. We must all keep our diplomatic priorities straight." He glanced at the filling floor and said, "Why don't you take Venuše and warm up with the Prince and the Space Girl? For the good of the God King, of course."

"Oh," said the younger man looking around and noticing people on their way to dance. "Yes, of course. Venuše, with me."

The thin woman with the spiked hair glided forward to take the Second Ambassador's arm. Then the two of them headed toward the dance floor.

———

THE MUSIC BEGAN with a Latin beat and Prince Alfred twirled her toward him. One arm slid around her waist as they clasped hands. Red's feet picked up the beat and the two of them began to move. He was a good dancer. At first they moved easily around the floor with the other dancers. When the beat called for it, she slid away and swayed her hips. Twirls made her dress seem even more like fire as it flew away from her.

At one point she caught sight of the two Xercian dancers.

The shaking of hips and shoulders had an angry intensity. Their determined movements cleared space around them. The bold colored skirts setting them out among all the black and white. When the music downshifted to a slower pace, both the couples pulled in close.

"You can dance, Red," said the Prince.

"As can you. Have you competed with the young ambassador before?"

"I have. He is quite passionate about it. I do not always win." The music continued as they talked. When the dance called for separation their conversation paused, only to continue when they were back together. Red's twirls and movements at the extension of the Prince's arms gathered more and more attention. As people became more interested in watching the dance than actually dancing she and the Prince had more and more room to move.

"What is your dance competition like?"

"It has a freeform start. All the competitors will assemble around the dance floor. Then music will start and two couples will enter the floor. They will dance back and forth—each doing moves and challenging the other to top them. Sometimes a couple will concede they cannot outdo a particular set of moves. In general, though, after a few times back and forth, the dancers will pause and the judges will decide who they think is the winner."

"Then the winners leave the floor and allow another set of couples to go."

"Yes, until only winners are left, then the winners will do it again." The Prince put one firm arm behind her lower back and she leaned back into the dip. The music changed and she moved in close and began to dance more slowly.

By the time the song had stopped, the floor had cleared. Only Red, the Prince, the Second Ambassador, and his assistant were still dancing. The Prince commented, "That will give them something to think about."

"Really? That old thing?" Red asked with a wicked smile.

"There is one other thing you might want to know. It is possible to challenge a single member of the other couple to a dance off. I've seen Venuše do it to other women of the court."

"Can only women challenge women?"

"That is generally how it is done, but there are no official rules."

The music came to a close and they bowed goodbye.

Then there was a general announcement of the dance contest and Red went looking for her dance partner. She strode up to a group of soldiers in fancy dress uniforms, among them the young Captain she had met earlier in the day.

"Soldiers, it seems I'm going to need a dance partner tonight," Red said.

The humans in the group looked excited at the prospect of dancing with her. Then she saw them looking over her shoulder at the Xerces dancers still on the floor. There was much silence then.

"For the Royal Guard you seem a little afraid of something as simple as a dance contest."

"Lady," a young human lieutenant said, "If you wanted us to fight hand to hand next to you against the Xercians we would volunteer with vigor. But we are not dancers of their standard."

"Then I need conspirators. Surprise may work for me tonight."

———

THE CONTEST BEGAN with two surprises. The first was only two groups came forward when it was time for it to start.

One group was, of course, Second Ambassador Drahoslav and his assistant Venuše.

The other surprise was the second group.

Space Girl Red stood on one side of the dance floor with three Kitchian military officers in full dress uniforms behind her. Captain Powell was the shortest and in the middle directly behind her, invisible to her opponents.

Across the dance floor stood Venuse Krozel and Second Ambassador Ctirad Drahoslav holding hands loosely. She was the picture of calm. Ctirad was trying to look calm, but could not steady the tremble in his hands and feet. Perhaps he's just excited, thought Red.

The two judges sat on tall chairs to one side at the middle of the floor. Opposite them were the Queen and a number of retainers. All around the dance floor, and crowded against the balcony of the second floor, the Kitchian audience waited.

Red's dress now split on both sides and she held one corner of each half in her hands. The groups stood across from each other and waited. Red and her partner had spoken to the Musician about what they wanted. He'd been excited to mix a beat and a theme for each of them, and almost bounced in excitement when they explained how they wanted to sync it to their performance. But their music wasn't the first to break the silence. Instead a more traditional, fast rhythmed, stringed song swelled over the floor.

As soon as it begin, the Xercians twirled into each other and took over the floor. Their dance was impressive. It involved fast footwork that intertwined in a way requiring keen observation to tell whose limbs where whose. They never completely separated or lost touch with each other. Ctirad was the perfect platform for impressive acrobatics by Venuše. Red recognized something in the way the woman moved, but couldn't quite place it.

The music got faster as the dance continued and the two dancers kept up easily. If anything they increased the difficulty of the movements, as if they were trying to make a point—which they probably were.

The Xercians used their entire half of the dance floor, following an unspoken rule about crossing into the other's territory. When it seemed the music had to slow down or the dancers would explode, their dance moved to the back of their space. Then they raced directly at Red as if getting ready to leap. At the last second, when the music reached a crescendo, Venuše launched into the air directly at Red foot extended in a kick. If Red had been nearer the front, her instincts would have forced her to react, but Ctirad held onto his partner's arm and the forward launch turned into a compact arch, ending with the tall woman wrapping herself around the man.

There was a second of stunned silence, then the crowd exploded in applause. The dancers untangled themselves slowly and stood almost at the center court line together as the clapping stopped. Ctirad had an expression of glee. Venuše one of challenge.

Red shrugged her shoulders and tilted her head. She lightly rotated at the hips and played with the skirt in her hand. The music started low with a deep beat like a human heart. She strutted slowly forward toward them, shoulders confident, hips sensual. As she got closer the galactic theme rose around the beat. Majestic, the music rose, space. She let her arms rise with it. The skirt also rose, each side becoming a triangular wing. Her long legs were exposed, muscles flexing, high heels confidently planting with each step, like her saucer settling for a landing.

At a point not more than a meter from the Xercians she began to move and sway to the music. She twirled and snapped to a stop, legs shoulder-width apart. Her stars lit up, starting where they disappeared into her skirt. The red matched her dress and hair perfectly as they flowed out of the lava and up to her head. Slow and strong she began moving left and right, executing perfect ballet movements: high kicks, pirouettes, frozen moments of balance—all in perfect sync to the swelling theme of the galactic part of the music.

Then the beat changed, becoming deeper, louder and faster. Her dance transformed as well. Becoming more primal and athletic. Her hands moved up and down her body. Hips pumped and snapped right and left. She swung to the ground, rolled into a kick one leg vertical. A quick fluid motion dropped her into splits, long bare legs to either side. Then, a couple meters from where Ctirad and Venuše still stood, she lay forward, face to the ground. Her hair flared around her head, and her arms tucked under her to arch her back. Her stars flared to a bright white.

Everyone's eyes were focused on her as the galactic theme disappeared and a crashing boom exploded into the room. The two human soldiers snapped to attention with a clash of boots on the floor. From the very back of the dance floor Captain Winchester Powell launched into a twisting double flip. He arched high over the prone glowing Space Girl, and landed on the beat with a bang. He was so close to the middle line, the Xercians flinched and Venuše moved in front of the Second Ambassador.

The beat hammered like a machine gun and Winchester moved through a series of martial movements. Red had noticed the silver pen of a Simia Fluxus practitioner on his dress uniform. He had immediately understood which form would be the most dramatic set to music. Simia Fluxus had been developed eons ago by ancient monkey masters in the mountains and deserts of Kitch 8. It took advantage of the unique double handedness of the monkeys, which meant Captain Powell seemed to be upside down a lot of the time.

As the beat became more coherent, a new theme could be

heard. It invoked the feelings of tree and forest. He continued to leap over Red's prone form, but when he landed there were smooth movements of his hands. His crouches were low and shifted from lower limb to lower limb. Finally he leaped over her once more, landing to one side and balanced on one arm.

The galactic theme of space rose again and Red seemed to levitate out of her position on the floor. She slid into a fighting stance on one side of the floor opposite the Flying Monkey. Then the two songs clashed together and combat began. It wasn't really combat. Too on the beat for that to be true. Contact was less about inflicting damage, and more about grappling in a way that propelled their partner. It was as dramatic as the Xercian dance had been sensual, but it only lasted for a moment. When the song stopped suddenly, they seemed less locked in conflict than united to watch each other's back.

Again the crowd roared applause.

On the side the two judges were deep in deliberation. Red and Captain Powell separated and bowed deeply to one another. Then they stepped together to within a meter of their opponents in the center of the dance floor.

The judges came to a conclusion and walked up to the waiting contestants. Prince Alfred turned to the Xercians and said, "Second Ambassador Drahsolav, you again produced a dance that was beauty to behold. Venuše, I am in awe of your ability and the raw sensual splendor you put into this piece. There is no doubt this was the best couple's dance I have ever seen on Kitch 10."

The two Xercians smiled and bowed to the Prince.

The First Ambassador said to Space Girl Red and Captain Powell, "It is beyond me how the two of you could have improvised such a performance so quickly. Captain Powell, who would have known you were such a dancer? Space Girl Red, you have only added to the mythos of your planet. Everyone who experienced tonight will indeed know the multifaceted talent of Space Girls, not just by legend, but unexpected demonstration."

Red and Powell bowed as well in acknowledgment.

"We are, though, left with a dilemma," said Prince Alfred. "Clearly the Xercian pair were the better couple dancers. But Space Girl Red and Captain Powell showed two individuals of extreme prowesses."

"We cannot decide a winner," said the First Ambassador. "So we are left with a choice. You may choose to take a tie, or there can be a dance off."

The Second Ambassador was chagrined. "How can you not rule for us? What that monkey did wasn't dance! It was combat."

The room fell silent and stared. It looked as if the First Ambassador was about to say something—maybe about being a sore loser—when Space Girl Red's voice cut across the silence. "As a Xercian, I would think you would be used to Flying Monkeys dancing circles around you."

The Kitchian crowd burst into laughter. Venuše slid into a fighting stance aimed at Red. That shifting of weight told Red a great deal about this woman. It was one of the 87 Steps of the Bloodway, a martial form that was a great secret taught only to individuals who survived the indoctrination of the Syndicate of Assassins. Venuše was more than she seemed, though really you'd expect an assassin to have better control over her anger.

Before things got really ugly, Red said, "I issue a challenge. For the dance off, I suggest we do the Home custom of mirror dancing."

"This sounds interesting," said First Ambassador Alexandr. "Please explain."

"If you want to know who the better dancer is, who has the best moves and raw talent, you do a mirror test. The dancers take turns. Each executes one of their moves. The other must match it. If they do, then they give answer with their best move for the other to try. This continues till one of the dancers cannot or will not do the movement."

Venuše smiled and licked her lips, anticipating competing against the Space Girl.

"I challenge Ctirad Drahoslav to a mirror dance with me," said Red.

"What! But you are a female!" said Venuše in surprise. "He cannot compete against you."

Red didn't even bother to look at her. She locked eyes with Ctirad, put a little baby talk into her voice, and said, "Is big bad Second Ambassador Ctirad Drahoslav afraid to compete with little old me?" She wiggled her hips at him, "because I'm a girl?"

It was really too bad the genetic engineering that gave the Xerces the matte, coal black skin didn't allow them to flush red any more. But the look in his eyes was even more murderous than before. "I fear no woman. About anything."

He turned to the judges. "I accept her challenge."

The judges looked at each other and shrugged. "Very well. Let the challenge begin," said the Prince. "Clear the dance floor. Musician, pick the music."

"You can go first, Ctirad," said Red and took a step back to give him room.

Ctirad looked her up and down, undoubtedly looking for a disadvantage in the dress she wore. Then his eyes got a far away look remembering what she had done in her recent dance. Finally he shrugged and executed a rapid set of footwork that tapped out a doubling of the beat.

Red let her mind go blank. She opened her senses to all experience. It would be too hard to see and analyze his feet. Instead she just experienced his movement. His whole body at once.

Then she mirrored the foot work. She stopped and looked at him. "And I did it in heels."

There was a smattering of applause. Then she stepped up directly in front of him and executed a spinning ballet move with one leg parallel to the ground, but as the rotation was almost done, she took the leg vertical and held it there for a few seconds. Then she relaxed back to standing.

Ctirad phiffted and mirrored the ballet with no difficulty. His answer started with the covering of his face with his hands, then his lower body began to move, looking disconnected from the top. His shoulders moved left and right perfectly parallel to the floor. He ended with a frozen seemingly impossible position of disconnect between upper and lower body. "Try that, girl," he said when he opened his hands.

Red gave him a nod and covered her face as her feet migrated away from her upper body. A few seconds later she opened her hands in the same position. Relaxing upright, she said, "My turn."

For the next 30 seconds she did a wonderful belly dance. He rolled his eye and said, "Easy girl dancing." And copied her. "Here's a better girl dance."

Then he grabbed his chest and massaged it. He finished by running his hands down between his legs and rubbing suggestively.

The Prince looked like he was going to intervene, but Red waved him back. She executed a parody of his dance and said, "You wish."

Red moved to the back of the floor then she accelerated forward and slid up to the line on her knees. There she made a series of 10 bows from the waist, arms extended in front of her. She stood, flipped her hair at him and walked off.

Ctirad furrowed his brow confused at the ease of the dance move. Then he stepped back and executed the slide to the line. In a quick motion, Red turned back around and stepped right up to the line. She stood over him and raised her arms to either side, like a queen accepting supplication. He had done three motions when he got it, and froze. She looked down at him kneeling before her, "I did 10. You've done 3."

He thought about it. Then hopped to his feet and said, "You. Win," through clenched teeth. He spun on his heel and walked into the crowd pushing people aside to get away. Venuše looked long at Space Girl Red and followed him out.

Prince Alfred and the Queen both walked to the center of the dance floor. The Queen said, "Well done, Space Girl Red. You have my favor."

"Thank you, Your Majesty."

The Prince took Red's wrist and lifted it over her head. "I declare Space Girl Red the winner."

———

AT THE SIDE of the dance floor the First Ambassador from Xerces stepped back into the crowd. Ljuba was at his shoulder. "Ljuba, I would like to speak privately with the Space Girl. Can you arrange that?"

"I take it you don't want the Second Ambassador nor Venuše to know about this meeting?"

"No, I do not."

"There is a pub on Canton Way in the city. They have a private meeting room I am familiar with. If you would retire there, I will convey your request to the Space Girl. I will send a messenger if she says she will not come." They both looked at where all the Kitchians were swarming around the victor. "But something tells me she will be there."

CHAPTER 9
MESSAGES FOR THE GOD KING

SPACE GIRL RED had gone to her saucer and changed on her way to the secret meeting with the First Ambassador. She wore her standard red jumpsuit and utility belt with a raygun. Then she threw a long dark coat over it and pulled a black ship's hat over her hair. Wraparound glasses that enhanced her night vision or protected her eyes in bright light finished the ensemble. In the night she could disappear.

Her dance contest exploits had gone viral on Kitch 10 and she was now something of a celebrity. So much so that there were newspapermen staking out her ship. Sergeant Major James and his troop were keeping them at bay, but she'd had to move Astroboy under the branches of the Flying Monkeys tree. This allowed her to walk out of the ship and into the building without the newspapermen asking questions or getting pictures. A private led her through winding passages and up internal branches that would have challenged most humans.

Finally they ended up at the end of a branch that stretched over the wall of the space port. She stood balanced on the very end of the slightly swaying branch with the monkey casually balanced gripping the branch a meter behind her. "There is a soft landing on the building below, Ma'am." He said.

She looked down 30 meters and back at him, "For a human?"

His blue face broke into a smile, "Yes, Ma'am. Even for a human."

"Okay," she took a deep breath and stepped off the branch.

Just as she did, the private added, "Bit bouncy though."

It took her a little under 3 seconds to reach the top of the building below and realize what the private meant. It was a camouflaged trampoline. The first bounce was a surprise, but after that it was fun and she did a couple extra leaps with flips. Finally landing softly on her back, she rolled off and found the door to the street.

———

IT WAS WELL into the middle of the night and the streets were mostly quiet. All of the bars and other establishments catering to spacers were near the entrances. Mostly this area was warehouses and repair shops, closed at this time of night.

She walked down the middle of the dark street so she could see anyone coming. It was unlikely the First Ambassador was setting a trap for her, but she didn't know the Diplomat Girl was telling the truth about the meeting. She seemed nice enough, but better safe than sorry.

When Red reached the street the pub was on, the lighting changed. It wasn't a party street but the lights were more regular. There were a few more people out, generally in pairs supporting each other on the walk home. She pocketed her glasses and walked down the sidewalk toward the pub.

The pub itself was about as lit up inside as the street was outside. There was a large man at the door who looked up at her as she walked in, but said nothing.

"I'm looking for Bohumil," she said giving the code word Diplomat Girl Ljuba had given her.

"Straight past the bar and through the pink door," he grunted and went back to staring at the wall.

She moved into the main room, which was sparsely populated. There was only one person at the bar, talking quietly with the woman behind it. Red walked past them looking for the door.

It was not pink like her mother's hair. Maybe it had been once, but now it was a dirty color Red couldn't bring herself to call actual pink. She walked up to it and pushed. Nothing happened. Locked. She shrugged and knocked.

The door opened a crack and a dark face with white hair appeared, looked at her quickly, and opened the door. It was Diplomat Girl Ljuba. As Red got through the door she could see a seating area taking up much of the small room. It held a couch and two padded chairs. Rising out of one of these chairs was First Ambassador Prazak.

"Thank you, Diplomat Girl Ljuba," she said.

"I'm not a Diplomat Girl."

"Then what is your title, so I can call you the right thing?"

The woman glance furtively at the ambassador then said, "We, Venuše and I, are servants of the ambassadors. And the God King, of course."

"I don't really want to call you servant girl. What would you like me to call you?"

The question took Ljuba aback for a moment and caused more glances at the First Ambassador who just looked bemused. "I guess you can call me by my name. Ljuba. Ljuba Reznicek." The white haired woman looked down, letting her hair cover her face. Then seemed to think better of it and looked Space Girl Red in the eye.

"I will do that, Ljuba. And you may call me Red."

The Xercian woman's eyes went a little wide at that, then she dropped her chin a little and said, "I must go and allay suspicion with Venuše and Ctirad at the embassy." Then she was gone.

The ambassador motioned to the couch across from him and Red moved to sit so she faced the door. The First Ambassador settled back into his seat.

"That was kind of you, Space Girl Red," he said after a moment. "I know to you it doesn't seem much of a kindness, merely polite. I have lived for almost 20 cycles on Kitch 10, where people are generally kind, or at least polite. Where a servant feels affronted if treated like one.

"It is not so on Xerces. Which is what I want to tell you about, because I don't think you understand what you are up against."

Then Alexandr Bohumil Pražak told the true story of the God King Bruno, which was probably an act of high treason.

———

THE HISTORY OF GOD KING BRUNO OF XERCES

Bruno's family settled Xerces Prime as a mining colony generations ago. The planet had a human breathable atmosphere, and plentiful deposits of XXXite. One of Bruno's great grandfathers had brought a colony ship filled with indentured human labor. These humans had all manner of skin and hair color, though where they came from is a mystery.

Xerces' star was a red dwarf with some unusual radiation reaching the planet. When they arrived Grandfather Bruno — his true name isn't known now as the current King Bruno erased all detailed history — discovered the planet to be inhabited. The native race are called Horsemen because they have the bodies of horses and the torsos of men. They also had coal colored skin and light colored hair, unlike the humans. They were primitive when the humans arrived and were quickly enslaved.

The colony ship had an extensive science section, as it was known they would have to develop technology to survive on the planet and mine its treasures. It was quickly learned a human would die if exposed to the natural rays of the red sun. But the clever scientists quickly came up with a plan. They took genetic material from the Horsemen and used it to modify the humans. It is where we got our black skin and white hair.

The Horsemen were useless as miners because of their size and shape, so they were used mostly for agricultural labor, while the modified humans did the mining.

The mining was a success and towns grew around mines on the planet. New humans were born and Grandfather Bruno got rich, while the lives of those in his colony improved. Even the Horsemen prospered from learning the agricultural techniques the scientists could teach them.

This went on for a while. Generations perhaps. Then we come to the time of the current God King's Father, King Max. King Max was a man who enjoyed his pleasures and didn't like to work too much or rock the boat. He was rich. His miner and Horseman slaves were content. It was all good to him.

His favored wife gave birth to a boy. There was much fanfare for Prince Bruno. He was a smart boy, if not brilliant. Inquisitive and ambitious he wanted to learn about everything on the planet. As he grew into a teenager, he became obsessed with the going ons of the science research center.

There was a young scientist there who had an idea for an intelligent swarm of nanites that could do the mining and build whatever was needed to accomplish the task. It was considered impossible but he figured out how to do it. He created swarms of semi-intelligent nanites in the lab and could get them to detect XXXite deposits, break them into individual molecules, bring them to the surface and reassemble them. But the nanites would break down quickly soon after. They lacked a true intelligence giving them purpose and direction.

Prince Bruno found the idea so fascinating he was constantly with the scientist. They would talk about how to get intelligence into the swarm. Then the scientist figured it out.

The swarm needed to be connected to a brain.

This brain would command them and keep them coherent even after the work was done. It could also give them direct ideas of how to build things. The scientist was eager to try it by connecting the nanites to himself. In his excitement he told the Prince about his idea. The Prince tried to talk him out of it, because it would be too dangerous to connect such a thing to his brain. But the scientist was most confident about the safety of that particular part of the plan. He showed the Prince his research and experiments to convince him it was very safe.

Once Bruno believed it could be done, he promptly had the scientist arrested and thrown in the dungeons of Prince Bruno's palace.

You may be thinking he did this to protect the scientist from himself. But in reality, clever Prince Bruno understood the implications of controlling a nanite cloud that could create or disassemble anything. That was not something for a commoner.

It was something for a King.

But not his father.

Him.

The detailed lectures the scientist gave him were more than enough to tell him how to perform the connection between the swarm and his brain.

It worked perfectly. With a thought, the nanites would mine XXXite. No holes in the ground. Refined metal would just appear on the surface ready for use or transport. His nanites would produce more nanites to fulfill the Prince's wishes.

Within a week he was producing more XXXite than all the mines on the planet.

Prince Bruno was able to think things into existence.

This made Bruno's family very rich and impoverished every one else on the planet. The miners had nothing to do, and lived in abject poverty. He could produce any food he wanted without the pesky Horsemen farms.

King Max was proud of his boy's new powers, but he realized the chaos this was causing to the society and culture of his planet. He made rulings to protect the people. He required the Prince to only make food for himself and his household, letting the Horsemen continue to grow food for themselves and the miners. He ordered the mines to stay open to give the people jobs, even if meaningless ones.

He funneled some of his resources into education, trying to give the miner's children something else to do than the dead end of following their parents. He created the first space fleet of Xerces to explore the system and visit their trading partners, which was mostly Kitch because of the disadvantageous location of Xerces in the portal network.

At first the Prince was fine with all of this. Money meant very little to him when he could create anything he wanted with a thought. He mostly kept to his castle and created things. Some of these were good, like the space fighters and scout ships he made. Others were darker. He made a whole race of mechanical little men and played games of war with them. When he got bored, he loaded the lot into a spaceship and shot them off into space.

He had created a self-sustaining race. That was when he first thought himself a god. He turned himself to controlling humans then. He experimented with sending his nanites into people's bodies and changing them. This turned out to be more of a problem than anticipated. Most biological beings have extensive defenses for stopping tiny nano machines. Because isn't that what bacteria and viruses are?

King Max was shocked when he first encountered a Horseman marked by Prince Bruno. The Prince's swarm couldn't live in a person's body, but they could live on the surface and burrow in to leave marks. These were the God King's marks, and you still see them today.

The King ordered his son to stop the tattooing and to stop experimenting on people, both human and horsemen.

Bruno acquiesced without complaint.

Within a month King Max came down with a painful infection. It lingered for weeks twisting him in pain. The Prince and his mother spent every day at his bedside until he died.

His mother, who would have been Queen, abdicated and ran to a convent in the desert on the opposite side of the planet from the capital and the Prince's palace.

Bruno ascended to the throne and twisted all the benevolence his father had begun.

He closed the mines and compelled the humans into the military. The Horsemen's food would supply his fleets.

Ruling one planet was not enough for God King Bruno. He wanted more. He looked for systems to conquer. Unfortunately for him, Xerces was located out in the boonies of the galaxy. The only system close via portal was Kitch. So they became his target.

It was then he learned the limits of his powers—the planet of Xerces Prime itself. The nanites could not leave. The one time he took a trip off world he realized his powers were gone as soon as they exited the atmosphere. He ordered the ship down before anyone else noticed and he never left again.

On the planet his nanites could build ships. His human population could be compelled to man them.

Then he threatened a very young Queen Natalie. Actually at

first he tried to woo her. She wasn't interested. Plus God King Bruno couldn't leave his planet, so it was hard to court the queen. After she sent him a message explaining in less than kind details all the reasons she would rather marry a squirrel than him, God King Bruno declared war.

He sent his fleet to attack Kitch. The Xerces Navy was brand new and inexperienced. The ships they had were not great because they came primarily from the mind of the King, and they had to be built in atmosphere. There were no huge destroyers, or mega-craft carriers.

They burst through the portals without warning and attacked any habitation they could find. There was no plan of attack and little intelligence. It was just the berserker rage of an oppressed people who had a chance to make a better life away from their home planet and their God King if they could control the Kitch system.

They outnumbered the Kitch forces two to one.

Everyone on Kitch knows the story after that, though few on Xerces do.

The Flying Monkeys were experienced pilots. They literally flew circles around the Xercians. The Kitchians had battleships and craft-carriers. The first wave of Xercian ships came through the portals and did damage. But as Flying Monkey fighters powered into the outer system, the battle ships blocked the portal from Xerces. Nothing that came through lasted long under the cannons of the battleships.

It was at this point the Queen asked for a neutral mediator to get God King Bruno to agree to a ceasefire. Kantar agreed to send their best diplomat, Cynwrig Pembroke. Kitchian intelligence had learned from prisoners how powerful God King Bruno was on his own world. So Cynwrig and the Queen required Bruno to come to them.

He refused.

The Queen ordered her fleet through the portal. The craft-carrier's fighters destroyed everything in space. The battleships bombarded Xerces from orbit—outside of the power of the God King.

Finally God King Bruno agreed to negotiate, and sent two ambassadors to Kitch. The First Ambassador was his most loyal servant, Gustav Krall. The Second Ambassador was Alexandr Prazak, a trusted advisor to the king who managed to ride the line that kept him in the King's graces while also allowing him to tell the king what he needed to hear.

The First Ambassador was all bluster and demands. He was the voice of God King Bruno, demanding everything from surrender to the Queen's loins, threatening the God King would rain fire on every planet in the Kitch system if his demands weren't met.

It wasn't until Cynwrig discovered the Second Ambassador's abilities that peace was even given a chance.

In the end Second Ambassador Alexandr was able to convince God King Bruno to accept a peace treaty.

———

"ON XERCES it was a disgrace for us ambassadors," said Alexandr to Space Girl Red. "Gustav was sent to the mines, and I was exiled to be the only ambassador to Kitch."

"Sent to the mines?" asked Red, "I thought you said there were no longer any mines. That the nanites just brought the minerals to the surface a molecule at a time."

"Yes, and that is how poor Gustav was taken to the source of XXXite. One molecule at a time," said Alexandr. Red shuddered. "It is the most common punishment for those that anger the God King."

"There are two ambassadors now."

"Yes, I am old. I will soon need a replacement. So the God King, in his wisdom, sent one of his most loyal servants, a former captain in the Navy, to be my second."

"Ctirad Drahoslav."

"Yes, the one you so humiliated in the dance battle tonight." Alexandr smiled. "I am sure he has already sent a scathing report on you to the God King. Ctirad will use a private courier. There are a number of smugglers and the like available at the space port."

"Why are you telling me this? Why this secret meeting?"

The older man leaned forward, "Because you need to know it. You may be the hope of the people of Xerces."

"We Space Girls, and Home itself, do not get involved in other people's wars. Everyone must fight their own battles."

The man leaned back showing his age as he closed his eyes. "Then let us hope the Queen is more convincing than I am."

"You think the Queen will try and get me to intervene in your war?"

"We know she wants to meet with you. I expect it will be about this war/non-war she is fighting with the God King's pirates."

"So you admit they are yours?"

"Not in public. But to you, here, yes, they are ours. I expect they are part of some larger plan on the God King's part, though I am not privy to it. Don't forget he is clever."

———

"NO ONE MUST KNOW the contents of this data coin," said Ctirad Drahoslav, Second Ambassador of Xerces. "I'm trusting you to put it in the hand of the God King yourself. The symbol on it will gain you audience."

Space Girl Blue stood in the deep shadow of the space port.

She wore a black skin tight jump suit. One hand she extended to take the coin. The other held a black raygun behind her back. "Of course. It is safe with me. For a price of course."

"The God King will pay you plenty when he reads this."

"He had better, or I will be back to extract payment from you, my friend."

Ctirad shivered at the tone, but he was unworried. Either the God King would pay her handsomely, or she would end up in the mines. Either way she wouldn't be coming for him. Still he was glad Venuše was with him. Her assassin skills would protect him should this smuggler turn hostile.

"You can go now," said Blue. "And take your girl friend with you." Her hand moved from behind her back and pointed to an alley opening a couple of meters to his right.

Venuše slipped out of the opening. She wore nothing but black shorts and a hood to cover her white hair. In each hand she held a wicked looking curved blade etched with arcane symbols. With skin that reflected nothing, she looked like a shadow as she slid up next to the Second Ambassador.

"She's not my girlfriend. She's my guard."

"Whatever. You are leaving first and if I see you again, I'll show you why you don't bring knives to a gunfight, assassin." Blue's muzzle never wavered from the dark woman's eyes.

Ctirad wanted to say something more, but he was tired and defeated. It had been a long disappointing night, with the dance contest and now a secret meeting. So he just turned from the smuggler and walked away. Behind him Venuše looked at the woman's gun for a long moment, then made a quick pattern of movements before turning to follow her charge.

Two steps later she turned to check on the other woman, but Blue was gone.

———

SPACE GIRL BLUE didn't think she would ever stop laughing. There were tears running down her face from watching the dance contest video. It was the primary part of the message on the Xercian's heavily encrypted data coin. Buck was still gloating about his ability to figure out the key so quickly.

"Well done, Red," Blue said to the screen as she rewound to watched the part with the monkey dancing. "Simia Fluxus. As dance. That was smart too. Must have met the Flying Monkeys before." Which reminded her, "Buck, any sign I was detected?"

"Naah. The jet bike got you out of the city without coming up on anyone's scans. Nothing on the military or police bands."

"And at the space port? Did the monkeys catch I'd used their secret trampoline to get into the base?"

"Don't think so. They made no changes when you came in or out."

"Ok. Guess I got away with it." She turned back to the video message. "Dark spot here really wants this God King Bruno guy to do bad things to our Rainbow mate."

"Yeah. He was quite detailed. Almost as if he knew what the God King was capable of, Blue."

She nodded thoughtfully and stared off into the distance thinking. Her flying saucer was parked under a canopy of trees on the shoreline. It was a good thirty kilometers from the furthest outskirts of the city. They had come down using the cover of night and hid. She'd use her jet bike to get into the city to look for work. Smuggling wasn't her first choice, but this particular job had looked easy and very lucrative.

"A God King, huh," she said. "Sounds extra pretentious. Know anything about him?"

"According to local sources he is the ruler of a system one portal away that Kitch fought a war with a few years back. The local government thinks they are responsible for the pirate problem they have now." He paused a moment for dramatic effect, then continued. "He's quite rich. The only ruler of one of the biggest sources of XXXite in this part of the galaxy."

"Now that does sound interesting," she got a big grin on her face. "I have an idea that could make us a lot of money and give Red a little bit of payback for the World Heart thing.

"Plot a course to the Xerces portal. We'll lift as soon as the sun sets."

"Sure, babe," Buck answered. "What ya going to do for the rest of the day?"

She unzipped her jumpsuit and said, "I think I'll get a bit of a tan. The beach looks lovely." A couple minutes later she was running toward the water with the sun glimmering off her olive skin.

———

IT TOOK Buck about an hour to develop a voice profile for Second Ambassador Ctirad. Then he developed a speech profile based on how the Xercian had attempted to persuade God King Bruno to have Red rendered into pieces. Buck could now gush about something just like the Second Ambassador. Once he had all of that knowledge, he and Blue came up with a new voice-over for the dance contest video.

"Great and mighty God King Bruno, I believe I have finally found a woman worthy to be your queen. She is beautiful, with the body of a goddess." The video cut to Red walking down the stairs in fluid motion. He continued to gush on her good looks over a montage.

"She is wanted by all the men that see her," over video showing her and Prince Alfred whispering to one another. "You would be taking from the future king of Kitch if you were to secure her as your bride."

"But she is not just an incomparable beauty, she has unparalleled grace on the dance floor." More images of her dancing with the Prince, then her solo dance at the beginning of the contest. "As I have so many times before, I competed against these Kitchians in the contest of the dance. But even I had to bow before her talent." Careful cuts made his final kneeling slide into an act of worship.

"While you have no need of martial talent being a god yourself, my lord, Space Girl Red is a match even for the dreaded Flying Monkeys." The video made Red and Captain Powell's Simia Fluxus dance look like a fight to the death.

As the short film went back to images that had been enhanced to make Red practically glow with beauty, the Second Ambassador's voice gave the call to action. "I have found one of her sisters from her home world, who can explain their strange customs of marriage. You, God King, make your own rules, but as an ambassador I implore you to grant her minuscule requests. They will prove your worthiness to the whole of the Woman World, because you can give gifts from your great riches.

"I expect that if you conclude these negotiations quickly this spirited beauty will be yours, very soon."

———

"BLUE, you are a without parallel in your vengeance," said Buck when they were finished.

"No, you have outdone yourself, Buck. No other flying saucer could have faked it so well," said Blue. "You have reencrypted it on the data coin?"

"Yes, of course."

"Well, then let's get on our way." Minutes later Blue's flying saucer slid out of Kitch 10's atmosphere and headed for the portal leading to Xerces.

CHAPTER 10
THE PROPOSAL

"RED, YOU MUST MARRY ME," said God King Bruno of Xerces. He sat on his palanquin carried by four Horsemen. Bruno was a slender man with obsidian skin and shockingly blonde hair that would cascade to his waist if he were standing. His muscular chest gleamed in the light of the Red sun. Little red atoms spun lazily around the points of his platinum crown.

"Ummm, no," said Space Girl Red. A hundred meters behind her was her flying saucer. She'd come here to deliver a message from Queen Natalie as a special envoy. God King Bruno had only glanced at the peace proposal and then moved on to this command.

"Why not? You would be Queen of Xerces. Every luxury would be yours. You could settle down here and do what ever you would like. Plant a garden. Make art. Study the great writings of the universe."

"I'm a Space Girl. I could have stayed home and done all of that. I'm just here to deliver that message. You've got it. I could stay a little while if you want to send a reply to Queen Natalie."

God King Bruno's brow furrowed. He tilted his head. "I just proposed marriage to you. You can't just say no."

One side of Red's mouth rose. "I can't? I'm pretty sure I just did."

The Horsemen moved slightly as if their footing was suddenly unsteady. A flush came to God King Bruno's face, but he put on a smile. "No, I am king."

"I know that. That's why I just gave you a data coin addressed to God King Bruno." Red replied. "Mail delivery doesn't make me one of your subjects nor your girl friend."

"You are on my planet!"

"King, I go to lots of planets. That's what the flying saucer is for," she said, motioning back to her ship. "I'm not about to marry you 10 seconds after meeting you. Why do you want to marry me anyway? You don't even know me."

"But I have heard so much about you. About your beauty, wisdom, talent, and splendor. Your beauty lives up to everything I had been told. So the others must be true and you are the only female on this planet worthy of me."

"Who told you that?" Red said with a chuckle.

"Why your sister, Space Girl Blue. She who knows you best."

Red started shaking her head and rolling her eyes. "Of course it was Blue." She smiled in spite of herself. "Let me tell you a couple of things about my 'sister' Blue. We've been rivals since we were kids. If she told you I was beautiful and wise she had some reason for doing so, but it won't be for your - and especially not my — good."

When Red paused for a long moment, God King Bruno broke in, "She was right about your beauty. You are the most succulent of females. Your breasts are like full gangla fruit hanging on the tree. Your waist like the neck of a Tulon bird. Your hips like the curves..."

Red raised a hand and interrupted, "Whoa. Whoa there, big guy. Let's stop with the frankly disturbing description of my body parts. Let me tell you the second thing about Blue by asking you a question.

"What's missing?"

God King Bruno was perplexed, "What's missing?"

"Yeah, which of your greatest treasures is now gone. I assume Blue is also gone by now, and she probably took the most valuable thing or things she could load into her saucer."

"Are you implying she stole from me?"

"I'm just saying it, not implying it."

"She left two days ago and nothing is missing from the royal treasury."

Red look suspicious. "Nothing? Have you checked? Just look for the most valuable thing to an off-worlder. That's probably what she took."

"Well, she did leave with that, but not in theft." God King Bruno replied and smiled. "It was the Esaul power crystal riviere. Glowing blue with the power of a dozen planets and the beauty of a galaxy."

"And you say she didn't steal it? Why did you give it to her?"

"Why for your dowry, of course."

"Of course," Red sighed. "All right King Bruno, I'm going to try and explain this so we can move on to the important stuff. My rainbow mate Space Girl Blue and I have a bit of a tiff going on. We both want to be the first in our Rainbow to achieve Womanhood you see. It is a very high honor. Recently we both did some big things, but in the end I succeeded and she got kind of embarrassed by it. So she owes me one.

"She has this whole rob from the rich, give to the poor thing going on. She did it with the Zoran recently. And now it looks like she's conned you, too." Red didn't feel it wise to point out Blue only stole from scumbags, and God King Bruno was at the top of that list. "You see there is no such thing as a dowry on Home. Our woman pick men worthy of them, court them mostly off world and only bring them Home to marry after we are sure of their quality and honor. Never would we allow one of us to be traded like chattel. But you don't know that out here in the backwater of the galactic arm. She saw a chance and took advantage of you. If you want to get some kind of revenge for that, take it up with her. Me, I'm not involved in this con. I'm just here to deliver that message from Queen Natalie."

Red settled back on her heels, with her hands on her hips. *That should get through to him,* she thought.

"You are saying that your sister…"

"Rainbow mate. Not sister."

The King waved this away, "…your sister lied to me about you marrying me. You then came here and decided I wasn't worthy to be your husband. Rejecting me, the God King of Xerces, on my own world—a world I have total domination over and where my magic makes everything happen."

Again the Horsemen jittered ever so slightly. The hairs on the back of Red's neck rose, and her tattoos tingled as even Astroboy a hundred meters away caught the angry change in God King Bruno.

"Space Girl Blue lied to you. I had nothing to do with it."

"But you don't consider me worthy of you." He stood on his palanquin. The tiny red atoms zipped back into his crown in fear. Red thought hard at Astroboy, *power-up the impellers and prepare to lift fast.* The God King continued, "That is not for you to decide. I will no longer make you my queen. But I will keep you as a concubine. You will learn your place in my service." He waved his hands dramatically in her direction. "And my power on this world."

Her jumpsuit started to dissolve. She could see the nanites like a mist in the air around her. She pulled her rayguns off her belt, flipped the selector to disintegrator and waved it at the cloud. But that was a useless gesture. Trying not to point the muzzle where it would hit the King or his guards was never going to get a cloud of pests.

"Oooo, the famed Space Girl raygun. My magic will enjoy analyzing and copying that," said God King Bruno.

She was naked now and she could feel the nanites crawling over her skin like a million ants. *Forget the nanites. Go for the source,* Red thought and pointed the gun at Bruno. She pulled the trigger and realized it was no longer there. Looking down she saw her guns were slowly disintegrating like a time-lapse of decay. *When they breech the plasma chamber we're in trouble.* She hurled the crumbling guns, which were now a dark grey shrinking silhouette, toward the God King. Then she turned and sprinted toward her Flying Saucer.

Astroboy had the shield up and it was visible. Which it shouldn't be, but it was covered in a light grey film. The nanites trying to get at the ship. She sprinted harder. She could feel through her tattoos Astroboy anticipating her arrival. "If I don't make it, you run, Astroboy," she willed in his direction.

Then her feet went cold. Looking down they were covered in the silver metal XXXite. It was flowing out of the ground and up her legs. Her ankles went stiff and she stumbled, but she was so close. She bent at the knees and leapt for the shield, flattening her body into a dive. The silver flowed over her chilling all of her body as it covered her skin. She could feel tendrils working through her hair. It encircled her throat and sealed her mouth closed. At the top of her trajectory, just when she realized she might not make it to the shield in time, the world went black as the metal covered her eyes.

Then she accelerated way too fast as the plasma bubbles of her rayguns exploded behind her.

———

ASTROBOY DROPPED his shield for just a second as he saw her leap toward him. It was the worst possible second because the plasma explosions happened right then and the bubble of nanites collapsed toward him. He watched in horror as the blast propelled his Space Girl, now completely encased in XXXite, inside the bubble of the shield. Her new velocity carried her out the other side of the shield as he raised it back up.

She was gone and he had other problems to worry about.

The Flying Saucer had taken a big hit from the two raygun chamber explosions. Those guns were powered with the same energy that ran his repulsor engines used for the fastest sub-light travel he was capable. Even as small as they were, they were enough to blow the entire saucer off the ground. Because he had the impellers on already and his mistress had ordered him to run, he used the explosion to launch. The heat scorched his hull black on that side, which was mostly cosmetic. It was just soot from the things burned by the explosion, including all of the nanites on that side of the ship.

But the nanites on the other side were now free to go after him. He could feel them already starting to crawl over his skin. Many of them just started burrowing into his hull, eating at the XXXite and unobtanium alloy. A contingent of them went straight for the repulsor pods at the top of his fins. He could feel them eating through the casing, which was much thinner than the hull. If they got in there and breached the repulsor chamber, he was never going to be able to rescue his mistress.

He knew the trajectory she'd been launched into and easily calculated her landing point, but with great regret he poured power into the impellers and rocketed upward, desperate to get out of the atmosphere before he was destroyed.

———

HALF CHARRED AND PITTED, Astroboy looked like just another piece of debris floating in the ring of Xerces's nearest moon. The nanites had stopped working the second he'd reached orbit. They hadn't gotten through the repulsor's power chamber which was a good thing, but they had destroyed the control circuitry.

His repair drones were crawling across the hull doing what they could. There was no way the repulsors could be repaired outside of a shipyard with a Home engineer guiding the work. His Space drive was intact, but with just impellers it would take him a week to get to the only portal in the system.

The other casualty of the nanites had been his antenna array. That left no subspace bursts to call for help, and outside Spaceways there was no instant communication anyway.

There was no getting help for Space Girl Red.

She was alive. He could still sense her presence on the planet, but just barely. The distance was part of it, but there was something else in the way. She'd been completely cut off once the metal had encased her and the tattoos that were her antenna array among other things. Her signal had returned weakly about the time he was halfway to his hiding place. He considered turning around right then and getting her, but the signal had gotten weak immediately.

They must have taken her prisoner and put her somewhere underground. All that was left to him was to wait and depend on her to get free. Then he would go get her and she'd know how to get them out of this system.

———

"WAKE UP, SPACE GIRL," which was accompanied by a hard slap across the face. Space Girl Red's head exploded in pain. Not from the slap so much as the movement it caused. She had the mother of all headaches. Probably from oxygen deprivation and impact. She remembered the world going black as she leapt for her flying saucer. Covered completely in hard metal, there was no air. Probably a good thing though considering the explosion around her. She had hit and bounced which hadn't hurt much because she was encased in metal. Then it had seemed like forever before she'd passed out from a lack of air.

Red opened her eyes so whoever the speaker was wouldn't hit her again. *This must be the dungeon,* she thought. It looked almost stereotypical with the rough stone walls and fire burning torches lighting the room. Her arms and legs were attached at wrist and ankle to a large X of something cold and smooth. Metal or stone maybe. She was naked of course and the person in front of her was the cause of all this.

God King Bruno. His hair was different, she thought blearily. Wasn't it longer before? Must have lost some of it in the explosion. How had he survived? She wouldn't have if it hadn't been for the metal he encased her in.

"Something is wrong with your hair," she said trying not to move her head much.

"My hair! That is what you have to say? You blow-up the entire party sent to greet you because you don't want to marry me. And now the first thing you want to talk about is my hair." He grabbed his hair and pulled it over his shoulder in front of him. She could see the end was black. "My magic protected me, but not all of my *hair* survived. Though more than yours."

Red tried to feel her hair, but her head hurt. How do you feel your hair anyway? "You blew us up. Not me. Shouldn't try to take apart a raygun unless you know what you are doing."

God King Bruno looked perplexed for a moment, then it passed. "All of this is your fault. If you had just acted like you are supposed to, none of this would have happened." He reached out and grabbed her hair, though it didn't feel right to Red. Like he was having trouble getting a grip on it. Still he got enough to pull her head painfully back.

"You could have been a queen. Then a concubine." His face was almost nose to nose with her. He brought up his other hand and ran a sharp fingernail across the cheek he had slapped red. "Now you will be a new kind of plaything for me. Your time here will be only as long as you beg for it to be, and a day longer."

"Huh?" She asked. "You mean if I beg you to stop torturing me, you'll only do it for one more day?"

"Yes. I know you are a proud Space Girl. I know you will resist and I will enjoy making you beg. Beg for my mercy. Beg for the pain to end." He shook her head by her short hair. "I will enjoy breaking you."

"You make weird rules," Space Girl Red slurred. "Ok. Here we go."

The woman hanging from the stone cross looked the God King of Xerces in the eyes, pursed her lips and said in her sweetest little girl voice, "Oh, please stop. Please don't torture me anymore, mister God King man. Stop. I beg you, stop."

Bruno released his grip and jumped back like she had suddenly become piping hot. "Wait. What?"

"OK, now that that's out of the way. You've got one day to do your worst. Get after it." Red said, "Do you mind if I nap while you torture me?"

God King Bruno screamed in inarticulate rage. Then he started slapping her. All over her body his slapping stung, but wasn't particularly painful. She passed out when he hit her in the head again.

————

HOT WATER SPLASHED in her face woke her. It scalded and turned her skin red everywhere it touched. The skin that wasn't already red from the God King's attacks. She screamed at the shocking pain of it.

God King Bruno let the water run off her for a moment before stepping in close. "You destroyed my Horsemen. So I thought you should spend some time with one of them." He motioned and Xercians in nothing by shorts dragged something over near her. It was the blackened corpse of one of a Horseman. She assumed one that had been carrying the King's palanquin, though it was impossible to tell now. Everything was black from the fire. Much of the flesh was gone and you could see bone and organs. The stench was horrible. She gagged involuntarily and her head exploded again in pain.

God King Bruno held out his hand and a gas mask materialized in it. He pushed it onto his face and it stuck without straps. He came back over to her. "I would have let you spend time with one of my guards, all of whom have horrible stinking burns as well, but they need medical care. I go now to check on them. While there I will ponder what should be done to you to make up for their burns and pain."

He turned and walked out of the dungeon, followed by the servants. She was left alone with the dead Horseman.

THERE WAS no sense of time when she was alone. The cross seemed custom made for her because her feet just reached the floor in her shackles. But if they were flat on the cold stone, her shoulders were pulled and the wrist manacles cut into her wrists until her hands went numb. She could relieve it by pushing up onto her toes, but could only hold that for so long before the muscles in her feet burned.

She looked up at her wrists. Metal manacles were cinched on her wrists with a chain that went out to the end of the steel cross. There was spike there and it passed through a link in the chain. By changing the link the spike went through they could customize the length of the chain.

When she looked down, she couldn't see her feet. The loops that encircled her ankles we tight against the bottom of the cross and caused her to lean forward slightly. Her chest kept her from being able to see them but she felt there was a little more give in them than her wrists. Probably because they had to be loose enough to let her move her calf up and down when she stood on her toes. She shuddered to think there was someone who had figured all of this out. Probably by trial and error. Someone else's painful experience.

Could she pull her foot free if she pointed it and pulled? She started to try it when she heard noise from the door.

God King Bruno strode into the room. He was dressed in a new orange skirt and his hair looked freshly cleaned and styled. But the first thing she noticed was his hand. He held it weirdly while waving it slightly, but it was the glow around it that caught her attention. Angry orange tendrils of mist swirled around it a little like flame, a little like smoke.

He stopped in front of her. "I visited my guards. Two of them had already died and I had to put two more out of their misery." He opened his non-glowing hand and it held a small bottle. "These are them." He held the bottle close to her eyes so she could clearly see the black dust inside.

"Their deaths are on you," he said, popping the lid off the bottle with his thumb. He took the bottle and shook the dust out on her. "And now you will wear them forever."

He made a fist with the glowing hand and punched her hard in the stomach. The impact was considerably less than sparring with Space Woman Black, but where he struck burned even after he pulled back his hand.

He examined his handy work with a smile on his face. "Yes,

that will do nicely. It would say something to anyone who sees your belly in the future." Then he looked back at her, "But you aren't going to live long enough for that to happen."

He walked back a little. The servants he had brought with him pressed themselves against the walls. Between two of them there was a wooden rectangle that had not been there before. Had they brought it in when Bruno came in?

Red, you are not being very observant, she thought to herself.

Well, the glowing hand and all the torture pain is distracting, she answered herself.

Stop being a wuss. You are a Space Girl.

Like you are any better. We haven't even heard what he's been saying because you wanted to have a conversation in your head.

Red brought her attention back to the God King. "So I am going to mark your body. Then everyone will know whose you were before you died."

Her eyes weren't focusing so well. She let her head roll around on her shoulders for a minute and then rested it against one aching shoulder. *Maybe if I only use one eye it will be better.* She tried by closing an eye and trying to focus on her torturer.

The glow in his hand hadn't been diminished by the punch. How did it glow anyway? Wasn't the point of his God King powers that he could summon nanites anywhere on the planet? So why power some up and then carry them to the dungeon?

He was monologuing again. Something about how great he was. How the whole universe was going to know it one day. He was going to send a message to all the women of Home. Make an example of her. How all the woman would fear him. Blah, Blah, Blah.

Must mean he can't summon nanites everywhere equally, she thought. Had he done any magic here? She didn't really want to relive her tortures, but she didn't think anything had involved nanites till he burned her. This place must not allow it.

So to do whatever it was he planned for her — not paying any attention to his words meant she wasn't getting a preview — he had to bring special nanites with him.

The God King started moving back toward her and stopped. "Wake her," he snapped. One of the grimy servants grabbed a bucket and filled it from a spigot on the wall. Then she splashed it on Red. She had been expecting more hot water like last time. Which probably made the cold water feel even more shocking. She squealed in surprise.

He didn't say anything as he walked up to her with his flaming hand held just so. She found this more disconcerting than all his lecturing. A little less than arms' reach away he stopped and extended the hand toward her bare chest. She tried to pull her body back, to move away from the hand, but her weak legs and bonds made this impossible. Right at the midline of her chest he extended a finger and touched her sternum.

Her heart stopped.

Electricity, or something that felt like electricity that was liquid fire, coursed and jittered in all directions from his touch. It climbed up the bone toward her neck. Over her chest in both directions. Down her belly fanning out as it went.

It hurt beyond imagination. And all the time, which was probably seconds but felt like years, she knew she was dead. He had killed her. Stopped her heart with his magic powers. *And early*, she griped a little to herself.

God King Bruno pulled his hand back and looked at her chest. Red's eyes were closed, her head back, desperately feeling for her heart beat.

Then there was a thump in her chest, which rapidly started pumping blood to her battered body.

God King Bruno's hand had stopped burning. He grabbed her hair again and pulled her face up. "You are mine now. Not as Queen, which you threw away. Not as concubine, which you rejected. But as prisoner. Plaything. Exhibition." Holding on to her head, he pivoted around to be next to her and said, "Show her."

Two of the gaunt servants grabbed the wooden rectangle she had noticed earlier, carried it closer, and turned it around. It was a mirror. In it God King Bruno stood next to a battered and dirty woman. His hand was in her short bright red hair, holding her tear streaked face up to the mirror where she hung from the X-frame. But it wasn't her face or hair you noticed.

It was her chest. She remembered the smooth pale skin that covered her chest. Now it was covered with a black explosion of jagged lines. Not carefully drawn perfect lines like her stars, still visible at shoulder and waist. Like branches of a tree or tendrils of lightning, these lines spread over most of her upper torso, with one line going further in each direction. One went up her throat to almost her adam's apple. Another arced across each painfully red nipple and down the other side of her breasts. The last ran down, over, and through her belly button. Below her belly button there was a dark black fist print, with small tendrils radiating from it.

"Someone take a picture," God King Bruno ordered. "I want the universe to know I captured and killed a Space Girl."

The servants rushed around frantically looking for a camera. Apparently they had not anticipated that request. Red continued to stare at her reflection. She noticed in particular that the thrashing of her legs had actually pushed the restraints almost to her knee. Over the thickest part of her calf. *They open when stretched.*

God King Bruno dropped her head and started screaming at the hapless servants, berating them for not having a recording device in the dungeon. "Fine, we will do it tomorrow before we finish her. Get out of here all of you." They rushed to comply and soon it was just her and him in the dungeon. He came up to her then and ran his hand lightly over the burn mark on her chest. "You are mine." His body was so near now she could feel the heat of it aggravating every wound. "I would take you now, except you are so disgusting," he sneered and turn away from her. "Must remember to send a copy to that imbecile Ctirad. Let him see you now. How could he recommend something like you to me?"

Then he was gone and she was alone.

CHAPTER 11
THE ESCAPE

FOR A LONG MOMENT she just hung there. Finally she raised her head and thought, *Light, give me strength.* Across the room the mirror leaned against the wall. Not at a perfect angle, but she could see most of herself. It was not a pretty sight.

Space Girl training included SERE — Survival, Evasion, Resistance and Escape. The training was brutal and thorough and included resistance to torture. It was early in your training before the Space Girl HQ did their even more savage training. She remembered thinking then she was pretty sure they weren't allow to actually kill or maim her. That had gotten her through. It wasn't until the last year of training a Space Cadet got her implants.

She took a deep breath and concentrated. Her tattoos flashed and much of the pain floated out of her consciousness. She discovered her legs worked, and stood on her toes to rest her shoulders. Once that ache was lessened she started pulling her left knee toward her right hip. First slowly, getting the manacle off her calf. She pointed her foot like a dancer and jerked hard again. The first time it didn't get over the heel of her foot. The second time it did, and one leg was free.

She repeated the action with the other leg till it too was free. With her legs no longer forced apart she was able to stand up, releasing all of the tension on her arms and the chains. With a flipping motion she got the chains off the spike at the top of the cross. The shackles were still on her wrists, with a length of chain attached, but she was free. It felt so good and hurt so badly to hang her arms at her sides. She stumbled to a wall and slid to the floor next to the door.

She must have dozed off because she startled awake at a feeling. Was someone coming? No. The feeling was inside her. It was Astroboy. The feeling was faint, but worried. Moving to the door must have let him connect with her tattoos. If he was getting bio-metrics, he was probably distraught.

She eased the door open and saw a staircase. She forced herself upright and began to slowly and, as quietly as possible, climb the stairs.

———

ASTROBOY HAD DONE everything he could to fix himself. He was airtight and could use his impeller engines. Then he waited. Xerces Prime had two moons. One a small pitted ball of rock about 4 light seconds from the planet. The other even smaller, but surrounded by a ring of debris and 2 light seconds from the planet. They rotated opposite each other. On maximum impeller he could be back on the planet in 20 seconds give or take, depending on where on the planet and its rotation's relation to the moon.

What had he learned from the previous days terrors? The nanites could not get through his shields. It was only when he'd had to drop them that they had been able to attack him. When Red called him, Astroboy figured he could get to his Space Girl in half a minute and be safe. Picking her up would mean letting the nanites have another go at him, but he could be back out of the atmosphere in just a couple of seconds. It had taken considerably longer the first time because of the blast and his own surprise at the attack. Sitting alone in space waiting for a sign, he ran simulation after simulation.

Flying saucers couldn't fire their weapons without the pilot giving them permission. Space Girl Red had told him to run, not to fight. This meant he couldn't just go back in guns blazing to rescue her. There was some grey area when it came to defending himself, but he wouldn't know if weapons would be available until the moment. Then some subconscious part of him would let him use the weapons or not. Luckily there didn't seem to be much, if any, Xercian Navy activity near the planet. Which seemed odd, but he was thankful for any luck he got.

Then he could sense her. The signal wasn't strong; he couldn't even locate exactly where it was on the planet. Once second she just barely existed to him, the next he could sense her being.

The signal was getting stronger. He started powering the impeller drive. Waiting till he knew where she was. Planning his run.

Bio-metrics came through first. She was damaged. She'd accessed her pain block, and still he felt her hurting. That was not good. *Where are you, Space Girl Red? Let me know and I'll be there.*

———

SHE'D THROWN the chains over her shoulders to keep them from rattling which meant she had to keep her hands near her body. This made climbing hard without hands to support and hurting legs. She extended her senses as much as she could. The dungeon area seemed empty. A floor up from where she had been held, there was a large open area with multiple cells on either side. They were all empty. A little surprising because she figured God King Bruno would keep lots of playthings around. There was a bench with some tools on it, including a chisel and hammer she might be able to use to get the chains off. But it would make too much noise and she didn't risk it.

Another set of stairs lead to a large round room. It too was empty, but no longer seemed to be a dungeon. There were windows periodically around the perimeter and a glance showed her it was night. Looking up she saw balconies around the sides about where you would expect floors to be.

It was a tower, which appeared to be about 6 stories tall. Red looked around for a way to get up. She noticed a staircase across the room. She wanted to just run across, but felt too weak and exposed. So she eased around the edge of the room. At one point she passed a closed door possibly leading out, but ignored it.

She could feel Astroboy more strongly. Her mind started planning how to climb to the top of the tower. Hopefully there was an opening to the top of the building. From there she could call for the flying saucer, and if she was very lucky, and the Light shone on her, she could get away.

Every step on the stairs was a victory. The pain still throbbed, but it was the raw weakness of torture and captivity that were eating at her. As she climbed, Astroboy became more and more real to her.

She heard a noise from below. The door on the first floor banged open and a loud group of people came into the tower. They were laughing and talking excitedly. A quick glance down showed a group of well dressed Xercian men and women moving behind single tall figure, God King Bruno.

She froze trying to be small for a moment. He was leading them toward the dungeon. *Probably going to show off his captured*

Space Girl, she thought. Looking desperately around she saw a ladder leading to a trap door a few meters ahead.

Below the noise quieted.

In her head Red thought, *Come get me now, Astroboy*, then she ran toward the ladder and started to climb. Her chains banged against the ladder as she climbed.

A sonic boom shook the whole building. Astroboy had come in hard and decelerated just above her. *He must be at the roof waiting for me now*, she thought. She pushed on the trap door and nothing happen. It was locked.

Below she heard an infuriated scream. "She's escaped!" It was God King Bruno. The burned pattern on her chest began to itch. *The nanites are waking up. He's ordered them to find me.*

The trap door seemed more locked the more she pounded on it. Then she yelled, "Astroboy, get me out of here. Use your weapons!"

———

IT HAD TAKEN 17.14 seconds to go from the moon's ring to hanging above the tower his Space Girl was escaping from. Her biometrics were the worst he'd ever seen. It was a miracle she was even standing, much less climbing toward him. She wasn't alone in the building, a group had entered just a few seconds before he hit atmosphere. God King Bruno was one of them.

With shields up, the nanites hadn't been a problem. Hanging there he could feel an increase in their number. They were swarming against his shield. He could sense them through Space Girl Red's tattoos. They had just activated somewhere on her skin. This was very bad, and he could do nothing. There was no way to open the hatch she was under. So close and yet so far away.

Then he heard her yell.

Inside him the restrictions on weapons released with a feeling of relief and angry power. After she yelled, she'd backed down the ladder to let him do something with the trap door.

That was not going to be enough.

The flying saucer moved from directly over the tower, to one side of it. He applied a strong tractor beam to the roof of the structure. Then he fired the main rayguns at the walls just below the roofline. In seconds he'd flown a circle all the way around the building, cutting the top off like an electric can opener. He flipped saucer and the tractor beam up, flinging the roof away.

———

"THAT WAS A BIT OF OVERKILL," Red said as the top of the tower flew away. She wished she had the energy to realize how cool it was. Astroboy looked like the most beautiful thing in the world hanging there. His shields were covered in grey nanites. The ship rotated to put the opening gangplank directly in front of her on the balcony. As it did, the anti personnel rayguns fired, clearing a small space for just a few seconds on the shield. The gang plank was there. The shield was down and she stumbled forward toward it. The ship's maneuver scooped her up as she fell on the metal entry way.

Her skin burned all over as every nanite began to eat at her skin.

She could tell the ship was already lifting and the gang plank was closed. Still the God King's curse was eating her. "Four seconds till we are out of the atmosphere, Ma'am. Hang on."

"Astroboy, shock me."

He understood immediately and despite the readings of torture on her biometrics, he sent electricity through her skin.

All of the nanites eating at her immediately died.

The Astroboy did the same thing to himself and sent electricity through his hull even as he climbed. The grey film eating at his hull turned to black and two seconds later they were out of the atmosphere. He pushed the impellers to maximum and headed for his hiding place.

———

"MA'AM, you need to get into the med pod," said Astroboy. Two of his repair drones scurried out of small hatches in the entry room. They moved to the battered woman sprawled on the floor. With quick use of their repair lasers, the chains and manacles fell off her wrists.

Red knew he was right. She was at the end of her strength and it was unlikely she'd survive much longer without medical help. She tried to push herself off the floor, but only got up a few millimeters before her hands slid out from under her. She opened her eyes and realized the floor was covered with blood. As was she.

Astroboy neutralized the ship's gravity. "You are weightless now, Red," he said quietly. "You don't have to go far. Push up again and grab the drones. They will get you to the medical pod."

One more time, she thought and pushed. She could feel herself float. Opening her eyes again, she found one of the drones directly under her hand now. She grabbed it.

The little drone moved slowly, not made to move her mass, into the central room of the saucer. Then to the left where a panel had opened next to the entry hall. Inside was a white area shaped like a bathtub stood on its end. She reached out and grabbed the door, using it to pull herself up. Each move left a sticky red hand print. Once vertical she pushed herself backwards into the space and the door closed over her.

A screen on the door lit up in front of her. Showing an outline of a human figure. A female voice that reminded her of Space Girl Green said, "Scanning. Please remain still. All will be well."

Red thought about the voice. The pitch was wrong for Green, too low. Closer to where Purple's voice was. Why did she think it sounded like Green? Then she got it. It was the tone and pace. This was healer talk.

"Scan complete," said the medical unit. The screen changed from a humanoid outline to a picture of an actual red human being. It took a second to realize that it was her. She was covered head to toe in blood, from a myriad of micro-wounds the nanites had given her. "Space Girl Red, you have experienced a great deal of physical trauma, especially to your dermis and involving blood loss. I recommend you be rendered unconscious while this unit attempts to heal you. Please understand, some of your injuries are beyond this unit's abilities. I recommend you seek a full medical facility as quickly as possible.

"Do you consent to being anesthetized?"

"Wait," she answered. "Astroboy, status. Can you take me to a hospital? Are we under attack?"

"Ma'am, I sustained damage to my repulsors and hull during the first attack and explosion. Additional damage was done to the hull during your rescue. Hull integrity has been maintained. Life support, power systems, and weapons are all functional. I recommend you allow yourself what healing my med pod can give you. I am very afraid for you."

This made her smile in spite of herself.

"I have found a safe hiding place as floating debris in the rings of the near moon. There is surprisingly little navy traffic here."

Red realized it wasn't going to matter if she gave consent soon, because she was going to pass out. "You are a good saucer,

Astro. Thank you for saving me." Was there anything else she should do? "Astroboy, you have full use of ship systems, including all weapons, until I awaken. Keep yourself safe."

"Yes, ma'am. I will. Now rest and leave it to me."

"Med pod, I consent to be treated for not more than 24 hours. Do your best in that time and wake me when it is over. I need the sleep," Red commanded and was asleep so fast she thought the med pod may have jumped the gun.

CHAPTER 12
RIDING A ROCKET

SPACE GIRL RED sat in the command chair of her flying saucer eating a huge, high protein sandwich. She was wearing a standard ship jumpsuit in her signature red and her feet were bare. It was zipped all the way up to the neck with only a single tendril of the God King's mark visible. The explosion had cut her bright red hair to a uniform 2cm all over. She'd shaved one side completely and clean up the other, leaving the top long. The new pixie cut showed off the silver comm snaking into one ear. It looked more like a piece of jewelry than communication equipment, even piercing her ear in two places. She would not be without Astroboy again.

"To recap, we've got no repulsors and the nearest portal is over 8 light hours from here. Which means at full impeller it would take us 80 hours to get there. That's across open space, to the only way in and out of the system, which would be the place most likely to have a Xercan Navy presence," Red said.

"Yes, Ma'am. Also there is no way to connect to the com-net from here and Xerces is not a system that allowed the gate transmitters. We have no way to send a message other than to get onto the Spaceways."

"Which we can do easily enough if we can get to the portal." She took a moment to gulp from a large mug of some green goop the med pod insisted she drink every three hours. Didn't taste nearly as bad as she'd expect it to. It contained collagen to supposedly rebuild her skin. Orange would have understood that better than she did. Red had found herself thinking about her rainbow mates a lot since she'd escaped. Well most of them.

"Has anything changed since I escaped? Did Bruno do anything to try and recapture me?"

"Not that I have noticed, Ma'am." Astroboy had also changed through this experience. She noticed he was more constantly in her presence. His voice was less formal and more careful. "But I have limited my scanning as not to give away our position."

"We can't sit here forever. Do a sweep. First of the rings, then the lunar system and then Xerces Prime orbit. Display and pause between each." She shifted in her seat and tossed her empty cup away. There wasn't much to see out the canopy, just astroids floating and the glowing moon in the center. You couldn't even see stars because of the reflected light.

The screen materialized in front of her and the moon and its rings were drawn in a red that quickly faded to black. "Next," she said.

The display zoomed out and she could see the other moon far away from the first one. Nothing else new appeared. "And now planetary orbit."

The moons got smaller and the planet drew in as an arch at the bottom of the screen. Then three red dots appeared. "What are those?" she asked.

The display zoomed and they took on the shape of rockets. Curved fins on the bottom of cylinders that ended in a point. "They appear to be rockets. I don't remember them being there when I went down to get you. Though we are about a quarter rotation away from where you were held."

"Mmmm, can you get anymore information on them? Are they missiles? Bombs?" She asked, "Maybe they are Collector ships, like the one my rainbow mate was trading with."

"They do not seem to be as large as that ship. I also cannot tell what kind of drive they may have. We are just too far away to get good information. I fear if we get closer, we will be detected by the planet."

Red thought for a moment, "Are they under power? They seem bunched up. Why are they even in orbit?"

"They do not seem to be under power. Actually if we assume orbit wasn't their aim, but rather just shot from the ground," Astroboy was calculating and dotted lines appeared behind the rocket and curved back to the surface, "it appears they were launched from where you were, though it could be anywhere on the planet depending on when they were launched."

"So maybe Bruno got mad and made some rockets to shoot at me, but they gave out as soon as they exited the atmosphere." She leaned back and spun her chair around thinking. "They could also be a trap. Something to lure us back near the planet. Might be booby trapped. So us making another speed run isn't going to happen."

Red stopped spinning suddenly and snapped her fingers. "You know I'm not Yellow, but I think we need to build something." She jumped up and headed down to her workshop.

———

"WHAT DO YOU THINK, ASTROBOY?" Space Girl Red said excited. "It is like a little you." Sitting on the workbench was indeed a little flying saucer. With the iconic shape, but this one was only about 2 meters in diameter and lacked the fins for repulsors. OK, and the canopy for the control room was replaced with a tractor beam emitter.

"While I can understand your thinking that, Ma'am," said Astroboy, "even in my current damaged state there are many differences in ability."

"Of course, it's a baby." Red patting the little ship affectionately. "And don't worry, you are still my favorite. What should we name it? Astrobaby?"

"What about Ass?"

She laughed, which felt good. "Ass, it is. Though I have to say that is a little juvenile on your part."

"Yes, Ma'am," he said, but she noticed he didn't offer another name.

"Okay, it has pretty strong impellers with lots of torque if it needs to tow the rockets. And tractors to do the actual towing. Have you finished melding the flight program with the drone brains?"

"Yes, Ma'am, and I believe it will be easily controlled from here."

"Great. Let's launch this and find out if those rockets work."

"Ummm, Space Girl, how do you plan to launch it?"

"From the entry room. Just open the gangway and throw it out."

"Yes, but how will you get it there?"

Red looked at the entrance to the workshop. It was a standard door, one meter wide and three meters tall. "Well, poop," she said.

"Indeed. Poop."

"Why didn't you warn me about this before we started building? I could have done assembly in the entry room."

"I thought you had a plan."

All she could do was laugh again. "OK, here's a plan. I'll roll it. Can the impellers withstand being rolled on?"

"Yes, Ma'am, they are quite sturdy. Though the friction will be significant."

"Hey, what if we turn off the AG again? Like you did for me when I needed to get to the med pod?"

"I believe that would allow you more leverage options."

"Great. Let me go change real quick. Might as well do the launch as soon as we get it moved. I'll put on my pressure suit."

———

AN HOUR later Astroboy had many new scrapes on the inside, and it was possible some of the vaults might not open again without a visit to a repair shop. Still the new drone saucer was in the entry room. Space Girl Red put on her bubble helmet and said, "Ok, Astroboy, close the hatch and pump the air out of here."

"Yes, Ma'am," he replied and the door behind her closed.

Anti-grav was still off and she floated at the top of the gangway. She stared at the floor while she waited for all the air to be recovered. The floor was clean, of course, but she still felt like she could see it slick with her blood.

She shook her head to clear it and started calculating how she was going to get the saucer out the gangplank without causing further damage to Astroboy. In the end it was just a matter of getting above it and pushing. She managed to not even scrape the sides of the gangway entrance.

The drone exited the ship vertical and drifted away till that orientation meant nothing. Then Astroboy took over and its impellers engaged.

The door slid shut and her external pressure gauge started rising.

"Astroboy, get your Ass over to those rockets," she said with a smile.

"How droll, Ma'am."

"Get your Ass in gear," she said while waiting. She laughed. "This is never going to get old."

———

IT TOOK the drone about 15 minutes to get to the rockets. Red had stripped out of her pressure suit and changed into a turtleneck and shorts. She was back in the control room by the time the drone started its survey. "What are the sensors saying?" she asked.

"Density shows they are mostly fuel tanks, Space Girl. There does not seem to be any part of them consistent with explosives. Though if someone were of a mind to, the fuel itself could be quite explosive."

She nodded. "Let's find out. Lock a tractor on one of them and let's see if they let us move them."

"Locking tractor."

The Space Girl could see what the drone saw, but tractor beams are invisible. Nothing seemed to happen, then she realized the planet behind the rocket was moving slightly. The drone had locked on and started moving.

"There seems to be no reaction to moving the rockets, ma'am."

"Then tell your Ass to bring me a rocket."

"As you wish, Ma'am."

———

I DON'T KNOW *why I bothered to change*, she thought, having changed back into her pressure suit. She was floating in space next to the rocket. She'd already sent the Ass back for another one. Under one arm she had a ship's drone. She put one hand on the rocket and gave it a very slow spin. She looked up and down it for some kind of access panel. But there were none. *Guess you don't need to work on the insides of something you think into existence.*

"No access panel, Astroboy," she said. "How does it even work, him thinking complex things like this rocket into existence?"

"I don't know, Ma'am. There must be some intermediate intelligence involved with some encyclopedic knowledge of how things work."

"Your ship's drone still going to be able to work on it?"

"It should, Space Girl. Please set its wheels on the rocket. They are magnetic."

She did as he asked and the little drone started sniffing around the rocket and sprouting arms. "The rocket's fuel tanks appear to be mostly full." Astroboy commented as he received detailed data from his drone. It scurried up and down the rocket for a few minutes. Then it stopped near the top and cut a hole in the hull with a laser. Another appendage held on to the scrap of metal. Then it stuck a number of appendages, including a light, into the opening.

"This is quite strange," mumbled Astroboy in her ear. "There doesn't actually seem to be a control computer."

"What?" Red used her jet pack to move over next to the hole. Then she rotated and wrapped her legs around the rocket to hold her in place. She looked into the opening. Indeed there was nothing but bare wires where a controller should be.

Curious she reached in and felt around. Then she pulled out her hand and looked at it. It was covered in black dust. She shuddered. "I think there were actual nanites controlling it. When they left atmosphere, they just stopped working."

Ass appeared near by and dropped off another rocket. "Do you think you could rig up a controller to fit in here?"

"Maybe to make the engines fire, but steering would be difficult."

Red noticed that if she shifted her weight right or left the rocket started to rotate under her. "Mmmm. How much thrust can we get out of one of these rockets? Enough to tow the ship?"

"Based on the fuel load, one rocket would tow me, but only about as fast as my impellers."

"What about three?"

"Obviously that would be three times as fast."

"Which would mean we could get to the portal in only 26 hours. Still moving pretty slowly."

"Actually, Ma'am, impellers just give the ship velocity. They don't accelerate. These rockets will give us constant acceleration, about a full G. Do that for a few hours and our velocity will be significant when we near the portal."

"Is it a problem to being going that fast when we enter the portal?"

"Not on the Spaceways. Though coming out we will have the same velocity we went in with, and no way to slow ourselves without repulsors."

"But we will be in the Kitch system and can call for help. Actually we can ask for help before we exit the Spaceways. Tell them we are coming."

"Indeed."

"I need some metal beams and a lot of cabling. And a welder."

———

"SPACE GIRL RED, are you sure about this? It is crazy even for you."

She had to smile. It was crazy. She was straddling a rocket. That rocket was attached to two other rockets in a triangle.

Between her legs and slightly in front of her was a big lever. All it did was control the thrust of the rockets. Using her jet pack, she could move the whole assembly side to side a bit. But the real steering was done by leaning.

"Just like riding a jet bike. Nothing to it."

"Except a jet bike doesn't have 40,000 newtons of thrust and isn't towing 50,000 kilograms of flying saucer."

"I thought you said you could handle keeping yourself in line."

"I can, Ma'am, as long as you aren't too crazy in your steering."

"What are the chances of that?"

"Not very good. In my experience, Ma'am."

She laughed and began to edge the lever forward. "Guess that depends on how you define crazy."

The cables went taut as the rockets moved away from the flying saucer. For a moment it felt like she had stopped moving. The flying saucer oriented itself directly behind her and she pushed forward. A throaty roar was transmitted through the hull. The rocket rumbled and vibrated between her legs.

Looking directly forward, the display in her helmet showed a cross hair. No matter how she moved her head, it always pointed in the direction the rockets were pointed. If she looked to the left, it disappeared to the right. There was also an arrow floating around the parameter of her vision. When she looked where it pointed a white dot appeared with the word *Portal* under it. That was where she needed to go.

They were moving now, slowly but surely. She leaned toward the arrow and the crosshairs started moving. Soon, by leaning left and right she had the portal dot in her field of view, but low. She leaned forward to push the nose down. When everything was lined up, she yelled, "Yahooo!" And pushed the lever all the way forward.

———

HOURS LATER RED THOUGHT, *So this is what saddle sore means.*

It had been a lot of fun at first. Then a little tricky/scary to keep the points together as they picked up speed. But for the last half hour the cross hair and portal dots had been locked together. They were moving so fast now, any movements she made didn't cause a course change at all.

"How are fuel levels?" she asked Astroboy. One of his repair drones was wired into the sensors of the rockets.

"We are almost out on rocket C. The other two have 20% but I don't think we want to try maintaining control with only two rockets."

"I agree. So we better prepare to separate," she said and pulled the thruster back. The rockets all slowed and then stopped. "Come here, drone," she said and motioned to the repair drone near her. It dutifully cut its wires and rolled over to her. She took it in both hands and pulled it to her chest.

Then she slowly spread her legs and released the rockets. She floated upward away from them for a second. Pulling her legs up almost to her chest, she put her boots on the side of the rocket and pushed. Her back arched as she went one direction and the rockets the other. Her body slowly flipped over until her feet were oriented toward her flying saucer. "Release tethers, Astroboy."

On the hull of the ship there was a spark and the cables holding the rockets slithered away from Astroboy. She engaged her jet pack to slow her approach to the saucer's top. Touching down she felt the magnetic clamps attach her to the hull. She bent over and placed the drone down as well. She walked toward the canopy of the ship, which slid back to greet her.

CHAPTER 13
GREEN TO THE RESCUE

SPACE GIRL GREEN hung in space thousands of kilometers from the Kitch-Xerces portal. In the distance she could see the Kitch Destroyer *Cynwrig* hanging dark in space. As if coming out of an invisible doorway, a flying saucer zoomed across the stars in front of her.

She engaged her repulsors to full and curved off to match trajectories with Astroboy and Space Girl Red. Her Kitch fighter escort were left quickly behind as she poured on the power to catch up with the other craft. They were going fast, but it didn't take long till the two saucers were side by side.

Green could see Red through her canopy. She triggered her comms and said, "Hey Red, you changed your hair. How do you want to do this? Tractor or dock?"

Red looked over at her with a slight smile. "Dock. Astroboy is a little worried about his hull's ability to take a tractor at this velocity. I did, not completely by choice. Long story."

"It looks good, like everything on you," Green replied. "A dock is going to have to be hard, not umbilical."

"Yes, we know. Even then it will be a stress turning both

ships with just the docking coupler holding us together," Red said.

"Perhaps Mistress Red would have Astroboy lock his tractors on my hull once we are coupled. That should hold us together, relieve some of the stress, and put the tractor stress only on his tractor mounts," said Halamar, Green's flying saucer. His voice was a clear tenor with just the kind of melodic flow you'd expect in a forest glade.

"An excellent suggestion, Halamar," replied Astroboy. "I should have thought of that myself."

"Worry not, Astroboy. You seem to have been through the fires of testing. You made it through and now need a time of rest. Let me help you, bold companion," Halamar said. It made Green smile broadly and even Red thought it a nice way of comforting her ship.

"Do you want me to do the matching maneuver, Green?" Red asked, "Or will you?"

"While you are an Ace Pilot, Space Girl Red, I feel confident I can mate our two ships. You two just hold your course."

"Of course, Green. I never doubted your ability."

"I know, Red. Rest, 'bow," Green said, using a the shortened form of Rainbow that Red hadn't heard in a long time. Then she pulled her stick to one side and down, performing a barrel roll. This roll ended with her flying saucer directly underneath Astroboy, their bellies pointing at each other.

Halamar automatically changed the forward display to a view from inside the bottom docking ring. It had crosshairs superimposed on it, one for her ring's center and the other for Astroboy's. She got them generally lined up and flipped a switch to make her controls more precise. She used the foot control to move the ship slowly downward.

Halamar counted off the distance between the ships: "10 meters. 9 meters." As the two ships eased toward each other. "1 meter. 500 centimeters." Then the magnetic couplers on both ships reached out and pulled them together. There was a grinding noise as the two ships locked together.

"Astroboy, if you would be so kind as to engage your tractor," asked Green as the connection indicators went white.

"Engaged, Space Girl Green."

"All right then," said Green. "Let's change course before we completely exit the Kitch system. I'm going apply a vector force slowly at first to get us turning. Thought we'd hang on to as much of your velocity as we can till we're on course for Kitch 10. Then I'll use my repulsors to slow us as we approach. No need for it to take forever to get there."

"Sounds good, Green," said Red. "I'll just sit here and read a book or something."

"You do that, but take a picture because I want to memorialize you sitting still," Green said as she eased back on the still sensitive stick. Halamar had displayed a course and vector for her to follow. He also had a gauge bar showing the stress on the docking rings of the two ships. It went from white to black as the pressure increased. Too much and the couplers would be damaged. Right now it was in the white and even as she increased the turn, the meter didn't move much. "Astroboy's tractors seem to be relieving a lot of stress on the docking ring."

The two ships ascribed a slow curve in the sky outside the outer planets of the Kitch system. Soon they were heading back in toward the sun, a distant light. "Ok, we are on course for the inner system. Let's just hold this velocity till we get inside Kitch 12. Then I'll engage the repulsors to slow us and approach Kitch 10."

"Green, I'd like to bring Astroboy into port on my own impellers," asked Red. "If you don't mind."

"Of course. We'll be sub-impeller well out from Kitch 10." Green flipped some controls, and jotted off a message to the

Flying Monkeys explaining their course. Their fighters couldn't achieve the velocity the two Flying Saucers were going, but they could provide an escort from the capital. "Auto-pilot engaged." Green stood up and stretched tall.

Space Girl Green had an athletic frame, but unlike most of her rainbow mates, she seemed delicate. Her green hair flowed down her back to her waist. It was parted in the middle and two small braids wrapped her head in a crown. A long braid pulled the sides away from her face and lay on a bed of straight hair. Her skin was light and her features pointed. She had wide green almond-shaped eyes and a long, thin, slightly upturned nose over a small pink lipped mouth.

She wore her standard uniform, all in green of course, with gold accents. Form fitting trousers tucked into dark boots with metallic bands at the top. The trousers came up to her waist, but were covered in a wrap around skirt. The skirt was slightly longer in the back than the front and ended mid thigh. A wide belt in gold held the normal Space Girl gear. Her top was sleeveless, form fitting and of a leather like material. There were golden metal bracers on each arm. The left held advanced medical sensors and the right, a miniature chemical lab to produce healing elixirs.

"Red, I'm coming over for a visit." She said, telling not asking. She understood her friend needed more than a tow, but would never ask for it.

"You don't have to do that, Green."

"No, I don't, but I'm going to anyway," she said and thought, *Something is definitely up because that was token resistance.* Green went down the ladder from the control room. Halamar opened the normally closed floor plate so the ladder continued all the way into the lower level of the saucer. This circular room had panels around the sides that opened into storage and some saucer systems. With all of them sealed and the floor plate to the main core closed, it became an airlock. "Tell Astroboy to open up."

The floor glowed a pretty green, which meant there was air on the other side. Halamar must have pumped air into the space between the ships.

"I have already opened my side, M'Lady. And I have neutralized gravity, which you need to do as well," said Halamar.

"Of course," Green said. The floor plate above her closed and she was weightless. Then the floor below irised opened and she was looking into the matching airlock on the other side. She rotated in place, her green hair fountaining above her as she moved. Then she pushed off her floor plate and floated into the saucer. Once on the other side she stopped her motion with her hands and tucked her legs next to her chest.

Astroboy closed the outer door behind her. There was a pause while he scanned her for foreign bodies, then gravity came on and she was standing on the outer door. *They are being very careful.*

The door above her opened and she could see Red standing on the level above her. She clambered up the ladder and the floor plates closed beneath her. Red was wearing high waisted trousers with transparent sides that exposed skin on the sides of her legs. Above that she wore a sleeveless mock turtle neck zippered in the front. Her short hair, shaved close on one side, seemed brighter than ever and was coupled with dramatic makeup of deep red lipstick and smoky eyes. Her dark eyes glistened as she smiled at Green.

"It is good to see you, Green," she said, standing there tentatively.

Green knew Red was never tentative about anything, which made her eyes burn. Green grabbed her in a deep, hard embrace. "I'm here, 'bow." Something was wrong. Green could feel it and it brought tears to her eyes.

For a moment Red was stiff. Then she relaxed and wrapped her arms around her friend.

They stood there for a long moment, just soaking in the closeness. Green had always looked up to Red. She had always wanted to be like Red and Blue: strong, fearless, and capable of anything. They had told her she was strong in a way they could never be. It wasn't until her recent adventures Green that was true.

"Thank you for being here," said Red, not letting go. "Why were you in the Kitch system anyway?"

Green relaxed her hug and held onto Red by her shoulders so she could look in her eyes. The was something there, but she couldn't figure it out yet. "Tis the season," she said with a smile.

Red laughed. Which released something in Green's heart. The laugh told her Red was hurt, but not broken.

"You know I'm kind of in the middle of something right now," Red said.

"Yes, and Astroboy needs to have some work done," Green tilted her head and looked hard at Red. Then she looked past her friend and said, "And I think maybe you do too."

With a confident motion, she stepped around Red and up to the med pod. She pulled up a history on the display. Behind her Red did nothing to stop her, which told Green a lot. On the screen text scrolled up one side explaining all the things the med pod had done the last time it was used, but the other side was all Green was seeing. It showed the image of her rainbow mate as she had looked when she got in the med pod.

While the healer part of her digested the horror and information in front of her, she said without turning, "I found us a great mystery to solve on Keblr. The elves are behind on production of Scout Girl Cookies because something's wrong in the forest. You know how the Scouts depend on those things for sustenance while out in the reaches. If it is the forest, I could handle it on my own, but if there is someone in the forest... that is probably more your kind of thing."

Her brain clicked when she'd absorbed it all and dealt with the horror, so she turned.

"Show me."

Red took a deep breath, planted her feet and squared her shoulders before unzipping her top to reveal the spider web of lines the God King Bruno had burned into her.

Green tapped her scanning bracers and pointed her hand at Red's chest and waist. She looked at the results a little confused. "How was this done? What was the mechanism of injury?"

"God King Bruno has power over a swarm of nanites. His hand was glowing with them. He touched me here," she pointed to the center of her chest, "and it felt like electricity coursed over my skin and left these marks." She motioned to the punch mark, "For these he first put ash on me. The ash of his guards a raygun explosion had killed. Then he punched me and it left his mark."

Green traced some of the lines on her chest and belly, looking at the results on her scanner. "You blew up your rayguns to kill his guards? Where you there? Must not have been, since you are alive."

"No, I was there. He did it, not me. He told his nanites to analyze the guns by disassembling them. I threw them and ran for Astroboy, but he covered me in XXXite before I could get there. Which saved me from the explosion, but also cut off most of my hair."

"Space Girl Red, you do know how to get into it." Green looked again at her read outs. "Do they hurt?"

"Physically, there's an ache. Not too bad," Red said.

"I can do more than your pod did to fix them. Time to visit my med-lab."

Red raised an eyebrow. "You've got a full med-lab on your saucer?"

"Don't you have a full armory on yours?" Green replied.

Red smiled and pointed to a closed door off the core. "Of course. The natures of our vocations and purposes, huh."

"The nature of our vocation, yes," Green said.

Half an hour later Red lay on the med bed where she'd been scanned and probed by her rainbow mate. Green held a huge syringe in one hand. "Good news, bad news kind of thing. This," she wiggled the syringe she held, "will remove the nanites under your upper body mark. Won't work on the ash marks, but I've got a cream you can apply every day for a month or so and those will gradually fade and heal completely."

"What's the bad news?"

Another wiggle of the syringe, "This won't remove the scar tissue. Those nanites did a number on your skin. It changed its very composition to make those marks. Which means you'll have the pattern, but it won't be as obvious because the scars are the same color as your skin."

"OK," said Red.

"Don't give up hope, Red. I'm pretty sure the school of beauty on Home can remove the scars. It's possible Orange might have something in her med bay that would do it."

"Orange has a med bay in her saucer?"

"Yes, it is part of her art studio," Green smiled.

"Like your garden is," Red said motioning her head toward the plants growing up one side of the room.

"Yep," Green said smiling. Another wiggle, "now about this. It's gonna hurt. It has to be pushed in and through the places the nanites went. Then I have to suck them out. Neither will be a fun experience."

"Can't be worse than when I got the marks."

Green nodded and stroked Red's hair. "Undoubtedly not. But I'm not Bruno. So you are going to sleep through it." Then before Red could react, she pressed the narco-disc she'd palmed to Red's forehead.

"Shouldn't you have asked for consent before knocking her out, Lady Green?" asked Halamar.

"Pfft, I'm next of kin. And she wouldn't have given it for no good reason."

Halamar was silent.

"And Astroboy, I noticed the ear comm. You have anything to say about my treatment methods?"

"I do not, Ma'am. I agree with your assessment." Then he paused, and added, "Thank you for your care."

"Of course, Astroboy."

———

"WAKE UP, SLEEPY HEAD," said Space Girl Green giving Space Girl Red a poke.

Red blinked and looked around. She was still in the med bay, but the table had changed shape into more of a lounge and rotated toward the wall of greenery. Green stood next to her wearing a short green silk robe and rubbing a towel through her wet hair. In one hand she held a rolled up piece of paper she had used to poke Red.

Red looked down at herself. She was nude and the semi-reclining position let her see both of her wound sites easily. Her chest was still a web of ridges, but they were no longer black. The punch mark was still dark, but shone with some oily substance. She ran her fingers over the scars on her chest. There was a feeling or pressure, but not of touch. "They look better," she said to Green.

"Yep, and I already gave the removal cream to Astroboy. Use it every day on your belly."

Green dropped the paper in Red's lap. "Message came for

you. Read it; then get back to your ship. We're parked on the far side of Kitch 10's moon. You wanted to fly in on your own."

"Hey! You knocked me out!" Red said remembering. "How long have I been out?"

"A few hours. You needed the rest," she twirled around and headed out of the room. "Get a move on. We have places to be. I believe there is an escort of Flying Monkeys waiting."

Red muttered to herself and opened the paper. It was a message from Yellow.

Dearest Red:

I'm still on Kenix learning how their World Heart works. It is a-maz-ing. But I think they are ready for us to leave.

I hear you have damaged your beautiful flying saucer. Luckily Engineer Woman Aquamarine is still here with her cruiser. They have spare parts for flying saucers and I grabbed a pair of new repulsors for you. Also a few other things while she was busy and left me alone in the parts bay. Blue would be proud.

I'll be leaving for Kitch 10 today. Might even beat you there.

Light,

Space Girl Yellow

P.S. They are building a statue of you here. Quite pretty.

Red shook her head and folded up the letter. No pockets, she thought and got out of bed. The ache in her chest was gone, which made her smile. Soon she was climbing the ladder back to Astroboy.

———

THINGS WERE different at the Kitch 10 spaceport thought Red as she walked down the gangplank to the tarmac. There were a lot more ships visible. Two other flying saucers were lined up next to hers. There was a full wing of Kitchian fighters which had come in as her escorts. In the distance was a light cruiser, apparently the personal craft of Prince Alfred.

At the bottom of the gangplank Sergeant Major James had his troop formed up at attention. Behind them was a truck she assumed went with the repair group. Standing in front of them was Captain Powell.

"Hello, Captain. It is good to see you again," said Red.

"And you, Space Girl," she could tell he wanted to salute, but they'd settled that last time he'd done it. "Our fighters told us your ship had significant damage. We wanted to make sure you knew the Flying Monkeys are willing to do what ever we can to repair him."

"Yes, Astroboy does need some work. My rainbow mate Space Girl Yellow was supposed to bring new repulsor engines." She nodded toward the other two flying saucers. Green's was right next to hers and in the distance was Yellow's. Even as she was talking she saw a panel open on one side and boxes start unloading. A dark-skinned, yellow-haired Space Girl was walking toward her, hair rippling in the wind. She wore a brightly colored long vest with many pockets. A thick utility belt at her narrow waist gleamed with gold colored tools.

"There she is."

As Yellow strode past Halamar, Green came running down the gangplank and jumped on her back. Despite probably 40 kilos of gear strapped to her, Yellow started running in circles and you could hear Green's screams from where Red stood with the commander of the Flying Monkeys.

"Don't worry; they do that all the time." She smiled at them and added, "Looks even weirder the other way around."

"I wouldn't think the little green one could carry the other," said Captain Powell.

"We Space Girls are stronger than we look."

Yellow had run half the distance to Red and Powell when Green started pounding on her to let her down. Red could almost hear her yelling something about looking crazy to the monkeys.

With a casual shrug Yellow tossed Green over her shoulder forward onto the tarmac. Someone in the troop gasped at the move, but Green landed and rolled to her feet in a motion so fluid it looked like dance. She casually brushed at dust on her green skirt, then synced her steps to walk next to Yellow.

"And more acrobatic," said Sergeant Major James.

Captain Powell said, "I take it you've seen the video of Space Girl Red's dance off, Sergeant."

"I'm pretty sure there isn't anyone on Kitch 10 that hasn't seen that video, sir," answered the sergent. "Just didn't realize they were all like that."

Yellow stopped in front of the group, but only had eyes for Red's saucer. "Oh, Astroboy, what has she done to you?"

The saucer's external speakers answered, "I'm afraid all of this was God King Bruno's doing, Space Girl Yellow. And he did as much to Space Girl Red."

They all looked at her where she stood. After Green's ministrations she'd put aside hiding her scars. She was wearing a tight long sleeve red jumpsuit with a scoop neck. It showed almost half of the scars.

Captain Powell said, "Those scars look like the ambassador's assistants' tattoos."

"I understand it is a mark God King Bruno puts on women he thinks he owns. Mine were black, until Space Girl Green removed the color."

"So are we rid of the so-called God King now?" asked Sergeant Major James.

"Thank you for the vote of confidence in my abilities, but it was all I and Astroboy could do to escape their system."

There was silence then.

"Another day then," said the Captain.

Red nodded. "I need to talk to the Queen. Captain, I'm hoping you, the sergeant major, and Space Girl Yellow can make a plan to bring Astroboy back to new, while I'm gone."

"Will do, Space Girl," said Captain Powell.

"I'll look him over," said Yellow. "I've got some parts, and new repulsors. If the Kitchians have raw metals for the hull, I think we can get it done."

"The Queen told me we are to expend whatever is needed to repair Space Girl Red's ship," said Captain Powell. "The Prince added we could dismantle his cruiser if we need to." The monkey's blue face curved into a wide grin.

"Great, I'll leave it in your capable hands." Red turned and started walking back up the gangway into her saucer. "Better clear a path, though. I'm taking my jet bike to the palace."

———

"HOW IS SHE?" asked Space Girl Purple as she walked up to where Green stood on the tarmac. Red was disappearing on her jet bike heading to talk to Queen Natalie. Green smiled at her rainbow mate whose saucer had landed while everyone was distracted. Purple had long layered hair in many shades of purple with some blue and red subtly mixed in. Her lips were dark and full, accenting her light brown skin and high cheekbones. She wore a dark cropped jacket over a low-cut lace edged camisole. You could just see saucer control tattoos curving over the top of her chest to disappear under her jacket.

But all this was secondary to her eyes. One was a light red and the other a striking blue. When you looked at them you immediately felt known. Purple's slow fluid movements, soft touches, and feathery voice made you want to tell her everything. It was her gift to instantly be anyone's friend. She dressed like a punk rocker and from a distance you might fear she would kick your ass. Which of course she could do, but once you looked into her strange eyes you knew it was unlikely and would only happen for your own good.

Green didn't ask why she was here. Purple had always sensed when she was needed. "I'm giving her the healing I can," she said watching Red disappear around a corner. "But soon..."

"She'll need the healing I can give," Purple finished. "I don't think she is ready for that yet, do you?"

"No, and Blue is going to have to start it," Green said looking into those eyes and enjoying the sensation. "Red says it's no big deal, but it is. I don't think Blue thought her mischief would lead to Red getting tortured. It did, though. She needs to answer for that."

"Yes," Purple paused. "Those two. From the beginning."

"Yes, but it was never hate."

"Oh, no. The opposite really. They were the closest of us. A bond of sister love the rest of us just got a shadow of. Even if it did manifest in the constant rivalry."

"Which made them the best of us."

Purple looked more deeply at her green sister. "Do you think so?"

Green laughed at her. "Of course. And so do you. Life and love do overlap you know," she said referring to their respective purposes.

Purple grabbed her in a fierce embrace. "Of course they do. It is why I love you so much, 'bow." Then she let go just as quickly.

"You love us all," said Green, still feeling all warm and crinkly inside. "That is your purpose after all."

"You have it backwards, Green," said the tall woman in leather and chains. "It is my purpose because I love you all."

Purple looped arms with her rainbow mate and started walking them back towards where the four flying saucers stood. "What do you have in mind? I hear Astroboy is grounded for awhile." That particular flying saucer had monkeys all over it, and a strong black woman with yellow hair giving them a run for their money.

"Tis the season," Green said.

Purple laughed, "That old thing. I thought it ended with graduation. It annoyed Red so much."

"I know, but it makes my year. So I just assumed it would continue. A good thing I did, because I was here to tow her in from Kitch's portal." Green continued, "We are going to Keblr to help the elves. Seems something is interfering with the production of Scout Girl cookies." She got a wistful look on her face as she said, "Those forests and their factories inside the trees themselves, without any damage at all. It's magical."

"And for Red?"

"I'm thinking the problem is with the eco-system, but it may be with some inhabitants of the forest knocking it out of balance. She can figure that kind of conflict out better than I. Along the way, I'm hoping to be able to do something about what the God King did to her body." Green's eyes flashed at the mention of his title.

Space Girl Purple, the Space Girl of Love, also reacted at the name. Her eyes went black and the visible tattoos strobed. It was not a good thing to see love angry. "I wish you luck with that. Is it as bad as I heard?"

"The main mark covers almost all of her chest and belly."

The other woman nodded. "I haven't been to Keblr, but I've heard there is a special being in the forest there—some princess of the inhabitants you don't see. She is said to have incredible healing powers."

"I will look for her then, if I have not succeeded by the time we get there." Green said as they got to Merlin, Purple's saucer. "And you?"

"I'm going to find Blue."

CHAPTER 14
A QUEEN'S FRUSTRATION

THE PALACE GUARDS were expecting her and Space Girl Red was able to zip right through the gates. There were more guards and they were better armed than the last time she was there. At the top of the main stairs, Prince Alfred stood. He was wearing his military uniform complete with side arm, which on Kitch 10 was a recoilless pistol that shot rocket bullets.

"Prince Alfred, good to see you again," Red said as she climbed the stairs toward him. His eye were locked on her chest. "At any other time, Prince, I would tell you my eyes were up here."

The Prince started, then said, "Sorry. Did he do that to you?"

"'Fraid so, but it was black when he did it. Space Girl Green was able to remove the color." She was up the stairs and next to him now. "I didn't think it was visible from that far away," she said looking back to where the jet bike was parked.

"I have pilot eyes. They give me more distance vision." The Prince shook her hand, holding it just a little longer than strictly needed as he looked intently at her face. "We are greatly sorrowed at what happened to you while delivering our message." Then he turned quickly and said while walking, "But

I will let my mother express that sentiment in more depth. This way."

He led her into the palace and immediately turned onto a side corridor that led away from the throne room she had used last time. As they walked he asked about her saucer and the Flying Monkeys repairing it. She thanked him for the resources and explained Yellow. After a few more turns, they arrived at a simple door with a uniformed and armed Space Marine standing in front of it. He snapped to attention when the Prince approached. The Prince nodded to him and said, "Space Girl Red to see the Queen."

"Sir," said the guard. Then he opened the door, blocked the doorway, and announced them. There was a feminine voice answer, and he stepped to one side. "The Queen will see you now."

Inside Queen Natalie rose from her desk as they approached. She wore a simple, knee-length black dress. It had cap sleeves and a short contrasting insert in silver that slashed from her left shoulder to right side of her chest. She wore black cap-toe pumps with silver speckles and 100mm heels. Her blonde hair was pulled back in a bun. A sliver and black band encircled her head with a simple glowing stone in the middle of her forehead.

Red stopped a few meters from the Queen and the Prince moved off to one side where there were a group of chairs near a fireplace. While the Queen's dress made her look put together, her expression was weary. She took in the younger woman in front of her from head to toe as she walked around the desk to stand next to Red.

Red said nothing, still not sure where she stood with the Queen. She would have said the Queen thought her a novelty when they first met. Then useful after the dance contest. Now there was something else in her expression. Regret? Worry? Sorrow?

The queen reached out a hand toward her head, then stopped and asked, "May I?"

"Yes, Ma'am."

She lightly touched the shaved side of Space Girl Red's head, her finger running over the silver device entwined with her ear. "Was your hearing damaged?"

"No, your majesty. That is a more permanent connection to my flying saucer."

Queen Natalie nodded understanding. "But this is his work," she said with menace in her voice as she lightly ran a finger over the scars on Red's chest. "Ljuba has one like it."

Red had forgotten the Ambassador's assistant's tattoo until that moment. "Yes, I'd forgotten that. Now that I think about it, Venuše had one too, but it was on her arm at her wrist."

"The first Ambassador said it was a mark of former concubines," said the Prince and then realized what he had implied. "I'm not…"

"I think it is more of a mark of ownership to him," Red said cutting him off. "Their's are white to contrast with their skin. Mine were black, but Space Girl Green was able to remove the nanites causing the color."

"Will she be able to remove the scars, too?" asked the Queen stepping back and motioning to the sitting area where the prince sat. "I will call the best cosmetic surgeons we have, if you would like."

"She says it is beyond what she can do on her saucer, which is quite a lot. But she thinks they could remove them on Home." She settled into a seat that faced the royals and said, "But I choose to wear them now. Enough about me, I noticed a significant uptick in security on Kitch 10 since I left. Has something changed?"

The queen ignored her attempt to change the subject and leaned forward to lock eyes with the Space Girl. "No, not enough about you. You went on a mission for the monarchy of Kitch. You were captured by our enemy, tortured, scarred, and God only knows what else. We are in your debt. Whatever you need to return you to your former state we will provide.

"I believe your ship was heavily damaged as well. Space Girl flying saucers have an AI I believe. Is it alive? Do you consider it a person?"

"The AI in flying saucers are the most advanced Home has developed. Whether they are people is a matter of debate for philosophers. You will find Space Girls and Women are quite close to their ships. I certainly consider mine a friend. His actions on Xerces undoubtedly saved my life."

"What is his name?" Queen Natalie asked.

"Astroboy."

She smiled at that. "We shall be passing out medals as Queens do and we will make sure Astroboy gets his own. I know, if you are anything like your father, those medals will be of little importance to you. Nor will being designated a Friend of the Royal Family, but I am going to do it anyway."

Red merely nodded. "Now give us a report on what happened," said Queen Natalie, settling back in her chair.

"Your majesty, I landed and delivered your data coin to God King Bruno."

The Queen interrupted her and said, "Friends of the royal family do not have to use our royal titles except on formal occasions. This is not one of those."

———

HALF AN HOUR later Red finished her story. Queen Natalie and Prince Alfred had listened quietly only asking a few questions for clarification. When she finished, Red leaned back in her chair.

"Is Space Girl Blue an enemy of yours?" asked Alfred.

"No," Red answered. "Far from it actually. We are rainbow mates, which is very much like being sisters. We are rivals, but not enemies."

"But her actions led to your torture," said Queen Natalie.

"I'm sure that was not her intention. She thought she was getting back at me for taking something from her a few weeks back. If she had known Bruno would do that to me, I'm pretty sure she would have done something horrible to him first."

"So she is not a bad person," asked Natalie.

"No, I don't believe so."

The two royals looked at each over. Then the Queen asked, "What do you think the reaction of Home will be to this incident."

Red understood they were asking if Home might help them in their conflict. "I expect there will be none."

The others looked surprised at that. "Why? He intended to kill you. They would just let that stand?"

"It is the way of the Space Girl to put herself in danger. In times of peace, Space Girl is the most dangerous of the vocations. Space Girls are lost often on their adventures."

It was obvious to her that the royals did not understand this viewpoint. "What has changed since I left? It hasn't been that long, but security is much higher."

"There was an assassination attempt on the Queen, and a nano-bomb attack in the capital. The assassin got the wrong room in his attempt. He broke into one of her suites but it was not the one she was using that night," said the Prince. Red was interested to find out the Queen did not sleep in the same place every night—even before the increase in security.

"Yes, we have some murky video, but were unable to pinpoint who it was," said Natalie. "The nano-bomb was a much bigger deal. It went off in a crowded market. Are you familiar with nano-bombs?"

"I am very familiar with what nanites can do now, but I don't understand how they can be a bomb."

"There are lots of ways to deploy nanites. Often they are sprayed in some way. A bomb disperses them rapidly via an explosion. In this case that was a high pressure gas explosion. No heat or flame, but canister fragments did injure those near by. It was the nanites themselves that were pernicious." The queen made a motion at the wall and a screen appeared. It showed a crowded street market suddenly break into chaos. "If a person got nanites on their skin, they began to burrow and eat their flesh. The more nanites, the worse the condition."

"Nanites are not very robust in the open air," said Alfred. "It is one of the unique things King Bruno is able to do. But in this case they quickly killed the 10 people nearest the explosion. Another 63 were hospitalized. By the time haz-mat teams got there, the nanos were inert on surfaces."

"On Xerces I experienced similar effects. We found an electric shock to the skin neutralized them. Also getting out of the atmosphere. Do you think this was Bruno?"

"I do," said Alfred. "My mother isn't ready to jump to that conclusion."

"At least not publicly," the queen added. "After hearing your story, it does seem his style, if you will." She stood up and began to pace. "We are also sure our pirate problem is his doing. But like the assassination and bomb, we have no proof. I am reluctant to start another war with him. He's tricky and has had time to prepare for us if we just send ships through the portal to bombard the planet."

"After what he did to our messenger," Prince Alfred said indicating Space Girl Red. "We would be justified in some show of force. Perhaps see if we can learn something about his defenses."

"What do you think, Space Girl Red? You have a unique perspective on our conflict and the enemy."

Red thought for a moment. This was just the kind of thing Space Girls figured out for Home, but this was someone else's fight. Also she was too close to Bruno and her emotions would compromise her judgements. "Natalie. Alfred, I would like to help truly, but right now I am too emotionally involved. I fear I'd recommend you bomb Xerces lifeless, just to get revenge for myself. And I know that would be wrong."

The others nodded understanding, and Red continued. "While in their system we saw nothing. No ships at all. That seems strange, especially if King Bruno is running a pirate operation. There should have been something. It is possible we missed something, being injured as we were. I will share with you Astroboy's scanner data from the system. But for myself, I have another mission I must go on with Space Girl Green. Perhaps afterwards I will have some perspective and be of more help."

Red stood, suddenly anxious to be on her way with Green. The other two stood there for a moment as if to say more, then they both bowed. "Thank you for all you've done, Space Girl Red," said the Queen. "We will do everything in our power to repair Astroboy while you are gone. I look forward to talking with you again when you return." She reached out a hand and shook Red's.

"I will walk you back to your jet bike, if I may," asked Prince Alfred.

———

WHEN THE PRINCE returned from walking Red out, he found his mother back behind her desk. But she wasn't reading any of the many reports on her desk, nor working on her terminal. She was staring into the distance.

"Thinking, Mother?"

"Yes," she said and sat up to look at him. "Do you think you could get a message to this Space Girl Blue? The one who stole from King Bruno?"

Prince Alfred was surprised. What did his mother have in mind? "Perhaps. There is at least one Space Girl staying with us. I could talk to her."

"Do that and tell her we would be interested in paying handsomely for the riviere."

"What do you have in mind, mother? Instruct me."

"I was thinking our biggest problem is we can't see the pirates, nor know how they are getting into our system. What if we give them a reason to show themselves?"

"Like this stolen object from the God King. He will want it back."

"Exactly."

Prince Alfred bowed to her wisdom. "I'll head to the port immediately."

CHAPTER 15
RED & GREEN GO TO KEBLR

"I FEEL HORRIBLE LEAVING YOU," said Space Girl Red as she packed weapons into a jump bag. There was a much smaller bag already in the entryway with her clothes.

"I will be fine, Ma'am," said Astroboy. "Space Girl Yellow is here to support the repairs. I'll be good as new in no time."

"Yes, but I should be here in case you need me."

"I will miss you too, Red." This brought a smile to her face. "I have also taken the liberty of giving Halamar the transmission code for your new ear piece. He has promised to 'guard you with his life and honor'." Red could have sworn there was a smirk in his tone.

Red zipped the bag closed and slung it over one shoulder but its weight almost caused her to lose her balance, so she set it on the floor.

"All right. Before I leave, I need to give you some orders."

"Awaiting your command, Ma'am."

"Astroboy, you are to stay on Kitch 10 until your repairs are complete. During that time, you are to take orders from Space Girl Yellow concerning those repairs."

"Yes, Ma'am."

"In the event of an attack on yourself or the planet, I authorize you to defend yourself and your allies with all of your weapons and capabilities. You may defer to Space Girl Yellow for orders regarding how much you should be involved in their conflict."

"Yes, Ma'am. Thank you, Space Girl Red."

"As always, you are a representative and servant of Home, and will conduct yourself according to their orders and protocols. No need for worry there."

"Acknowledged."

"Finally, and this is the big one, once your repairs are complete, to your and Space Girl Yellow's satisfaction, I want you to join me on Keblr."

"Ma'am, it is irregular for a Flying Saucer to navigate by themselves."

"Did you not navigate and even engage in combat operations just days ago in Xerces space?"

"Of course, Ma'am, but that was under very special circumstances. It also did not involve Spaceway navigation."

"Tell me, Astroboy, if your repulsors had not been damaged, would you have gone through the portal to get help?"

"Yes, at least to send a Spaceway transmission."

"And you would have done this without authorization to use your weapons."

"I may defend myself, Ma'am. It seems unlikely God King Bruno's forces would have waited for me to fire first."

Red smiled. "True, but they didn't give us any trouble. I sometimes wonder if we could have done without the rockets and just taken the slow road."

"The system seemed very empty, Space Girl."

"Anyway, that is an ongoing mystery, and I need to get going. You are authorized and ordered to join me on Keblr when you are fighting fit. You may use your weapons to make that happen as needed."

"Yes, Ma'am. Anything else?"

Red hauled the heavy bag over onto her back, sliding the other arm through the strap to carry it like a backpack. She was wearing her pressure suit just because that was easier than trying to pack it. She gave the ship one more long look, then she sighed. "Nope, that will do. Get well soon."

"Stay as safe as you can, being you, Space Girl Red," Astroboy said as she exited the saucer.

———

"SHEESH, Red. What the heck is all of that?" Asked Green as Red got to the top of the gangplank and started dropping stuff willy nilly on the floor. Green wore a halter top one piece with a short skirt. The top wrapped around her neck and met at her belly button. Then it seemed to cross and meet at the back, with the fabric forming a skirt that reached to the top of her thighs. With the front so open from neck to belly button, there was a white bra visible in the front and the open back. She had on her Space Girl utility belt with one raygun on her left hip. She also wore her gold healer bracers.

The bubble helmet had landed first and Green grabbed it before it rolled back out of the saucer. The small bag Red dropped first made a soft thump. Then a louder clunk with lots of metal on metal sounds as the big duffle dropped off Red's back to the floor. Her short red hair was drenched with sweat from the walk over with the heavy bag.

"My gear," said Red. "Where should I put it?"

The other Space Girl looked at the piles, then at her friend. "By gear do you mean weapons? You can hang your pressure suit over here." She turned and hung the helmet on a hook next to where her own helmet and suit hung.

"Of course, but only my non-standard weapons. I figure you have all of the regular necessities." Space Girl pressure suits were designed to be skin-tight, allowing no air between the wearer and the suit. This kept them from ballooning up and making it almost impossible to move. She pressed a toggle on the collar and the suit split in a T shape down the front. This allowed her to lift the neck ring off and shuck out of the rest of it. Her skin glossy from sweat, she walked over and hung her suit under the helmet. The cool air of the ship felt good and the flush of exertion started to fade.

"Where am I bunking for the trip?" Red asked, then picked up the smaller bag and tossed it to Green, "That's my clothes."

"You've got two choices," said Green shouldering the bag and stepping into the central core of the saucer. "You can use the med bay lounge, which is quite comfortable as you already know. Or you can bunk with me. The bed is plenty big enough for two."

Red shrugged and said, "Think I'd rather a proper bed."

"Okay," answered Green and tossed the bag across the core, through the open door, where it landed on the green silk covered bed.

Red, still standing in the doorway, asked, "And my special gear?"

"Here's my armory," Green said and the panel opened. "You can decide what will fit in there. I can also clear you a locker in the med bay if you need more room."

"I think I can fit most of it in here," she said looking at the locker. "You are under-armed. What happens if you lose one? You know I lost both my rayguns on Xerces."

"That why you are carrying that old thing?" She motioned to the sleek silver pistol in Red's hand. She was carrying it after taking it off the pressure suit since she had no belt or holster.

Red held up the silver and gold weapon, inspecting it as if she'd never seen it before. The main body of the gun was a silver lozenge with a gold fin coming out the top. The fin had circular holes in it. The front of the gun had three metal disks spaced half a centimeter apart that got smaller at they approached the gold tip. "Hey now, don't talk bad about the Atomic Atomizer Mark IV. It's a classic."

Red stepped back into the entry way and unzipped the duffle. "It is this thing I'm not sure where to store." Then she pulled out the astroid mining laser. It was a meter long, silver with a cone shape at the end of the barrel. The back end was a large power pack.

"What the..."

"It is an astroid mining laser. I saw Blue use it on Zoran and decided I had to have one, too." She tossed it around trying to get a comfortable grip but it was smooth all over and she had trouble resting it against sweaty skin.

Green just shook her head. "Of course Blue would come up with something like that, and then you'd have to have one." She thought for a moment looking around the entry room. "Halamar, do you think you could fabricate a wall mount for Red's big pet?"

"I believe I can." There was a pause while the ship did some scanning and planning. "It is fabricating now. Lady Red, I created two mounts one for the laser and one for its power pack. The power pack mount will have built-in recharging."

"Cool idea, Halamar. Have to tell Astroboy about that one."

"Yes, my lady. I will send him the plans. Now, if you wouldn't mind, could you remove the power pack from that thing? An accidental discharge could cut sizable holes in me."

Red smiled and rested the gun's nose on the floor while she

disconnected the power pack. "Where should I put these for now?"

"Just leave them there if you will. I'll have my drones put them away once they've installed the mounts."

"You got it," Red said. "Now, Green, when are we leaving?"

"Ready to get going, huh? I can lift as soon as your stuff is secured. Don't want weapons flying all over the place."

"Sounds good. I'll store this stuff and get some clothes on." Red shouldered the now much lighter duffle and headed toward the refresher, as Green headed for the ladder.

———

"WHERE ARE YOU GOING TO LAND?" Red asked. She was standing behind Green in the flying saucer's cockpit looking at the forest below. Keblr was the fourth of six planets surrounding a blue-white star. Its surface was 70% water and had two large continents. The one they were over seemed to be covered with trees—the whole 30 million plus square kilometers.

"There is a Scout beacon," the woman piloting said, waving at a map displayed in front of her. "It is labeled 'Forest Glade' and next to the elves' factory."

"Is that why you wear that getup?" asked Red. Green wore an overbust corset made of silk and decorated with gold brocade. Under it was a light forest green skirt of tulle. Green also wore round gold framed eyeglasses that probably did a great deal more than correct her perfect eyesight.

"You're one to talk, Space Girl Red, Warrior Princess. Did you steal an Amazon uniform?"

Red was wearing a dark crimson kevlar corset over a matching leather kilt and dark red boots with matching sgian dubh in the top. Wrapped around her shoulders was a red cape with hood. "Even I'm not bold enough to steal from the Warriors. Or wear one of their uniforms I didn't earn. And I'm not wearing a sword either."

"Only because you left yours on Astroboy." The saucer was now cruising above the giant trees. The Keblr giant trees could grow up to a 1000 meters high, though most were in the 600-800 range. You could see nothing below their dark green foliage. "And if I remember training right, Space Girls have a provisional rank in the Warriors."

"True, but only for use during war. Still I would totally have carried the Amazon sword I won during the games. When was that?"

The saucer was almost stopped now and Red still couldn't see anywhere to land. Then there it was, an opening in the canopy maybe three times the size of the saucer. The grass was just as dark green as the trees. They cleared the trees and Green changed the display to show down, there was now a glowing circle in the grass indicating where they should land.

"You were what, 16?"

"Yeah, that seems right."

"But they let us compete against a rainbow getting ready to graduate, two years our seniors."

Red smiled at the memory. "I'm pretty sure they did it because that rainbow was cocky and they wanted us to take them down a notch before they got sent off to be warriors."

"Which you and Blue did," Green said settling down on the glade.

"Hey, you held your own. The sniper women gave up trying to spot you after finding everyone else in both rainbows."

Green stood up and said, "Yeah, that was a good day."[1]

As the two Space Girls moved to the entry room, Green noticed Red's sidearm. "Red, you can't carry that thing here."

"Why not?"

"A de-atomizer in this forest? The elves would kill you if you used it and took down one of their centuries old trees." She toggled open the armory panel and pulled out her extra raygun. "Here use my extra."

Red looked down at the gun like it smelled bad. "Its the wrong color," which she and Green knew wasn't the problem. A Space Girl's raygun was hers—a right of passage. Each one was the color of the Space Girl, but it was more than that.

"Mmm," Green put the extra raygun back, understanding. Then she pulled something else out and said, "Halamar, can you connect the defensive bracer to Space Girl Red via her stars?"

"I believe I can tune it to connect. I am not sure how the interface will work, M'Lady."

"Give it a shot anyway," Green said turned to Red, "I made this awhile back, before I needed two bracers for my healer gear. It is a projectile shooter. You wear it on your forearm, obviously," she said and waited for Red to extend her arm. When she laid the bracer on the back of Red's forearm, it seemed to stick and then straps appeared and latched around her wrist. "Point your arm at what you want to shoot and make a fist." Green held onto Red's hand to keep her from closing it immediately.

"I have tuned the bracer's frequency to yours, Space Girl Red. Please attempt to reach out and feel it," said Halamar.

Red could already feel the thing as soon as it attached. There was an immediate understanding it would accept her commands. "I think it likes me. What do I need to tell it?"

"Point it that way," Green said, pointing out a target across the gangplank door.

Red turned and pointed her open hand at the target. A round tube levered out of the bracer.

"That is the launcher. It has several loads. Think target practice. Then make a fist."

She did and there was a pffitting sound. A dart appeared in the target across the room.

"You can also vary the fire rate by thought."

She closed her hand again and rapid fire darts sped across the room.

"Now think about putting it away," suggested Green. "You don't want to think about not closing your fist all the time. It takes an intentional thought to turn it on and off. Though after you practice some, you will find you do it without thinking. You just decide to shoot something and point at it. Then boom."

Red smiled looking at the sleek gold bracer like a little girl at Christmas. "That is sooo cool. Green, I never thought you a weaponsmith." She moved her arm around marveling at the thing. "What are the loads?"

Green curtseyed at her friend and said, "I built it to deliver drugs and tranquilizers. But I'm still a Space Girl and added a few mods. It defaults to shooting knock out darts, but it will also shoot regular unjacketed bullets of a couple of metals: lead, gold, silver. There is also an electric bullet that delivers a shock."

Red hung her Mark IV in the armory. "Thanks again. What do you say we go meet some tall, dark, and handsome elves?"

CHAPTER 16
PIXIES AND THE FAIRY QUEEN

THE ELF WAITING at the edge of the glade was definitely not tall, nor dark. Handsome wasn't how Red would have described the little white haired man. He was a just over a meter tall and wore bright blue pantaloons with dark blue hose. His shirt was a tan color and long sleeved. Over it he wore an apron knotted at the waist. On his head was a floppy red hat.

"Welcome, fair ladies," he said with a bow and a doff of his hat. "I can see by your craft that you must be Space Girls. Are you the ones the Scout Girls sent for about our problem?"

"We are indeed, sir," answered Green with a little curtsey. Red was fully capable of curtseying but stood silent to one side. "What is your name and what can you tell us about the problem?"

"I'm Wayne-Jo Wheatpicker, miss. I can explain the problem as we walk to the factory." He immediately began moving down the path into the tall trees of the forest.

Red looked around and noticed how quiet it was here on the edge of the forest. The trees were truly massive and the forest floor fairly dark. The sun was setting and warm lights hung along the path to light their way. It reminded her of Kenix, but with everything blown-up to giant size.

"As you know we make the Scout Girl cookies here. A tiny little biscuit that contains all the nutrition any humanoid could need while still being magically delicious. There are a lot of different ingredients in the cookies. All of them are sourced locally right here on Keblr. The forest is rich in everything from mint to cocoa beans to sugar in the form of various nectars."

He continued to lead them toward a large tree that was 14 or 15 meters across. "As you are no doubt aware, we keep our recipe very secret. Not even listing all of the ingredients or their source materials. For instance there is, of course sugar, in our baked goods, but it is not sourced from sugar cane or corn. It is sourced from various nectars of insects that live among the trees."

"Like bees," said Green.

"Like the bees of other planets, but different. They gather nectar from flowers and plants then produce a sweet liquid ambrosia. We then harvest this and distill it or just use them in their original form." Wayne-Jo had stopped at the base of the tree. There was a set of double doors perhaps two meters wide and a meter and a half tall. He took both handles in his hands pulled them open with a florish, "Here on the factory floor."

"Ooooh," said Green clapping her hands excitedly.

Red had to admit it was impressive. Warm light filled the space and a cacophony of sound washed over them. There was movement everywhere with elves in brightly colored clothes working on all kinds of equipment. As she ducked under the low door Red could look up and see multiple floors above them where elves were doing all kinds of mysterious cooking related things.

Wayne-Jo let them stand and take it all in for a moment. Then he walked them to the center of the room where there was a half cage about a meter and a half in diameter and connected to a thick rope that disappeared up the tree. He opened a door in the cage and stepped inside. "Bit tight for the likes of you, but I think we can all squeeze in."

They could get in, but Red did wish a little that she'd worn a slightly longer skirt. Wayne-Jo put himself right up against the rail looking out and at least seemed to ignore the girl flesh behind him. He flipped a toggle on one of the struts connecting the bottom of the cage. There was a rattling where the rope attached and they began to rise.

Wayne-Jo gave a running commentary about what all the machines did on each level as they rose, but Red only understood it at the most basic level. Green nodded and made interested noises as they rose. After they had risen seven floors, they came to a level full of big shinny copper kettles. It seemed much less active than the other floors. The elevator stopped and Wayne-Jo popped out like a cork onto a walk way.

"Now normally this would be a very busy level, but as you can see only about a quarter of the kettles are actually in use. This is where we take the blue nectar and distill it to an essence we use in the Scout Girl cookies. Unfortunately we are are only able to harvest 42.3% as much nectar as we could a year ago because of the dang pixies in the northern forest glades."

Red and Green looked at each other and then Green said, "Pixies."

"Yes, pixies. They are a curse. A pestilence. They buzz around the glades and scare away the Rozy Maple Bees. Rozy Maple Bees are very shy insects and easily frightened. Because the pixies are constantly buzzing around, they never pollinate the flowers and produce the nectar in their goo-pods." His little face had turned red with anger, which Red found adorable, though she hid her feelings. "I don't even think they are doing it for a reason, just buzzing around to be a nuisance, but that's pixies for you."

The two Space Girls looked at each other for a moment then Red said "And you want us to do what? Kill them?"

The expression on Wayne-Jo's face indicated that would be exactly what he'd like to do, but what he said was, "Of course we can't kill them. They are a part of the ecosystem. A very annoying and stupid part, but who knows what would happen if they were gone? Other than the Rozy Maple Bees could go about their business untroubled."

He had led them out a door and onto a branch of the massive tree that was the factory. Near the end of this wide branch was a small building. Wayne-Jo pulled a key ring from under his apron and selected a key. Then he unlocked the door. He paused before opening it and said to them, "We managed to capture one of them and put it in here. We're going to go through the door very quickly and lock it behind us so the thing doesn't escape." He looked at them very intently, "You understand?"

The two Space Girls nodded trying not to laugh at the serious little elf. *Be very careful of the big bad pixie*, thought Red. Still, she thought tranquilizer dart at her arm and the launch tube popped out.

The elf pulled the door open quickly and motioned frantically at them. Red was the first through the door, with Green right behind her. The hut had a high ceiling which meant it was a little more than arms length about the women's heads. Red held her arm at ready and looked at the rafters of the hut. The elf scurried through the door and was quickly locking it behind him.

"Oh it is so pretty," said Green. In the center of the room was a wooden table. In the center of that table was a clear glass cloche about 15cm in diameter. Inside it was tiny shiny little gold person with the wings of a hummingbird. She, for the figure clearly had a feminine shape, stood and hopped to the glass as soon as they walked in. Green went right up to the table and picked up the cloche. "Hello, my little pretty."

"No!" screamed Wayne-Jo, but it was too late.

As soon as there was space the little pixie shot toward the door. Wayne-Jo had already secured it though, and the pixie could only grab the door knob with its hand and push on it with her feet. Her wings buzzed angrily and her high pitched screams let every one know she was not happy. The screams were not coherent words, but conveyed plenty of emotion.

"Come here, little one," said Green holding out her hand. "I won't hurt you."

The little creature looked around and then leaped at the nearby elf's face. He swatted the air and covered his face as the creature dive-bombed him.

"Hey! Hey, now," said Green stepping over toward them. "Leave him alone. Come here."

The little thing hovered in the air for a second and gave a little lunge and buzz at the elf before turning toward the forest clad space girl. She flitted around the outstretched hand for a moment then landed on it and squatted.

"There you go that is better," Green said and then squawked as the pixie ran the edge of one delicate, but obviously sharp wing across her hand.

It leaped into the air with what could only be a shout of glee and started buzzing round the rafters.

"You ok, Green?" asked Red, keeping her eyes and arm trained on the little menace.

"Yes, I'm fine," she said scanning the wound with her scanning bracer. "Unfortunately all my salves are on that arm and a little hard to apply to the same hand." She turned to the elf and asked, "These things aren't poisonous, are they?"

"No. Why did you let it loose, you nidget! Do you have any idea how hard it is to catch those things? Took a dozen elves and an hour to catch that when it got into the factory." The little pixie gave a swooping buzz and laughed lightly.

It swooped at Red, who ducked quickly and said, "Oh no you don't." Then she shot it with a tranq dart. Despite it being barely 10 centimeters long and moving quickly, the dart hit it right between the wings.

There was a tinking sound of metal on metal and the thing wavered for a second, but then quickly flew up to the rafters and crouched half hidden on a joist.

"Huh?" She said still watching the creature.

"They are made of metal," said the elf.

"Metal? They aren't organic?"

"No, though we've never cut one open to see. Nor have we caught a pair to see how they reproduce."

"Are there any other metallic beings on Keblr?" asked Green. She had dispensed some healing lotion into her opposite hand and was rubbing it on her wounded hand.

"No," answered the elf a little confusion in his voice.

"How long have the pixies been here? This problem seems new, but how long have you know about them as a species?"

The elf rubbed his chin for a moment and then said, "I'd have to consult Grace-Lynn Natureknower to be sure, but I don't remember much about them before a couple of decades ago."

"Red, think Splat and shoot that thing please," said Green. She looked up at the pixie and said, "You need to come down right now, or else."

The pixie stood up on the rafter and made a rude noise complete with hand gestures. Red didn't know what splat meant or did, but she made a fist and thought *Splat!*

A spherical glob of something shot out of the tube expanding and losing its shape as it flew across the room. Then it hit the pixie and knocked it off the rafter. Unlike the dart it didn't bounce off the metal, but rather enveloped the creature in a sticky mess. There was a half soft, half metalic sound when the creature hit the floor. Parts of its wings, arms, and legs sticking out of the goo. It could move enough to try and push itself upright, but it was now stuck to the floor. Its wings were also useless.

Green walked over to the creature and squatted down next to it, "I tried to be nice, and I warned you."

The creature made a rude hand gesture and tried to drag itself out of the muck.

Red and the elf walked over. "Cool," said Red.

"Aye," said Wayne-Jo. "Wish we'd had such a thing when we went to the grove they are terrorizing. Doubt any of our catchers could shoot that well though."

They all just squatted there for a time watching the creature try to free itself. Then Green said, "I developed the splat to capture insects on Bugworld 7. It works, but is something of a pain. Getting the bugs out of it just requires a solvent, but that generally kills the bug."

The pixie had been valiantly trying to free itself, but froze at Green's comment. "Oh, don't worry little one. Bugs aren't made of metal like you. I can free you anytime. Then what will I do with you? You willing to cooperate and get back in your cloche?"

The pixie made its now trademark rude gesture.

Green sat down and pulled her green leather bag around in front of her. She rummaged around and pulled out something that looked like a little blow torch, shook her head and laid it aside. Then a pair of tweezers, at least 20cm long, and snapped the opening at the monster. It buzzed and swatted. "Not so nice when people snip at you, is it?

"Red, if you would be so kind as to grab the cloche. We'll just put it back on her here."

Red got up and returned with the glass dome.

"I'm going to spray," started Green then looked at the creature, "Don't suppose you want to tell us your name do you?"

It crossed its arms and shook its head, which had the side effect of gluing its arms to its chest.

"Not real bright, are you?" Then she turned back to Red and said, "I'm going to spray Sparkles here with the solvent. Then you put that thing back on her before the goo dissolves. Don't worry it takes a minute or so. Then, Wayne-Jo, we'll lock back up and I'll go get the gear we need to catch the rest of them."

———

THE NEXT AFTERNOON the Space Girls walked down a forest path. Green now wore an outfit very similar to Red's 'warrior princess' outfit, complete with green cloak. Attached to Green's belt and floating above their heads was a semi-transparent balloon. It was about 20cm in diameter and buzzing around inside of it was a very angry golden pixie.

Red felt a little weird holding the device the other Space Girl had given her. It was about a meter long, with the top third a large loop. Inside that loop was a slick membrane that reflected the rainbow in the light. As Green had demonstrated in the cabin prison of Sparkles, if you waved the wand bringing the loop over a buzzing pixie, a bubble formed. Once formed the bubble contracted slightly and began to lose its transparency. More importantly, the pixie inside of it couldn't puncture or damage it. Then through some mysterious science of Green's enviro-lab, it would make its way to the master bubble. Once there the two bubbles would merge to make one larger bubble with more undoubtedly angry pixies inside.

After traversing the path for about an hour, they came to the clearing Wayne-Jo had told them used to be full of the Rozy Maple Bees. The sun was low in the sky when they arrived. The clearing was about a kilometer long and covered in flowers of many dark colors: red, blue, yellow, green, and more. In the center was a still pond about 20 by 15 meters.

"Wow," said Green as they reached the end of the path and continued out into the glade.

"Yeah. I know it doesn't look like it, but this reminds me of home," said Red.

Green turned to her as they walked and said, "Really? How?"

"I think it is all the color."

"Mmmm, ok."

They continued walking till they came to the edge of the pond. Everything was quiet in the clearing. They could see a few insects buzzing around, but not nearly as many as you would expect in a field this big. As they stood there a large pink and yellow bee flew by them to a flower. Another followed it and landed on Red's cloak.

"I guess this is the Rozy Maple Bee," Red said.

"Ooh, they are so cute!"

Then there was an angry hiss and a silver pixie zoomed out of the brush and toward the two women. The Rozy Maple Bee immediately flew for cover in the grasses where the pixie circled above it tweeting angrily.

Red swiped her bubble loop over it. Then it was really mad as it realized it was trapped. Its squeals got louder and it seemed to be calling out for help.

The meadow seemed to explode with flying metallic shapes, and the game was on.

Green pulled a spike out of her bag, thrust it into the ground, and tied the master balloon's lead to it. Then the two Space Girls, agents of change and some of the most bad ass females in the galaxy, frolicked in the field. They ran, leaped and swiped at the pixies. Bubbles floated across the pasture full of angry pixies.

The pixies weren't completely at the girls' mercy. A group of them grabbed on to Green's cloak, which she ignored until she leaped at another pixie and they pulled her cloak backwards, spilling her on the ground. That elicited laughter from everyone, the pixies at their victory and the Space Girls because it was funny.

This went on as the sun set, and the Space Girls were competing on who could catch the most in one swipe when they heard a high melodious voice in the center of the glenn.

"What are you playing at with my pixies?" said a woman floating a few centimeters above the water where a moment before there had been no one.

The two Space Girls froze and turned toward the pond. The fairy queen was a slender woman with pale blue-white skin and shockingly blonde hair that flowed away behind her as if blown by a wind no one else could feel. Her bare torso glowed in the twilight as the moon rose. Small wisps of glowing gold and silver sparks floated away from the points of her platinum crown. Her skirt of pale blue tulle billowed out behind her as she float to the edge of the pond. One small pale foot touched dry land and she walk through the flowers to the balloon full of pixies.

Red was the first to get her wits about her and turned toward the woman. She shifted the bubble wand to her left hand, leaving her bracer arm free. Then she asked, "And who are you, lady?" The tone of the last word could have been respect or hubris.

"I am Iveta, Queen of the Fairies. I created the pixies and they worship me." She turned her face toward the balloon, her crisp, achingly beautiful profile revealed in the last of the sunlight. All of the pixies in the balloon stopped ping ponging around the now quite large globe and attached themselves to a side and bowed their heads. The ones on the bottom even knelt.

"I understand their impish nature, but I would have no harm come to them."

Something was bugging Red about this Queen. She couldn't put her hand on it, but the woman made her angry for no reason.

"As you can see, fair queen," said Green stepping forward, "we have been careful to capture and not harm the creatures. We were asked by the elves to get the pixies to stop frightening the Rozy Maple Bees that inhabit this glade. You see these bees pollenate all of the flowers and then produce a sweet nectar the elves use in their Scout Girl cookies. They are essential to the work of exploration the Scouts do."

The queen made a motion of her hands and the cloud of gold and silver mites sprang off her to the balloon. The balloon sank down until it almost touched the ground. The Queen's light, and it was now obvious she was in fact glowing, shone over the globe which was as tall as she was. The pixies inside wiggled around nervously.

"Why, my children, have you be tormenting theses poor bees?" she asked the creatures as if she might get an answer. Red was surprised when she seemed to get one.

"Because they are prettier than you are. Really?" She made a buzzing sound and out of the grass a dozen Rozy Maple Bees rose. Each was accompanied by a little mote of white light so they were plainly visible. They flew around the Queen for a moment in a curious pattern, then settled on her up turned hand. "They are cute, my dears. But in the way a puppy is cute. All fur and bumbling. Nothing like you in your beauty. You do not have to be jealous of them."

The Space Girls had approached and were now inside the glow of the Queen's light. From here they could see the pixies inside the bubble plainly. They all seemed to be trying to hide their faces by looking away or just burying them in their hands. Some hugged each other and looked like they might be crying.

They were close enough to the Queen to see that her pale skin was so fair as to be translucent and you could see blue veins in it like marble. There were also lines of gold and silver winding over her like the veins, but these lines were on the surface and moved. Looking at them made Red's scars itch.

"Yes, yes, I know you are sorry." The queen blew toward her hand and the little pink bees all took off looking for a flower. Their matching motes of light drifted down to the Queen's hand and formed a new line of silver. "But really you have upset the elves. They do so care for our forests and do good for the galaxy. You mustn't interfere with them."

She looked at the two Space Girls and said, "I could burst this bubble with my own powers, but expect one of you has the power to do that without its destruction."

"Yes, ma'am," Green said and started to raise her bracer so she could get to the bubble controls.

Red thought the Queen was making a point by mentioning she could burst it. "Wait a minute. You aren't going to just let those things free are you?"

Both of the other women looked at her surprised. The Queen's hands suddenly became brighter. Orange tendrils of mist swirled around them a little like flame, a little like smoke. "I assure they will obey my commands. Won't you, my pretties?"

All the pixies Red could see nodded enthusiastically.

Red pulled on her corset, which was really itching. "I don't know, Queen Iveta. There is something wrong about you."

The itching got to be too much for her, she growled and stepped back. Red pulled the cord at her neck and the cloak fell off. She yanked at the hooks in the front of her corset. It quickly came off and dropped to the ground.

The Queen, Green, and even the pixies in their bubble gasped.

"Red, what happened to your scars?"

Red looked down. The formerly pale scars God King Bruno had left her with now glowed gold. She looked up, saw the glowing of the Queen's hands, the blonde hair, the bare chest over a long skirt. It all clicked and she raised her arm to point the gun at the queen.

"What have you done to me?" she yelled.

The Queen took an involuntary step backwards. The balloon popped quietly like a soap bubble and the pixies flooded out of it. They gathered in a mass between the Fairy Queen and the angry Space Girl.

"You're a Xercian! The hair, the clothes. Yes, the skin is wrong, but you all changed it once, you could do it again." She motioned at the glowing hands, "And the powers. Just like him."

The Queen uncovered her mouth, her shocked expression changing to one of pain. "Oh, you poor thing. I am so sorry he hurt you."

Green had moved over next to her rainbow mate, her raygun aimed at the Queen. The other she had raised, reading off a display on her bracer. "She's right; you are Xercian. There's some variation, but the genes are mostly there. And you are crawling with live nanites like the dead ones I removed from Space Girl Red." She dropped the scanner arm, but not her raygun. "I think you better explain yourself, quickly."

There was a long moment filled only with the sound of pixie wings and Red taking deep breaths. Then the Fairy Queen shook herself, squared her shoulders, and said, "I don't believe I have to explain myself to you."

Red almost shot her then. She half closed her hand. Oh, she wanted to so bad, but that wouldn't get her what she really wanted which was an explanation. She looked down at the scars on her chest, now covered in golden nanites. They no longer itched and she had to admit that if she had to have a crazy pattern of lightning on her chest gold looked almost elegant. "What are you doing to me now?"

The queen looked intently at Red's chest for the first time. "Ahhh, that was involuntary, but they are trying to remove the scars. Do you wish me to stop them?"

Green leaned over to Red and said in a low voice, "Talked to Purple at Kitch and she mentioned there was some 'lady of the forest' who might have the power to heal you. This must be who she was talking about."

"What? Purple knows this person?" Red answered feeling that she was being left out of a lot of things. "Wait, Purple was on Kitch. When we were? I didn't see her."

"It's a story, but no she doesn't know her. She just heard rumors. Yes, Purple was there while you were talking to the Queen. She was checking on you. I said you were fine. She had to go on another mission. Is this really the time for this?" Green said, nodding toward the Fairy Queen.

Red thought she was right and looked down again at her bare chest. Truth was, more than anything she wanted Bruno's mark off her, but could she trust this woman? "What will it cost me? I understand nothing is free with fairies."

Queen Iveta smiled, "As you have noted, I am not a true fairy. But I am a Fair Woman, or was. My magic is tuned to me and the golden motes on you reflect my desire to help and heal. They are practically acting on their own, because I certainly wouldn't have helped you at this point in our discussion. What with you having imprisoned my pixies and now pointing guns at me."

Red understood and dropped her arm. Green though, was having none of that. With her raygun unwavering on Queen Iveta she said, "We did capture your pixies because they were a danger to the forest and the rozy bees. But we captured them and did not kill them, which would be within our rights and authority. Frankly I think they were enjoying the game there at the end. Weren't you, Sparkles? Where are you, little one?"

One golden pixie separated itself from the swarm and flew over to the Space Girls. She wove a quick figure eight through them and landed on Green's raygun. She nodded enthusiastically and her wings fluttered as she tried to push the gun down. "No, No, Sparkles. I'm not putting this gun down till your queen understands why it is there." She flicked her wrist and dislodged the pixie.

Red arched her eye brows at her rainbow mate. This was not the Green she remembered, fighting when she herself was willing to negotiate. Red kept her arm down, but was ready to back her friend if needed.

"Where we come from," Green continued, "it is assault to do something to someone's body without their consent, even to touch them. Perhaps where you come from that isn't so, Queen Iveta, but one of the reasons Space Girls exist is to correct such misconceptions."

Fairy Queen Iveta gave a smirk and made a flowing slight bow to Green. "As you say, Space Girl Green. As you say," she then turned to Red, and said, "Which brings us back to the question. Do you want me to call my magic back or heal your scars? I assure you there will be no obligation between us for that."

Red had accepted the scars as a trophy of her trials. To remove them would make it like nothing had happened. She had intended to carry them until justice was done to Bruno, which is what she told the queen. "I do want them gone, but I intend to carry them until God King Bruno is brought to justice. I don't know yet how that will be done, or when. Once it is, if the offer is still open, I would come back for healing."

"So fierce, you Space Girls. To have such done to you by one so powerful I ran from him, then vow to defeat him. Even to carry the mark until you do. That is something." The Fairy Queen stood for a moment with her hand on her chin thinking. "Tell me, Space Girl Red, do you like the golden color they have now?"

"Actually, yes."

"Then let us do this. Allow my magic to stay on you. Let it be a symbol that I too want your vow to be accomplished. When it is, tell Sparkles and she will see they do their work." She looked at both of the women for an answer.

"Yes, your majesty," agreed Red. Once she had Astroboy back, a trip to Keblr would be nothing.

Green just stood there. The queen looked at her meaningfully. "Oh, sure I agree too. Thought it was just between the two of you."

The Fairy Queen smiled again, "Oh, no. You made yourself part of this with your actions. Actions that will have consequences beyond my control. And the first of those consequences is that you - Space Girl Green - cannot leave Keblr until Sparkles comes to you. You named her and that has impact. She and you are not quite ready for the galaxy, but it shouldn't be more than a few days for me to prepare her. Wait."

As she said this the Queen of the Fairies of Keblr, along with all of her pixies, began to fade. When she said that last word, she stepped back and was gone.

The two Space Girls stood there for a moment, then Red bent down to retrieve her corset and put it back on. "So, Green, think we can find the path in the dark?"

Green laughed and pointed to the forest's edge. There the opening to the path glowed a slight golden color. As the two of them walked toward it a thousand Rozy Maple Bees burst out of the grasses they had been hiding in.

———

SPACE GIRL RED could be patient. She could. In training she'd lain in a sniper's blind for days waiting for a target to appear. She'd stayed undercover to break a crime syndicate for a month. She could be patient.

But after two weeks of waiting for Sparkles to show up for Green, she was going crazy. She'd tried to keep busy: running through the forests, learning to climb the monster trees from the elves. Even a couple of days of hide and seek with the rainbow of Scout Girls from a saucer in for supplies. But she was ready to go now.

She could tell Green was getting bored too. Despite having a whole, literally giant, eco-system to explore, Green was ready to go when a flying saucer landed.

Red was out on a run in the forest when she heard the familiar whirr of a flying saucer pass over. She did the last 5km in a record time, hoping it was Astroboy coming to get her. Green could stay as long as the Queen wanted, there was nothing that said Red had to stay with her.

But when she got to the landing field the saucer parked there wasn't Astroboy. Space Girl Orange was standing in the middle of the field with Green looking at something hovering between them. Red walked the last few meters to catch her breath and hide her disappointment before she greeted her rainbow mate.

The focus of their attention was a gold pixie struggling to stay in the air. Green held out a hand and the pixie put something there. After she did she could fly as fast a hummingbird and zipped around Green chittering with excitement.

The space girls noticed her as she approached and paused to smile. Green was wearing the standard leather outfit with cloak they had adopted as 'Keblr standard'. Red was wearing a sports bra and running skirt. All of which were drenched in sweat.

Orange, with the Purpose of bringing beauty wherever she was called, could have worn a burlap sack and looked good in it.

Today she wore a one shoulder jumpsuit with a ochre top and skirt. The skirt reached to her ankles, but only came partially around in front. The legs of the jumpsuit were a umber color and tucked into red Space Girl boots.

To cap it off she wore a wide brimmed white hat that kept the sun off her face and formed a frame around her head. The icon of beauty stepped toward Red with arms out for a hug.

Red put her hands up and said, "Just finished a run, Orange, and I'm covered in sweat. May want to save the hug for another time."

"Nonsense," Orange said, embracing her rainbow mate tightly. "I seem to remember in training you used to make it a point to get sweaty and hug me."

Red laughed at the memory, "That was just to give you a challenge in beauty class." She sniffed loudly, "And you still manage to smell great even covered in my sweat."

"I guess it is just the combination of our scents that you like," she ruffled Red's hair and said, "Love the new do. You'll be setting trends. Bringing short hair back."

Orange's hair fell to her waist behind her. Where Red's was an unnatural red, Orange's was a true ginger.

"Hey, what about me!" came a small voice from Green's still extended hand. It coincided with the normal tweeting from the pixie. "I brought gifts."

This got everyone's attention. Whatever she had laid in Green's hands it had given the little pixie a voice. Green pulled up her scanner and waved it at the two necklaces. They had gold chains with a pendant of silver and a flat, blue stone. The stone appeared plain at a distance, but up close there was movement inside. It reminded Red of the bubble where Astroboy lived.

"Sparkles, what are these?" asked Green. "My scanner's got nothing."

"They are translators' stones. They let you understand me."

She landed on Red's shoulder and peered into an ear. "Your ears seem to be broken. But my old Queen made these for you."

She flittered over to Green and landed on her shoulder. "Sparkles has a new queen now. Space Girl Green gave me a name; now I worship Space Girl Green." She stretched out the word worship swooningly.

Red laughed and said, "I guess that was the consequence the Fairy Queen was talking about. You named her; now she is yours. You needed to wait for the Queen to make something so you could be a good queen to her."

"Wait! I can't have a pixie worshiping me. I can't have anything worshiping me."

This obviously upset Sparkles a great deal. She knelt down on her knees and clasped her hands together. "Please don't send Sparkles back. I would have to give up my name. Sparkles is the only pixie with a name. Please let me stay. Please."

"Come on, Green. You could use a pet. She'd make a great accessory," said Red.

"So if you give a pixie a name you get to keep it?" asked Orange.

"No, if you name a pixie it gets to keep you," said Sparkles.

"You know about pixies, Orange?" asked Space Girl Red.

"Of course she does, Space Girl Red," the little pixie said. She flew down to Green's hand, grabbed one of the necklaces and took it to Red. "You should wear this. Maybe it will make you smarter. Why do you think she is here?"

Then the pixie flew over to the new Space Girl and said, "The Fairy Queen is expecting you at sunset. You just follow that path, past the elf factory tree and on till you come to the glade of the Rozy Maple Bees. They are cute like puppies, not beautiful like me." Then she flew over and landed on Green's shoulder again. "Or my Space Girl."

They all laughed. Green and Red slipped the necklaces over their heads.

"I guess I'd better be going," said Orange. "Though I lack you all's fashion accessories."

"Ask the Fairy Queen for your own," said Sparkles. Then in a conspiratorial whisper added, "It took her awhile to figure out how they should work. But once she did it was easy to make more."

Red said, "It seems we're free to leave now. So let's get in Halamar and head back to Kitch ASAP."

Then she heard the sweetest sound she'd heard in a very long time.

"Or you could ride back in me, Space Girl Red," said Astroboy in her ear.

CHAPTER 17
THE QUEEN & BLUE

QUEEN NATALIE of Kitch sat on her throne in the same silver on silver outfit as Space Girl Red's first audience. Space Girl Blue wondered if it insulated her against the cold coming off everyone in the room. There weren't many, but clearly none of them liked Blue one bit. Prince Alfred in his dress uniform had escorted her to his mother's throne.

For her part Blue wore her ship jumpsuit, a shiny blue one piece garment that covered her from ankle to neck. She wore her standard Space Girl utility belt and a raygun on her hip. Given their complete dislike of her, she was surprised they hadn't even asked her to take it off, although it wouldn't have mattered much if they had.

"I understand you have the Esaul Power Crystal Rivere that once belonged to the so-called God King Bruno," said the queen.

"I do, your majesty," said Blue. "I was led to believe you wished to purchase it."

"I do."

Ok then, no chit chat. "I am willing to part with it for 100 million quintars," said Blue looking the queen of three worlds in the eye.

There was an intake of breath somewhere behind her. The queen merely looked at her for a long moment and said, "For that I could buy a new star fighter."

"And for that I can give an entire race the chance to be educated to a level they can join the galactic civilization, which is exactly what I intend to do." She stood her ground, knowing the Collectors wouldn't pay that much because they were mad at her, but they would buy it. "Given your planet doesn't seem to need the power in the crystals, I'm thinking you intend to use it to start a war. So you must have all the fighters you need."

There was much shuffling of feet and murmuring around her.

"How noble of you, Space Girl Blue," said the queen. "I assume you know what your theft cost your sister Space Girl Red."

Blue had the good graces to look down before she answered, "I have been recently and forcefully informed by two of my rainbow mates and Red's flying saucer." She looked back up at the queen, "If it matters, I never knew that is what would happen. I underestimated King Bruno."

The queen took a deep breath, then exhaled and said, "As have we all it seems. May I see the necklace?"

"Of course," Blue said and unzipped the front of her jump-suit. A silver chain came around from the back of her neck and ended at each of her clavicles. A loop of jewels completed the arch of necklace, one line of sapphire colored gems above another. Three simple plain diamonds the size of her finger held the two parts of the loop separated at intervals. The center of the sapphires also anchored a line of glowing power crystals, one the size and color of Blue's eye. The last jewel ended at the top of her décolletage. These jewels were not simple crystals, no matter how fine. They held power that swirled and churned in its confines. They glowed brightly enough to color the Space Girl's skin from breast to chin.

Queen Natalie rose from her throne and walked down the steps to get a closer look. Blue could see the light of the necklace reflected on the queen's silver outfit. "It is beautiful," Queen Natalie said in awe.

Blue had probably looked exactly as impressed the first time she saw it. If Orange had seen it in God King Bruno's possession she probably would have grabbed it and fought her way off the planet just to get that beauty somewhere worthy of it.

"Prince Alfred," Queen Natalie said, "pay the woman. May I?" She asked reaching for the necklace.

"My Queen, it will take a few minutes to get that kind of money in a form the Space Girl can take with her."

"Space Girl Blue, will you trust me to pay you?"

Blue smiled and said, "Yes, your Majesty. Allow me." She reached behind her neck and seamlessly removed the device that would have hurt anyone else who might try unclasping it.

The silver clad woman took it in her hands and just experienced it for a long moment. Then she said, "Curator McLean, would you please take possession of this and prepare to display it in the Royal Museum of Kitch?"

A tall thin man with ginger hair stepped forward. He had a black box about 20cm on a side that he opened and allowed the Queen to place the necklace in. Then he motioned to a group of men off to one side and they headed toward the door. The group had 'guards' written large on them and bulges concealing armor and weaponry.

"Your majesty," Blue said glancing at the still attentive Prince, "majesties, I want you to know that I will make it right between Red and myself. I heard you gave her your highest honor and I thank you for that. If there is anything I can do to aid you, please let me know."

The queen had reseated herself on her throne, and looked at Blue, "Actually there is something you might be able to help us with, since you seem to have knowledge of burglary. If you would join my son and I for dinner tonight in the royal chambers, we would discuss it with you. We shall be inviting all the other Space Girls on port as well."

"I assure you we will also have your payment ready by then," said Prince Alfred.

"I would be honored." Blue bowed.

————

DINNER WAS an intimate affair in a small dining hall obviously set up for working as well as eating. The Queen was there in a conservative but attractive dress. The Prince was still in his dress uniform, as were the other two military men: the commander of the Flying Monkeys on Kitch 10 and the head of military intelligence. The three Space Girls had worn their dress dresses. "You got a promotion," was the first thing Yellow said when she saw now Major Winchester Powell.

"Yes, Space Girl Yellow," the blue skinned monkey answered. "The Queen has added quite a number of craft to the home port which changed it from a Flight to a Squadron. It wasn't appropriate for a mere captain to command it."

"And you have served well and deserve it, Winchester," Prince Alfred said joining the conversation. "Your liaison with the Space Girls would be enough to merit it, but you also have an impressive record of getting maintenance and repair done."

"Indeed, Major, you run a tight ship," said Yellow. "I've worked in a few shipyards and yours is top of the line. When I got here I was a little afraid I might have to tow Astroboy back Home for repairs, or call in an Engineer repair saucer. But you had everything we needed."

Across the room, Blue and Purple stood together watching the others mingle.

"So how you handling it, Blue?" asked Purple.

The Prince had just given her a Caladium ingot slightly smaller than her hand. One of the rarest of metals, the small ingot was enough to pay for the rivere. It was scored with a grid of lines to make it easier to break into smaller amounts.

"It is a lot to be carrying when I left my rayguns on the saucer. But I guess I'll trust the Queen's guards." She had already slipped the bar into an inner pocket of her jumpsuit and could feel it cool against her chest.

"Not about the money, about the reception you are getting."

"Ahhh, it's no big deal. I get why they feel that way. It's the price of being a Space Girl. Sometimes you rub people the wrong way when you do your job."

"You've gotten stupid if you think this is a normal reaction to a Space Girl 'doing her job'," Purple said, taking a sip of the excellent champagne. "If you think you can fain indifference to me, you are also full of it. Which, come to think of it, would also mean you were getting stupider."

Blue was having a problem with it on a number of levels. Red was some kind of folk hero on this planet. Even before Bruno, she'd won the dance contest that went viral on the planet net. Then she came back all shot up from Bruno, which to a planet on the edge of war made her a bigger hero. News services were doing daily reports on the progress of Astroboy's repairs. All that would have been enough to ruffle Blue's feathers, but then she'd landed and everyone wanted to know who she was. Yellow was widely known because of her work on Astroboy and the Flying Monkey mechanics thought she was a goddess.

Then they found out she was Space Girl Blue. Faces turned stiff and jaw muscles clinched. Last time she'd been here as a smuggler she could sneak around the city. Now she required an escort just to get back and forth from the port.

Finally, below all that was a feeling she deserved it. Thinking about what Red had gone through because of her prank made it hard to sleep.

"Isn't the Space Girl of Love supposed to be soft and squishy?" Blue asked.

"Punk love, that's my thing."

"What the hell is that?"

"I spent some time on a planet doing a tour where I gave advice on love. Weird place that one. Lots of couples and triads of males and females, but they got it in their head a girl from a planet of all women would have the answers. So I toured around and answered questions at town meetings. After they started bootlegging the recordings - don't have a planet net there, so they have to use physical media to pass things around - they labeled them Punk Love."

"Were you singing or something?"

Purple smiled, "Light, no. I just answered people directly. Got in their faces with they were being dumbasses. Wasn't afraid to ask if they were stupid or deaf or blind. They called it punk love." Blue could tell she actually really liked the term.

"So are you going to tell me how you are handling being the most hated woman on the planet?" Purple said.

Blue was saved from answering by the appearance of the head of Military Intelligence, Colonel Munroe Innes. One second they were alone and the next he was there. *Damn spooks,* thought Blue impressed. "Hello ladies, I'm Colonel Innes. We met when you came in. I was wondering if I could show you something, Space Girl Blue? Won't take a minute."

"Of course, Colonel. Catch up with you later, Purple."

The two of them walked away and Purple smiled.

———

COLONEL INNES LEAD her to a display screen on one wall, authenticated himself and called up a video file. "I know you have some expertise at sneaking in and out of the Kitch system, and, if I'm not wrong, sneaking around in general. We had an assassin make an attempt on the Queen's life. Or at least that is what we assumed he was trying to do."

"It is generally obvious when someone tries to kill you. How can you be unsure of an assassination attempt?" Blue asked.

"They got the wrong room. We have a protocol that has her majesty sleeping in a number of different place in the castle. It hasn't always been true, but in these troubled times it seemed wise." He did something on the display and a video of a dark bedroom appeared.

"And I take this is one of those rooms? A royal bedroom."

"This is the official one. It's location isn't known to the public, but I don't doubt it would be easy for a determined agent to find out."

Beyond the royal bed was a window and a head appeared silhouetted in it. It was coming from above and looked around slowly. Blue could think of a number of means to climb down the outer wall like that. Then more body appeared and one hand drew a line all the way around the glass. With more deft motions it eased the window's glass in and down to the floor. A swift flip and the dark figure dropped into the room. In the time between holding the window ledge and flipping in, to the crouched silent landing, two curved knives appeared in her hands.

"Impressive move. She's good," said Blue still watching as the woman moved around the room looking for a quarry that wasn't there. She didn't try to rummage through anything, so burglary or information retrieval were out.

"You think that is a woman?" Asked the Colonel surprised.

"Uh, yeah. Obvious isn't it?"

"Perhaps I don't have your cultural bias to assume an assassin is female, but I don't see how you could tell the difference here."

Blue looked at him a little shocked. "You mean you don't know who and what she is?"

"No, we've been stumped since it happened. Are you saying you can identify the person? You know who they are?"

"Yes, and you do to. Though I can understand how you might not have made the connection." She glided her hand across the progress bar at the bottom of the screen to rewind to the flip and landing. Then she froze it.

"Those knives are the give away. They are from the Tyfo sect of the Syndicate of Assassins. I doubt you have a whole lot of those on your planet, and since I met one here just a few days before this video was taken I'd be willing to bet it was her."

Colonel Inness was dumbfounded. "You met her when you were here before. I knew you'd been here and left the night after the dance contest. I did not know you'd met with anyone. And you met this woman?"

"Yes, she was guarding the idiot that gave me the data coin for God King Bruno. She's pretty good, but not Space Girl good. I called her out of hiding after he'd engaged me to take the data to Bruno. She came out of hiding and I saw her clearly."

She looked closer at the video. "Sure is handy having matte black skin. You don't have to wear clothes that would get in the way. See," she motioned to the moonlight on the assassin. "She's topless. That's a Xercian thing. She is wearing a mask, but I'm pretty sure she's the same one I met that night. I wonder how many assassins God King Bruno has had trained? Probably not many. The Tyfo are supposed to be pretty brutal and not many make it."

"OK, I give up. You are better than my whole building full of analysts if you can name the person."

Blue smiled broadly. It was good to be called the best, especially here. "That is Venuše Kozel, the ambassador's *assistant*. The guy who gave me the data coin for God King Bruno was the same person who lost the dance contest to Red, Ctirad Drahoslav, and Venuše was his partner."

"Oh my God," said the spook and turned to the room. "Your Majesty, I need your presence please."

Soon everyone was standing in front of the display looking at the frozen picture of the assassin in the Queen's bedroom.

"My Queen, Space Girl Blue has identified the assassin. I apologize that we weren't able to figure it out ourselves."

"Have them arrested at once then," said the Queen, confused that he hadn't already done it.

"She is Xerces's Second Ambassador's assistant, Ma'am."

"Ahhh." Now the Queen understood.

CHAPTER 18
NEW DANGERS DISCOVERED

CTIRAD DRAHOSLAV, former second ambassador and hopefully soon to be governor of Kitch 10, was not one to question the orders of his God King. But as his two-person craft circled slowly over the Zoran city, he began to wonder. It was a tangled mess of buildings with no true roads, only what seemed like the worn tracks of ants. The whole planet was a dark black mass with an atmosphere unbreathable by humans.

Why the God King wanted him to come here was a mystery. He and Venuše had managed to sneak out of Kitch 10 and back to Xerces when it become known that harlot, Space Girl Red, was coming back from Xerces damaged. He had thought God King Bruno had done as he suggested but the girl had escaped. When he got to Xerces and seen the damage she had done, he was worried. When the God King had begun to peel away his skin for lying to him, he thought himself for the mines. But Venuše had intervened on his behalf, though a little later than he would have liked. Then they had all found the extent of the lies Space Girl Blue had told.

Still, it had been the altered data coin that had given his greatness this idea and ultimately sent Ctirad and Venuše to

Zoran. There had been a list of Red's accomplishments that included pictures of the Zoran's attack on Kenix. God King Bruno had become very excited when he saw the creatures. He had created the monolith, then ordered Ctirad and Venuše to deliver it to Zoran.

Which was why they were circling this place looking for the space port or just spaceships.

"I think I have a lock on a Space drive unit," said Venuše at the controls. She rolled the small ship to port and said, "Don't know if there is a ship around it, but that's the closest thing I've found."

"I thought it would be obvious. I mean they invaded a planet not a few months ago, surely they felt the need to keep a fleet to protect their planet," Ctirad answered.

"You'd think, but they weren't really invading. More a smash and grab raid. Also still just garbage on the airwaves. Can't make heads or tails of it." She followed a dot on her scanner toward the Space drive's location. "If there is one thing these people are not, it is organized"

"Indeed."

In the near distance there was a tall tower with a globe on top. As they altered their course to go around it they could see it was gutted and damaged at the top. The Space drive, at least according to the sensors, was very close by. There was something that might have once been the fuselage of a spaceship laying on its side.

"That's where the signal is coming from. Don't see a ship, or a port, or really even a place to land," Venuše said as she started to circle the ship around.

"Mmmm, the God King said the monolith should be set up near their space port so they could build a fleet. This looks like as good as it is going to get."

"Still no place to land."

"Yes, and I don't like the look of that city, if you can call it that. I'm not sure I want to be on the ground."

"What about that tower?" she asked pointing the scouts nose back toward it. "It looks kind of central, or important. Perhaps we could put the nano-bomb, there."

Ctirad looked as her puzzled, "Nano-bomb? You mean the monolith? Who said it was a nano-bomb?"

Venuše did not turn to look at him. "Yes, of course, the monolith."

"Hey, if this thing is a bomb I need to know about it. Why didn't you say anything sooner? I could be killed placing it."

"You'll be fine. Just wear your spacesuit and keep it closed up. A nano-bomb is just something that produces a nano-cloud. The danger is in the nanos. The one we set on Kitch was nasty to humans. I think this one will have a different effect on the Zoran."

Ctirad still wasn't sure he liked the idea, but orders from the God King were orders. "All right then, let's put it in the tower. That will at least keep us away from those things while we set it up. Can you land the ship there?"

"Nope," said Venuše with a smile. "But I can hover it. You'll have to go out a hatch and place the monolith by yourself."

"What?!"

"Don't worry, you can do it, Ctirad. I have faith in you."

Ctirad grumbled but started moving aft to get on his space-suit. He noticed, not for the first time, she didn't use his title. Technically he didn't have a title, having abandoned his post on Kitch as Second Ambassador. But she'd really stopped being deferential to him while the nanos were eating his skin on Xerces. He would have to see what he could do about her once he became ruler of Kitch 10.

The monolith was about a meter tall, 50cm wide and 10cm deep. On the top there was a small lip that stuck out one side a couple of centimeters. His instruction had been to set the monolith on a flat surface near the spaceport, then pull the lip, which would open the top of the thing.

Ctirad triggered the cargo door and looked out when it opened. Venuše was holding the craft rock steady less than a meter from the top of the tower. The top of the ball was relatively flat and he expected that would work. After double checking his suits seals, he knelt and hugged the monolith. When it was in firm contact with his suit, he could feel it buzz and vibrate slightly. He straightened his legs and lifted the black object. It was not as heavy as he had expected, making him think it might be hollow. The light weight made his movements a lot easier and he walked to the door and stepped out.

It was an awkward fall, half a meter being too far for a step, and not far enough for a jump really. But he was sure footed from dance, and landed with nary a bobble. Gingerly setting the object down, he stepped back and looked around. The city didn't look any better from up here. Then he noticed vibration coming from his boots.

The tower wasn't empty. Something was moving on it. A lot of somethings.

Ctirad grabbed the trigger on the the monolith just as the first Zoran appeared over the curve of the ball. His surprise and fear seemed to levitate him back into the ship still holding the top piece of the monolith in one hand. "Get us out of there, Venuše!"

Dozens of little mechanical creatures in all shapes and sizes ran toward him and toward the monolith. Some sprouting saws and hammers from appendages.

The monolith changed.

A black liquid fountained out of the now open top. It oozed and spread over the top of the tower. The first robot man touched it and froze. A tendril of black goo would slithered up an appendage and disappeared into the body. Every Zoran seemed to keep its brain somewhere different, but the nanos always found it. Once the liquid got inside, the Zoran stopped trying to reach Ctirad. Instead they started climbing down the tower.

Venuše held the ship above the city and they watched the black liquid spread down the tower. It stopped moving before it reached the ground, but there were many Zoran still flooding toward the tower, and those on it were going to the fallen spaceship. They produced tools from their various appendages and began to work turning it back into a working interstellar spacecraft.

"The power of the God King," said Ctirad in wonder as he strapped into the co-pilot's chair.

"He made himself an army," agreed Venuše. Then tilted the scout ship skyward and engaged the thrusters. "One we had nothing to do with."

"Of course," said Ctirad. "Time to go home."

———

IT FELT SO, so good to sit in Astroboy's control seat. Space Girl Red was back home. Out the canopy she could see Green with her little golden companion perched on one shoulder, talking with Orange. Red had been seeing a lot of her rainbow mates lately. Space Girls could go months, if not years, without seeing each other. If it weren't for the Jubilee, some might never run into the girls they had grown up with. Red had seen every member of her Rainbow in the last month—except one, and that one had left her a message.

"Play it, Astroboy."

"As you will, Ma'am," Astroboy said. It was good to hear his voice again, which she had already told him multiple times.

The canopy went opaque and became one big display. In this case it showed a flying saucer control room. Since everything was red, she knew it had been recorded aboard Astroboy. The illusion reached down into the controls themselves and made it seem the whole room was twice as big. Standing a few feet in front of her was Space Girl Blue.

"First and foremost, Red, I'm sorry. I would never have conned 'God King' Bruno that way if I'd known what would happen. I figured he'd catch you and lock you up, then you'd escape and all would be well. I mean the guy is obviously an asshole, so the whole God King thing seemed like arrogance."

Red noticed that Blue was doing that thing she did when she was caught out during training. She'd look you in the eyes, head held high with complete confidence, but her feet shuffled and she didn't seem to know what to do with her hands.

"Then I heard you had escaped on the Rainbow net a couple of days later. I laid low and avoided you because, well, I knew you'd want payback. It's what we do." She shrugged and shuffled her feet.

"Then Purple called and said the Queen of Kitch wanted to buy the necklace. I'd heard you'd gone off with Green while your saucer was repaired, so I went to Kitch to make the deal." Then she broke eye contact for the first time, glancing off to the side for a second.

"I knew something was up when I saw your saucer."

"Both Purple and Yellow were waiting for me. Turns out Yellow could give Space Woman Black a run for her money in the chewing out department. I didn't even know she knew some of those words," Blue kind of smiled. Then her expression became grave. "Then she showed me the med-scan pictures."

The other Space Girl's eyes started to glisten and she had to look away from the camera. All the bravado was gone. "I couldn't believe it. I don't know how you survived."

She wiped her nose and re-squared her shoulders. "I wanted to turn around and take Buck back to Xerces right there, but it was Purple's turn to chew me out.

"You know Purple. She can give you a talking to, never raise her voice, sound like cold clean logic, and make you wish Space Woman Black was going to chew you out for a month."

There was a long pause, so long Red realized her own face was wet. When Blue again looked at her, she could see tears on Blue's cheeks too. "She made me realize this wasn't about Bruno. It was about me and you. Yeah, we push each other. We foil each other's plans. Argue about everything. But we don't truly endanger each other. Which I did, and, as Purple made clear, the first thing I needed to do to make it right was talk to you.

"I know this isn't face to face, but it is what I have. Probably easier for both of us. Not sure I could get past old habits if we were face to face.

"I was glad Astroboy's weapons were off line when I went to ask to record this in your control room. He said no, of course. It took both Yellow and Purple to convince him I should be let in." She paused to glance around the control room and said, "He's obviously got every control disabled, and only let me up here as long as the other two stayed just down the ladder."

"That's ok. I get it. But he won't talk to Buck either, and that's not fair," said Blue with some of her old fierceness back into her voice. Then she deflated again and said, "But I get it. It's my fault and Buck would tell me it served me right."

"All right," she said and wiped her face and stood up straight. "This has gone on long enough. Again, and most simply, I'm sorry, Red."

"I owe you. I made the sale to Queen Natalie and need to take the funds to Altar for the slugs. But whenever you are ready to bring justice to Bruno, you let me know and I'll be right there with you."

"Until then, know I love you," Blue said. Her stumbling voice added, "You're the best," stunning Red.

"For now," Blue added as the screen faded to black. Red had to smile.

———

ONCE ORANGE HAD HEADED off to meet with the Queen of the Fairies, Red had been ready to go. There was some kerfuffle settling Sparkles into Halamar's ecosystem so Red had gone ahead and lifted.

"Ma'am, I noticed some weird readings when I came in system today. Would you mind checking them out before we head back to Kitch?" asked Astroboy.

"Not at all. Matter of fact we don't even really have to go back to Kitch. I was just going stir crazy on Keblr. What have you got?"

"Mmmm, as you know, Space Girl Orange and Merlin arrived before me to the planet, but they didn't come in from the same vector as the portal from Kitch."

"Doesn't Keblr have more than one portal?"

"Yes, according to the charts it currently has two. KP-1 close to the star and unusable to most craft. KP-2 is outside Keblr's orbit, but inside the two planets further out. KP-2 connects to a long Spaceway with many exit portals, including Kitch. It is currently 3 AU from here and almost a direct line from the sun and the planet."

"OK, I get the layout. What is your point?"

"Space Girl Orange came in from a vector that doesn't conform to any known portal. And she came from further out than known portals."

Red thought about this for a moment and said, "Astroboy, have you been spying on my rainbow mates?"

"Ma'am?" Astroboy asked.

"You came in after Orange. Quite a bit after her really, and you are now telling me she came in system from way further out. Which I'm assuming you were able to observe. Which means you had to observe her come in from that distance even though you came in from a shorter one."

"I hear what you are saying, Ma'am."

"And that means, you not only hid from her to observer her, you waited to tell me you were here until she had landed."

"Yes, Ma'am," Astroboy said as his bubble turned pink.

"I'm thinking, Astroboy, that you may have trust issues, since Xerces."

The saucer's AI was silent.

"Mmmm, believe me I understand it. Me and Blue have some things we'll have to work out between us. I expect she and you may have similar things to work out. But you cannot change who you are to my Rainbow mates."

"I understand, Ma'am," said Astroboy.

Red had never thought how the things on Xerces had been for Astroboy. He too had been tortured by Bruno, in ways very similar to what had happened to her. Nanites eating into his skin, marking him. "I'm sorry for what happened, Astroboy. You do have an option I don't."

"I would prefer not to, Ma'am."

"I'm not talking about a personality reset, you know. I like you the way you are. But I can tell you to forget what happened."

"I know, Red, but if you are going to remember it, so am I."

"Very well. You need to treat my rainbow mates - all of them - the same as you would have before."

"Even Space Girl Blue?"

"Of course," then Red smiled. "We never really trusted her before."

A smile came in Astrboy's voice, "Indeed Ma'am. But what about her apology?"

"I believe it. I've known her all my life and she's never tried to kill me before. Even when it would have been to her advantage. We all underestimated God King Bruno. We went in cocky and unprepared and paid the price for it. We won't do that again."

"Yes, Ma'am."

"Now I take it you want to look into where Orange and Merlin were coming in from?"

"Yes, ma'am. Here is her vector." The display changed to show the system and a dotted line leading out of it.

"Interesting," Red said, changing the saucer's heading and engaging the repulsors. "This system's astroid belt is at the outskirts. That's kind of unusual."

They cruised in silence for a while. "Good to have the repulsors back. Is it just me or are you faster?"

"The new repulsors are 15% faster than the old ones. They were a gift from Space Girl Yellow. She had planned to put them on Victor."

"That was nice of her."

They arrived at the edge of the system and slowed as they encountered the astroid belt. Red dove into it and zoomed around the rocks for the fun of it. After a bit of a joy ride, she saw a large tumbling rock ahead and executed a difficult landing on it. There was barely enough gravity to hold them down, so she flipped on the tractor to hold them to the spinning astroid.

The rotation took them from light to dark and her display lit up.

"Space Girl Red," said Astroboy.

"I see it," she answered, looking at the spaceship a few hundred kilometers away. "Do you have an ID?"

The display in front of her brought up a schematic. Looking at it, she asked, "How did that get here?"

The schematic was for a Xerces PT boat. Small and light, like all Xerces craft since they were created planet side, the PT boat had a crew of just three. Its armament was a couple of atomic rockets. While they had a Space Drive, these craft generally didn't operate on their own.

As if reading her mind, Astroboy expanded his sensors. The screen in front of her opened a dozen new windows, and red outlines appeared all over the astroid belt.

Red cursed. "So that's where they went."

"Yes, Ma'am, it appears we've found the Xerces fleet."

"But how, Astroboy? I can understand them sneaking into the Keblr system. The elves don't have a space fleet, but to get here they have to go through the Kitch system. That portal has a destroyer sitting in front of it."

"Well, ma'am, perhaps the portals have changed for Xerces."

"That's not good."

"No, ma'am."

"Not for Kitch, but not for Keblr either. If the Xerces fleet is here, they could easily invade Keblr, but they haven't." Red wondered about that for a few moments. "I'm guessing their leader isn't interested in owning Keblr. Are they staging for an invasion of Kitch? They would be coming out of an unguarded portal, which would give them an advantage."

"Perhaps we would be best served warning Queen Natalie of the threat, Ma'am."

Red tried to think of something else to do, but couldn't. Three Space Girl saucers might be a match of the tens of Xerces ships she could detect from here, but no telling how many there where that she couldn't see. The best bet was to send a message to the elves and then go tell Queen Natalie. She could also let Orange know, so she could tell the Fairy Queen.

"Astroboy, plot me a course for the Kitch portal that will keep these rocks between me and the Xerces ships. As soon as we are out of easily detected range, I'll send Orange and Green a message, then we hightail it to Kitch."

"Yes, Ma'am," said Astroboy and a new plot appeared on her display. She waited till the correct time and powered away from the asteroid she had been parked on. Keeping it between her and the enemy ships, she engaged her repulsors.

They were not very far from the asteroid belt when Astroboy said, "Ma'am, I have located Halamar in transit to the KP-2. Space Girl Green will probably reach it before we do."

"I think Green will wait for me before transiting. I need to talk with Orange. Open a channel."

There was a pause then Astroboy said, "Merlin says Space Girl Orange is in the forest meeting with the Queen of the Fairies. Is that a real person?"

"It is indeed, Astroboy. I've met her. She's actually God King Bruno's mother. She's gene-modded her skin to blue-white, but still Xerces for sure. And she seems to have some of the God King's powers. She calls them magic and they don't seem to have the scope of Brunos."

"Could she have something to do with the Xerces fleet being here?"

"Don't know. That's another thing I'd like to ask Space Girl Orange about." She poured more power into the repulsors to get to the portal faster. "Ask Merlin to give Space Girl Orange a message."

"Yes, Ma'am. Recording."

"Orange, we have discovered the missing Xerces fleet in the Keblr asteroid belt. It seems there is a new portal out beyond the system. But I think you already know that. Since you are meeting with the former Queen of Xerces, I'm hoping you can get us some answers to if she's involved.

"In the mean time, I'm heading back to Kitch to warn Queen Natalie there is a whole Xerces fleet one jump from an unguarded portal to her system.

"Orange, talk to me. I'll be on the Spaceway in," she looked at the plot, "in 5 minutes. You can use Space Girl Net when I'm in transit. End message."

"Tell Green we are in a hurry and won't be pausing at the portal."

CHAPTER 19
ATTACK OF THE ROBOT ARMY

"MAYDAY, MAYDAY," growled the flying monkey around the stub of a cigar clenched between his teeth. "I am under attack by a robot army on final approach to the landing field."

As if to prove his statement a robot crashed into the armored window of the cockpit, shattering into nuts, bolts and a thousand fragments of metal. All around the troop carrier zipped small robots. Most of the robots were shaped like humanoids with two arms and two legs. On their jet packs allowed them to buzz around First Lieutenant Maxwell Tyson's plane like hornets.

They didn't seem very good at flying because they kept crashing into the larger craft. The plane was made for war and could take the non-explosive little robot's impact, though the same couldn't be said of the big jet engines. The first of the dastardly things that got sucked into the *Bella Banana's* port engine had made it cough. The second had made it start smoking. Now he was trying to land with only one of his engines working completely and the other at 50%.

"Mayday. I've lost one engine and the other is on its last legs, clogged with goddam robots. I can glide her in, but I'm not sure about stopping at the end of the runway." His hands were locked on the control wheel while his feet flipped switches and pressed the rudder pedals trying to keep the plane aimed at the landing strip in front of him.

One of the robot pests zipped up and plastered itself to the window in front of him.

"Get out of my way, you god forsaken animated can opener." As if to prove Lieutenant Tyson right, the robot's hand transformed into a circular saw, which it applied to the cockpit window.

How far did he have to go? A glance at the altimeter said he was still 50 meters up and he knew he was three klicks from the landing strip. Close, but that wouldn't help if he couldn't see the freaking runway as he got there.

He wanted to broadcast that he was carrying a troop of new flying monkey pilots and a very special royal secret. But of course that would be stupid in combat, and it wouldn't matter any way. He knew the local squadron was already in the air and had their own robot army problems.

The pesky saw-robot finished cutting a square in the cockpit window. Then promptly disappeared because he'd cut the hole all the way around himself. For a few glorious seconds, Maxwell had a chance to check the location of the runway and adjust his heading. A new robot landed on the wind screen and crawled over to the opening. His arm was a drill bit spinning menacingly as he started to crawl through the opening.

Lieutenant Tyson grabbed the control stick with one of his lower hands, crossdrew a revolver, and shot the robot. The craft bucked as his maneuver caused him to bobble the controls. He dropped the revolver and grabbed all the controls with the proper limbs.

"Hey, I could use a little help up here," he yelled back over his shoulder at the cargo bay. "One of you knuckleheads grab a side arm and climb up here. We're being boarded!"

There was a loud *bang, bang, bang* from behind him and a shout of, "Not just up there, LT." He could hear his sergeant barking orders as he moved closer.

Then the starboard engine went quiet.

"Don't that just beat all," Maxwell said. "Guess we're gliding in."

His controls were mushy and the altimeter was dropping too fast. "Mayday, Mayday, this is Flight Troop Museum. I have lost both engines and am losing altitude fast. Better clear the runway; we're coming in hot."

His sergeant had just climbed up into the cock pit with him and noticed their angle of descent. A couple of colorful words decorated the rushing air as the sergeant frantically buckled himself into the nearest seat before they crashed.

"Don't worry, Troop Museum," came a calm female voice over the radio. "I've got you."

Then something grabbed the plane and leveled them out. Someone was using a tractor beam and enveloping the whole plane in a forcefield that kept the robots from getting to the *Bella Banana.*

"This is Space Girl Red. Why don't you let me do the flying from here on in?"

———

RED WAS JUST SETTING the troop carrier down on the field of the space port when Green radioed her, "Red, do you still have your Rosetta Stone on? You have to check this out!"

She was in fact still wearing the necklace the Fairy Queen had given them. "Yes, I'm wearing it. What's up?"

The Zoran army were still banging themselves against her

forcefield trying to get at the heavily damaged troop carrier. Why was that so important to them?

"Sparkles noticed it first," Green said. "Halamar had turned on the frequency the Zorans are using and she just started yelling at them. Asking what they thought they were doing attacking her Space Girl."

"She what? How?"

"That's just it, she could understand them. And so can I with the Rosetta Stone."

"Astroboy, tune into the Zoran frequency."

"Yes, Ma'am."

Her cockpit was filled with a cacophony of sounds and voices. Just like the first time Red had heard Sparkles, she got some of the emotion from the sounds she heard, but the words came from the stone itself. In this case there were so many voices it was hard to pick out just one, but Red heard a lot of, "Get the river. Get the stones. For the God King."

The Space Girls had broken out of the portal right behind the Zoran ship and chased it all the way to Kitch 10. All of the Royal Space Force's major ships were out of pocket and the Space Girls were reluctant to open fire on the Zorans, so they had followed the ship that looked more like a derelict than battle ship. They had radioed ahead and the Kitch 10 fighter wing had launched. They had no qualms about opening fire on the ship as it started to descend toward the capital city and would not respond to hails.

Just inside the atmosphere the ship had broken into a thousand pieces. Possibly because of the fighters and anti-aircraft barrage that hit it, but it might have just been because all the robots inside of it bailed out. The Kitchians could see them flying toward the surface on a mission.

The debris from the blasted ship rained down on the capital. Luckily most of it was pretty small and burned up on reentry.

Still there was enough flaming debris that the city would be damaged.

As for the robots themselves, they had controlled flight and slowed their descent. Then, like a swarm of insects, they buzzed over the city looking for something. It wasn't until the *Bella Banana* crested the horizon they seemed to find it.

"They seem to be looking for something for the God King," said Red. "And apparently this troop carrier I just helped land is it."

"I think they may have found something else they want," said Green. "Light, she's going to have a big head. I'm at your 7 o'clock, Red."

Red rotated her seat to look where Green had indicated. Green's shield was set to a much smaller bubble than Red's as she was covering the troop carrier. Clustered all over the top of the bubble were a huge number of Zoran's. So many that Red couldn't even seen the cockpit of the other saucer.

"What do they want? I can't even see you, Green."

"They want me," came Sparkles voice. "I'm going to be a princess."

Below her, Red could see a platoon of Imperial Marines jogging out of a building nearby accompanying a vehicle with a very large weapon mounted on it toward where the Zorans were clustering.

"Sparkles if you are going to be a princess, you better give your subjects orders to lay down their arms, or you may not have many left."

"What?" asked the Pixie.

"I can see a platoon of marines - soldiers - setting up a high powered laser cannon right now. I expect they plan to burn all the robots off our shields." She paused as Astroboy displayed a message for her. "Yep, I'm getting a question from a Marine lieutenant asking how much heat my and Space Girl Green's shields can handle."

Sparkles was probably using her words in the frantic screaming that came out of the radio, but Red couldn't translate it. True to her word she must be a princess. Zorans started falling off the two flying saucers shields like dark melting snow. When they hit the ground, they all fell to their knees and bowed toward Green's flying saucer.

"Make a hole, you miscreants, I must land," came the little gold pixie's command.

———

THE ROYAL MARINES held their fire at Red's recommendation, but didn't relax until the Prince landed nearby and took command. When he walked toward the milling Space Monkey pilots from the the *Bella Banana,* the Sergeant ordered them into formation. That snapping into lines had apparently been an inspiration for Sparkles who took to flying around organizing her new followers into ranks.

Green had taken the expedient route and just opened the canopy and stepped out on the top of her saucer. She watched in amusement as her new companion took command.

"Always full of surprises, Space Girl Red," said Prince Alfred as he walked up to her. He was in his Flying Monkey flight suit and she in her Space Girl hard suit.

"That's my life, Prince," she said with a smile. "Though I had no idea this was going to be happening today." She looked over and watched the blur of gold squeal at any of the motley collection of robot Zorans who got out of line. There weren't that many left. Only about 18 were in three ragged lines.

"Who's Space Girl Green's gold little friend?"

"She is a pixie from Keblr. We ran into a swarm of them and

it turns out if you give one a name, it thinks it owns you. That's what Green did with Sparkles there."

"And you can understand what she and the Zorans are saying?"

Red reached into the neck of her suit and pulled the Rosetta Stone out. Immediately the Prince could hear the overlay of Sparkles's commands, which mostly seemed to be cajoling the poor robots to line up and not embarrass her. "A gift from the Fairy Queen of the Forest of Keblr, who, it turns out, is King Bruno's exiled mother."

Red and the Prince had reached the line of troops in front of Green's saucer. She was sitting on the lip with her armored legs swinging. "Green, what is she doing?" asked Red and motioned to Sparkles.

"Your guess is as good as mine. Hello, Prince Alfred, good to see you," Green said with a wave and jumped off the saucer landing next to them. "Let's find out. Sparkles! Come here, girl. The Prince needs some answers."

Sparkles froze in mid-air where she was talking intently with one of the robots. She zipped over to where the three stood. Red noticed some twitches in the ranks of Marines at the pixie's rapid approach to the crown prince of Kitch, but they maintained their position. The Prince for his part acted like he greeted pixies every day.

Sparkles managed a flying approximation of a curtsey and said, "Your Highness, I am Sparkles, companion of Space Girl Green and Princess of the Zorans."

Prince Alfred made a neck bow to the pixie. Looking straight at her, he asked, "Then, Princess, you are responsible for this invasion of Kitch?"

Sparkles flitted around for a moment, zipping around Green looking for answers. "Ummm, no, Your Highness. I didn't have anything to do with these... I actually just became their princess."

"Being a member of the royal family brings with it not just privilege but responsibility. Are you now going to take responsibility for the actions of your subjects? Or are you just playing at rulership?"

Red did her best not to laugh at the pixie's reaction. One minute she was a princess with all kinds of happy perks—the most important person to a group of robots willing to follow her anywhere. Now she was on the hook to an entire world for a hostile military invasion.

Sparkles hemmed and hawed for a few seconds, not knowing what to do. Green finally had mercy on her and said, "Sparkles, perhaps you should ask one of your new subjects what they were doing and why."

"Yes, yes. Thank you Space Girl," Sparkles said and zipped over to the captives. "OK, which of you is in charge?"

The robots looked at each other clearly not understanding. Finally Sparkles just picked one. Size mattered to Sparkles, just not the same way it mattered to everyone else. She pointed at the smallest bot. "You there. Come answer the Prince's questions."

The little bot had a square body made of wood, spindly arms of springs and gears, with a torpedo shaped head. His two eyes were white and there was a small rectangle of grill for a mouth. He tottered over to where they were and said, "What questions, Golden One?"

"Princess. You call me Princess. Or Your Highness," Sparkles corrected. "This is Prince Alfred of this planet and he wants to know why you invaded."

The bot looked at the tiny gold pixie and the humanoid in a flight suit then back again. "Princess? Prince?" Clearly confused.

Realizing just how long this would take if they left it up to the pixie, Prince Alfred spoke, "What is your name, Zoran?"

"Name? I don't have a name," it replied.

Red leaned over to the Prince and whispered, "Be careful with the naming." Then nodded meaningfully to the pixie now sitting on Space Girl Green's shoulder.

"How may I refer to you then?"

The robot motioned to his chest. There was a white circle with the number 55 on it. "I am Circle 55."

"OK, Circle 55. I am Alfred Morgan the Third, Prince and heir to the throne of Kitch, Captain of the Royal Guard, and a pilot of the Flying Monkeys. What you and your companions did today is an act of war. You invaded our planet by force causing much destruction and death."

Circle 55 just looked at him.

Sparkles wasn't having any of that. "Answer him!" She commanded.

"He didn't ask anything, golden one."

All the humanoids smiled, but Sparkles was not happy. "You need to get smarter, Circle 55. Explain why you did what you did."

"Yes, golden one. One moment, Alfred Morgan 3." Then the little bot turned and walked back down the line of robots behind him. He tapped two boxy bots and they stepped out of line. The three of them faced one another and Circle 55 said, "I need to be smarter. You are the most cognitive here. Please give me your smarts."

The other two looked at each other and nodded. Then they did something that surprised everyone but the Zorans. The two big bots, kneeled down, produced screwdrivers for hands, and began unscrewing part of their head. In a moment they had removed the top of their mechanical skulls and were feeling around inside of them. Each of the robots pulled out a number of components. But once they did so, they just stood up holding the pieces confused.

"Assistance required," said Circle 55. Another robot stepped out of the line and came over. This one took the components from the confused robots and ordered them back into line.

He turned to Circle 55 and opened a panel on the front of his chest. Then he inserted the components there. When he finished he got back into line. Circle 55 walked back over to the humans. He looked at the Prince and said, "Prince Alfred, I am Circle 55, and wish to ask forgiveness for the destruction we of Zoran caused today. We offer our services to help with repairs. I now understand and believe we did not act of our own accord, but under the compulsion of someone else."

"The God King Bruno of Xerces," said Red.

"I believe so. He was our creator, though he exiled us from Xerces many years ago." Then he told them the story of the black goo attack on their world of Zoran, and how all who touched it wanted to come to Kitch and retrieve something called 'The River'. "We can sense its location, though I don't know what it is."

"And it is in that craft over there," said Red pointing to the *Bella Banana*. "That's why you were swarming over it."

"It is not in that ship," Circle 55 said to her and pointed at the Prince. "He has it." The Marines and the other troops all made as if to move, but the Prince held up a hand.

"And do you intend to try and take it from me now?"

"No, Your Highness. We have been freed of the compulsion."

"How so?"

"She did it," he said and pointed to Sparkles. "Though I do not think intentionally." He turned back to the Space Girls and Prince. "You must again forgive me. This unit has never had so much cognitive capacity. I find when I remember things, I now understand a great deal more about them. Things I never knew before. It is quite startling."

"I imagine it is," said the Prince. "What are we to do with you?"

"We are prisoners of war. I assume you have protocols for this? I do not know them but if you give them to me I could see them implemented. The others will follow my instructions."

"And what does your Princess have to say about this?" Prince Alfred said intending for Sparkles to answer, but Circle 55 was faster.

"That one has made herself our Princess, but we've never had one before and our command structure - which I just realize we actually have, though I've never noticed it before." The robot caught himself and took a second to think. "Our command structure does not lend itself to hierarchy."

"Then why did you all bow down to me if I am not your princess?" asked Sparkles, sounding a little peeved.

And why did you make yourself a princess and not a queen, Sparkles? Thought Red, but decided that was a question for another time.

"You are very pretty," was the robot's simple answer. "Then we believed you gave us commands based on superior understanding of the context we are in. Which I still think is true, though given information, I believe I will soon surpass Princess Sparkle's understanding. In my current state."

"Very well. I will accept your surrender and take this group as prisoners of war," said Prince Alfred.

He looked around and met eyes with a particular Royal Marine. "Lieutenant, these Zorans are your prisoners. You are to confine and guard them until I figure out what to do next with them. Treat them as POWs under the Articles of Convention even though Zoran has not signed that agreement. We have."

The Marine Lieutenant saluted. "Yes, Your Highness."

During all of this Yellow had joined them. "Robot army huh? Boy, would I like to get my hands on that."

Red said, "Given their level of intelligence, I'm pretty sure what you have in mind might be a war crime."

"Ahh, I wouldn't do anything Green here wouldn't do to a humanoid. Maybe I'm the perfect doctor for them."

"She has a point," said Green. "I could go along, since one of us has to, if anyone is going to be able to talk to the Zoran."

"I had forgotten that," said Red.

"As had I," said Prince Alfred. "If the Space Girls wouldn't mind, I'm sure the Marines could use your help."

Green and Yellow nodded and started to walk after the Marines and Zorans. "Princess Sparkles, could I talk with you for a moment before you go?" the Prince requested.

Green said to Yellow, "Go on. I'll catch up. They understand humans fine. You just can't understand them."

The pixie was staying on Green's shoulder, one hand wrapping a lock of green hair around her. "Yes, Your Highness."

"Princess Sparkles, I quoted my mother to you a moment ago. 'Being a member of the royal family brings with it not privilege but responsibility.' You have a unique opportunity here. Almost nothing is known about Zoran or its inhabitants, though Space Girl Red here has run into them before.

"You have taken it upon yourself to be their Princess, and they have accepted. But now you must learn what that means. Being a royal in this age of the galaxy means many things on many worlds. Here my mother has ultimate judgement, but most of the law making and administration is handled by the Parliament. We members of the royal family are here to serve.

"It seems the Zorans have not given you ultimate authority, but they do defer to you. If you truly want to be a Princess, you need to serve them. Not just rule them. Do you understand?"

Sparkles had knotted Green's hair into a complicated pattern around her self. Red wondered if scissors were going to be needed to get her out of it.

"Not really, Prince Alfred. But I can be a good girl, and I think Space Girl Green will help me do the right thing," said the little golden woman.

The Prince smiled at her. "That is a good plan, Princess Sparkles. Now go see to your charges." He gave her a head nod. "And thank all of you Space Girls for your assistance." He gave a deeper bow to Red and Green. "Again."

Green laughed and curtsied, which was quite a feat in a hard suit. Red smiled and said, "My bet is our work isn't done. We have another crime that Bruno must answer for. Today was ultimately on his head."

"Indeed," said Prince Alfred. "It seems it is time for us to once again meet with my mother."

CHAPTER 20
OF QUEENS AND AMBASSADORS

QUEEN NATALIE SAT silent at the end of all the briefings. The Prince had explained the surrender of the Zorans at port. Then Space Girl Red had filled in all of the history concerning Bruno and the Zorans. She'd explained about the Fairy Queen being Bruno's mother. Then she had ended with her and Astroboy's discovery of a fleet of Xerces craft in the outer system of Keblr.

"And you say your rainbow mate Orange, is it, was in conference with the Queen when you left the system? You left her a message, but couldn't contact her directly," asked the Queen.

"Yes, Ma'am," said Red not willing to say Natalie. They weren't alone. The room held a number of high ranking members of the military and the Prime Minister of the parliament. She wasn't sure what she should say, so she went with ma'am. "I did receive a message from her via a limited communication system we have. It's slower, text based, and limited.

"She said, 'Working on it.'"

"And what do you take that to mean?"

"Frankly I don't know. She understands there is a fleet and

she is doing something about it. I'm not sure what. Perhaps something with the Queen."

"Is she the Space Girl of War? Could she defeat a fleet in a way you can't?" asked the Queen trying to understand.

"There is no such thing as a Space Girl of War. Space Girl Orange's purpose is Beauty. If one saucer could have taken on that fleet, I probably would have done it myself. But I couldn't and Orange can't. That leads me to think she has a more subtle plan, which would be like her. Beauty is subtle," said Red.

"Mmmm, if you say so," the Queen said. Then she turned to another person at the table. "General, I assume this will change our plans."

"Undeniably. I've already repositioned some of our capital ships to cover the KP-2 portal," said General Kingsley Compton. The leader of all the space fleet in the Kitch system was a lean specimen of the blue-skinned monkeys. He wore the ornate formal uniform with stars on his epaulets. "That is much closer to the inhabited worlds. Right now less than 10 light seconds from Kitch 8. We do not want to have to fight on two fronts at the same time."

"Our plan was," said the Queen, "to go through the portal and establish a strong presence in the Xerces systems. We need to find out if and how he was sending ships through the portal without our knowing it. Given the information we just learned from Space Girl Red, it seems likely the way he's getting his ships here is via the Keblr system. Since we don't watch that portal, we wouldn't see them come through. Then they can find lots of places to hide in our system."

"Are you sure the pirates are Xerces?" asked Red. She'd never been given proof, but she'd also never really had time to look into it.

"Almost all of the ships we've defeated or captured were of

King Bruno's design. They are pretty distinctive," the General said.

Colonel Innes of Military Intelligence added, "We've taken very few prisoners because of the nature of space warfare and the God King makes his ships destroy themselves completely when defeated. It seems to be an automated thing."

"And I assume you have talked with the ambassadors about this?" Red wondered about First Ambassador Pražak, who had been so helpful to her before to Xerces.

Intelligence glanced at the Queen, but it was the Prince who answered. "Your defeated dance competitors left the planet secretly about the time you were returning from Xerces. In case you didn't know, Space Girl Blue was hired to take a message from the Second Ambassador that very night. Apparently she changed its message quite significantly in order to run her con on Bruno."

"His partner, Venuše, is a trained assassin. She is the one who broke into the Queen's empty chambers," said the head of intelligence. "Space Girl Blue saw it right away."

"When Blue brought all of this to our attention, there was little we could do, but break off relations with Xerces," Queen Natalie said. "I gave the First Ambassador and his assistant the chance to return to Xerces, as was proper, but he chose to stay. Unfortunately that meant we had to put him under arrest. Given the unknown abilities of Venuše, we couldn't take chances with him or the other one. Nor could we just confine them to their embassy."

"They are in the tower," said the Prince. "Treated well enough, but under constant surveillance. Ambassador Pražak has been in ill health. He is quite old. But he has not given us any new information about the origin of the pirates. His assistant has been attentive to him, but closed mouth."

"The First Ambassador was kind to me before I went to

Xerces. I believe he was trying to warn me not to go, but that isn't the nature of a Space Girl and he knew it. So he gave me useful information." Red said, "Perhaps I should go talk to him, if you would permit it Queen Natalie."

"Of course, Space Girl Red. I'll give orders to let you in anytime you go."

"I would hurry," said the Prince. "Alexandr is quite frail now."

The conversation stopped then. Red had nothing to say about the waging of a war. It was neither her Purpose nor Vocation. Space Girls changed things, but not with battleships and armies. The others were unsure of the next step. They had come cautiously to the idea of moving into the Xerces system, now those plans were thrown into doubt.

Finally the general spoke. "Your majesty, you know the disposition of our capital ships: one carrier, one battleship, two destroyers. We had positioned them assuming an Xerces attack could come from only the outer portal. KP-2 is seconds away from here and the monkey's homeworld. When it led only to peaceful systems, the squadron here was enough. Now? It needs more. We've got to move ships around if a fleet could come through there. Which means our current plan to go through to Xerces would be underpowered.

"Though maybe we could, we could call up reserves on Homeworld and launch directly from there. That would put more craft near the new flank."

The General got lost in thought for a moment, probably thinking about how many flying monkeys had to return to Kitch 8, which its natives called Homeworld, and what craft were available.

"Continue, General," said the Queen.

"Oh, yes, ma'am. Sorry." He made a bobbing bow, then continued. "We can't fight a war. Going through the portal into

Xerces might just cause that. But we also may benefit from putting our guard ships in front of that end of the portal. Especially if they send ships to both of our portals from there."

"So what specifically do you suggest, General? We are keen to know," said Queen Natalie. "I can tell you truthfully there is no clear decision here. When we decided to send ships to Xerces it was a gamble. It appears an even bigger risk now with the other fleet and the Zoran invading. That's without accounting for a Queen from Xerces with powers like Bruno's. I fear doing anything will be a danger, but doing nothing more so."

"Quite right," said Colonel Innes. "To us in Intelligence, sending troops is a last resort, but my people see no other way. Unless you've reconsidered the other option."

The Queen took a deep breath and sighed. "I have not." She turned to Red and said, "It has been brought up that Bruno is only all powerful on the surface of his planet. We could park a battle ship in orbit and rain down destruction until there was little left of Xerces or its inhabitants."

"It is my job to bring up options, Your Majesty," said Colonel Innes. "I do not favor it myself, except as a last resort."

Turning back to the general, the queen asked again, "So what do you suggest, General Compton?"

The monkey's eyes went up and his lips moved for a moment in preparation. "Put the *Hattie Murphy* through to guard the Xerces side of the portal. Take the carrier *Bently Mclean* through and give them a wing of fighters. The Battleship can refuel that many, or we'll send a fueler with them. Then bring the *Bently* back. It will be uncomfortable for the fighters left with the battleship, but we need that carrier in our own system.

"Put a destroyer at each portal. Leave the carrier out system nearer the to fly patrols. Then fly patrols from Homeworld for the new portal. We'll need to call up reserves, and our fighters will be putting in a lot of hours. It stretches us thin. I wish we had some allies we could call on, but I can't think of any. That would be more your area, my Queen."

"Yes, I have already reached out to some of our allies, but so far have received no support. Don't depend on it."

"Yes, your majesty." He bowed low. "That is my suggestion."

"How long will it take to implement?" Prince Alfred asked.

"In theory I could order the *Hattie* through today and it would make the jump almost immediately, but if we did that, there would be a huge hole there and it isn't ready for long term operations. We could send through support ships to make up for our lack of preparation, but that is not really the preferred Flying Monkey way."

"We seem to be at equilibrium right now, General," said the Queen. "Let us do this right."

"Then at least a week," General Compton said immediately. "I'll start moving the fighters around and have already ordered destroyers into position. Actually the *Cynwrig* doesn't have to change position. We'll be protected in 24 hours, with a couple of days to call up reservists. The rest of the time will be getting the capital ships ready to deploy to Xerces."

"Very well then, we so order it," said Queen Natalie.

————

AFTER THE MEETING Red took a short walk to the tower. Ljuba answered the guarded door in the Queen's tower. It wasn't in the actual castle itself because putting your prisoners in your house doesn't seem like a good idea to any royal family.

"Hello, Ljuba," said Red, "it is good to see you again. I was wondering if I could see the Ambassador."

The dark woman couldn't hide her excitement at seeing Red, nodded a bow and stepped back, allowing her into the room.

"Of course, Space Girl Red. It is very good to see you as well. Please come in."

Red stepped into the small chamber. It was a simple living area with a small table, two chairs around it, and a couch in one corner near a fire place. There was only one door other than the one she had entered. Ljuba was clad in normal Xercan garb of a calf-length skirt and nothing else. Her long hair was pulled back in a horsetail. Her feet and chest were bare. Suddenly all Red could see was the mark on her chest.

"What is wrong, Space Girl?" said Ljuba.

"I didn't know before," Red answered. Then she unzipped the front of her jumpsuit, revealing her golden scars.

"Ahh," said Ljuba. She looked for a moment. "Those aren't the God King's mark though."

"They were. He left them black. Space Girl Green removed his nanites from them, but couldn't heal the scars. The Fairy Queen put her nanites in to heal them, but I took a vow to carry the scars until I have brought the God King to justice."

Red was gaining a great deal of respect for Ljuba. She took this revelation with hardly any reaction. She didn't say Red's vow was impossible, or inquire why or how she had been marked by God King Bruno. Instead she just looked at the golden marks.

"The Fair Queen?"

"Fairy Queen. She lives in the forest of Keblr, surrounded by golden pixies," Red said.

Ljuba seemed a little confused. "Fairy, not Fair. Was she Xercan?"

"Yes, but her skin was white, not black like yours."

"Then the Queen still lives, but she has abandoned the home planet completely. The Ambassador will want to know this. You said you wanted to see him." She seemed to have decided there was nothing more she wanted to say leading the Space Girl through the other door without a knock.

The room was small and dark, lit only with a few warm bulbs. It was dominated by a double bed with the First Ambassador sitting up asleep, a book held limply in his hand. Ljuba walked directly to him, gently took the book out of his hand, and said, "Ambassador Prazak, wake up please."

The old man woke with a start and snapped, "Not an ambassador, Ljuba. I told you that. Not any more. Just call me Alexandr."

"I know, Alexandr, but you have a visitor." Ljuba stepped back to let him see Red.

Red had forgotten to zip her suit closed and as soon as he saw the scars Alexandr said, "Oh Space Girl Red, I see our God King has marked you. I am sorry. I believe I tried to warn you."

"You did, First Ambassador, but we Space Girls are a foolhardy lot. Plus there were some shenanigans involving your Second Ambassador and my Rainbow mate Blue. Much has happened and I would like to get your advice on it, if you can spare me the time."

"And the strength. I know you are too kind to say it, but I am old and know my time is near. I very much want to hear your story, and all I have is time. Ljuba, could you get us some refreshments, please?"

"Really, Ambassador, I don't need anything." Red settled herself Seiza on the floor next to the bed. "I think it would be good for Ljuba to hear my story as well."

"Of course. She will soon be the ambassador for Xerces by default. Everyone else has abandoned us here." He motioned to Ljuba to stay and the woman sat down cross-legged on the floor next to the Space Girl.

Red told the whole story. The ambassador expressed a range of emotions from sadness to surprise as she spoke. Ljuba remained expressionless but attentive. She ended with the revelation given by the Zoran of their origin and why they had invaded Kitch.

She expected certain questions, especially about Bruno's mother, but they just nodded at the information. It was Lujba who spoke first, "So there will be war soon, if not already."

"Maybe not," said Alexandr. "Kitch doesn't have the navy to fight on two fronts. They may be cautious about starting a war."

It was Red's turn to say nothing; the Queen of Kitch's plans were not hers to share.

"If not now," said Ljuba, "then soon."

"Space Girl Red," said Ambassador Prazak, "you have had quite the adventure. What is it you want of us?"

"I came to check on you firstly, but I would like to know what you can tell me of Queen Iveta. I believe she could be key to a solution to this conflict."

"Do you think peace is possible with God King Bruno?" asked Ljuba.

"Do you?" replied Red.

Ljuba looked at the ambassador who just looked back, then said, "No."

"And how do you feel about that, Ljuba?"

There was a long pause while the Xercan woman thought about it. Her mentor and the Space Girl waited. Red felt that Ljuba could be key and, even if not, she represented a different generation than the Ambassador.

"God King Bruno is all I have ever known. I used to think he was all powerful, truly a God. When I was his concubine that was true. I don't remember a time without him. But when he discarded me and sent me here to be the servant of the Ambassador, I began to learn a different world. I see how the Kitchians see him: a distant evil, trapped on his own world; weak in his ability to project power.

"He is not a god. And I feel the way he rules his people is…" she struggled to say it. The others waited.

"Wrong."

"And gods can't be wrong. They define right and wrong," Alexandr said. "Once you understand that, Bruno becomes not a god but a devil."

The younger woman nodded.

Sensing Ljuba needed a moment, Red changed the subject. "Ambassador, did you know Queen Iveta?"

"Know her? I'm not sure that is the right word. I knew her in the way any subject knows their queen. I would say that I know Queen Natalie better than Queen Iveta. But that is not what you are asking. You want to know what she was like as a ruler."

The man leaned back, closed his eyes for a moment and thought. "We called her the Fair Queen. Mostly because she was quite beautiful as you would expect of a Queen. But also because she was an intellect, a thinker.

"As a junior ambassador I had little to do with her, but she did once give me stack of books on culture and Kitch culture in particular. She explained that to be an effective ambassador you needed to understand other peoples did not think the same way you do. They saw the world differently and valued different things. Understanding that was central to persuading them and getting along with them."

He opened his eyes and looked at the two women, "I think those books and that idea have made me as effective an ambassador as I am. My predecessor did everything based on power. He was always trying to determine how can we could force them to do what we want."

"Like King Bruno," said Ljuba. Red noticed she had dropped 'god' from the title.

"Yes, and like Ctirad," Alexandr said. "I think another evidence of her intellect was how quickly she abdicated when

King Max died. She saw before anyone else what Prince Bruno had become and recognized she could not fight him. By abdicating and joining the Fair Women, she protected herself from him."

"The Fair Women?" Space Girl Red asked.

"The Fair Women and their brother order, the Gentle Men, are philosophical communities. They separate themselves from the rest of Xerces society to focus on study, meditation, and spiritual growth. Their compounds are quite literally on the other side of the planet from the capital."

"King Bruno almost sent me there when he released me from my concubinage," said Ljuba.

"So he recognized your intellect," Red noted.

Ljuba looked surprised, "I had never thought of it that way. He just seemed to want to get me as far from him as possible."

"I did not think the Fair Women would accept a concubine," said Alexandr.

Ljuba shrugged. "The way I understand it, they take anyone who comes, but you are never seen or heard from again. Of course that may just be the perception of those in the castle."

"As you can tell," Alexandr said to Red, "very little is known about what goes on inside those societies. There is the idea that they've cut themselves off from society and that is that."

"Which is how Iveta could disappear from the planet and no one noticed," Red said.

"Yes."

"But can you tell me anything that would give me a sense of what the Queen might want? She may have a fleet of Xerces ships. If so, does she want to invade Kitch? Or are those ships there from King Bruno, aware his mother is there and a threat?"

The two Xerces looked at each other and shrugged. "The Queen always seemed like a good person to me. I believe she was an ameliorating influence on her husband King Max. She saw the impact Bruno's power had on our world's economy and what that would mean to the people. Many of Max's programs for the miners were probably a result of her persuasion," said Alexandr.

"Whether she did it because she thought it the right thing for a ruler to do for her people - like say Queen Natalie would - or because an unemployed and poor citizenry would be a threat to any ruler. I don't know. She could be coldly analytical, which is shown in the fact she ran from Bruno rather than fight him."

"She couldn't have won against the God King," said Ljuba.

Alexandr smiled, "Yes, I know, but some would have tried anyway, felt they must do something to help the people. By doing nothing how many people have suffered since then?"

Red watched the young woman. She was smart. That was obvious. She'd had a good teacher in the ambassador, so she understood there were other ways of doing things. But the idea of fighting the God King was still an impossibility to her.

"She is still the big unknown in this whole mess," said Red. "Could be a force for good or a bigger ill than the God King himself."

She rose to her feet and Ljuba stood as well.

"Thank you for your insight," said Red. "Both of you. Hopefully I will see you again soon when all this is resolved. Or I won't. It was a close thing last time I went to Xerces."

"You're going back?" asked Ljuba.

"Seems likely. But I will be prepared this time."

Ljuba just looked at her incredulously. What kind of preparation could you make to face a god or a devil?

"I fear, Space Girl Red," said the Ambassador, "I am unlikely to be here when you return. We Xercans are a hardy people thanks to our genetic modifications, until we aren't. It will be sudden and, I feel, soon."

Ljuba looked at the old man her eyes glistening, but she did not deny it.

"I hope it isn't so. But if you go before I return, may the Light That Is All Colors shine on you."

"Does your Light shine even on we dark Xercans?"

"The Light shines on all," replied Red her eyes wet. "We believe black too is the combination of all colors, just in a different way."

"We Xercans have no blessings, except maybe in the name of the God King, which I don't think would be appropriate. But know that I, Alexandr Bohumil Prazak, am honored to have known you Space Girl Red, and I hope you are successful at freeing my people."

"And I, too," said Ljuba, "wish you success." Then she bowed low in the way of the Kitchans.

CHAPTER 21

RAINBOW CAPRICORN REUNITES

WHEN SPACE GIRL Red arrived back at the spaceport, it was well into the night. The place was lit brightly and there was more activity than she had ever seen before. Flying Monkeys were everywhere and many Kitchian spacecraft were formed up on the tarmac.

She wove her bike through the commotion deciding to avoid the main area of the space port so she didn't get caught by anyone she knew. Astroboy was parked on the edge of the port. As she approached she was surprised to see he wasn't alone. There were four other flying saucers. Almost her entire Rainbow was here.

"Welcome back, Ma'am," said Astroboy in her ear as she parked the jet bike at the foot of the gangplank. "Your rainbow mates are in conference on McGregor and would like you to join them."

"Thank you, Astroboy," she said, and began walking toward Purple's flying saucer. The saucers were arranged in a loose circle as was protocol. She noted that Buck, Blue's saucer was on the opposite side of the circle from hers. Orange and Purple's were right next to her, which made sense from a rainbow point of view. She felt trepidation as she approached McGregor and the gangplank lowered for her. This would be the first time she'd seen Blue since, well since she had stolen back the World Heart. If you considered that "seeing" her.

In the saucer's entry room she could hear voices. The tone, as well as the back and forth, told her they were hashing something out. Solving a problem not arguing. She paused a second listening, but couldn't make out the words.

"Welcome, aboard Space Girl Red," said a husky male voice with a Highland accent.

"Hello, McGregor," she replied, killing time. "It's my first time here."

"Yes, but you are expected and always welcome," the flying saucer's AI said. "Do you need guidance?"

That made her smile. She did need guidance, but not to find the others in a flying saucer. Every Space Girl allocated a large piece of the pie to her work area. On Astroboy, that was her armory and workshop. Halamar's had been Green's med-bay and garden.

Of course on the Space Girl of Love's saucer it would be a meeting room. Red squared her shoulders and walked the few steps to it.

For a group of Space Girls it seemed to take a long time for them to notice a new armed person in their midst. Heck, Red could see a glow in one of Purple's tattoos peeking out of her camisole that must be McGregor's indication the hatch was open or someone new was onboard.

They were all in casual ship wear: shorts, camisoles or bandeaus, and bare feet or transformer heels in their various colors. Purple sat nearest the door leaning in saying something. Across from her was Green holding a tablet and studying intently. Yellow was the one Purple was arguing with.

Blue stood next to the table on the opposite side of Purple.

She wore shorts with a bustier in a dark blue, and was the first to notice her.

"Hello, Red," Blue said.

That brought all conversation to a stop. Green looked up. Yellow turned her face back and forth between the two. Purple leaned back in her chair and waited.

"Hi, Blue," Red said not sure how to start but added a greeting to the others. "Rainbow."

They nodded to her. Everyone knew nothing else was going to happen until Red and Blue had it out. Red knew it too and still didn't know exactly what to do or say. She didn't like that, but, in the nature of a Space Girl, just went with her gut and took action.

"Got your message," she said looking at Blue.

"Good."

"You mean it?"

"Yes, every word," Blue looked like she needed to keep talking, but Red stopped her with a raised hand.

"I don't know what to say here," Red said and looked at the other members of the rainbow.

Purple still sat relaxed and hadn't looked at either of them. "I forgive you?" she offered.

"Or you could punch her in the face," offered Green.

That got everyone's attention. Now they all looked at Green in shock.

"What? It is one of the ways you two deal with things," Green said putting the tablet on the table. "I mean, Red, if you and I have a problem we say nice things to each other. If you punched me, I'd be heartbroken, and our relationship would be in worse shape than you and Blue's is.

"But if you and Blue went outside and beat the shit out of each other for half an hour, you'd probably come back bruised but best friends."

Everyone had to smile. Green turned to Purple and said, "How's that for Punk Love?"

Purple nodded, and then said, "Green, you have grown. We should talk about what you've been through."

Green just shrugged.

"So, what's it going to be Red?" asked Yellow. "Cuz we got some shit to deal with. I'll ref if you two need to fight it out."

Red looked up at Blue, who stood there awkwardly. Not the defiance she would have had in the past that required forgiveness by combat. "I think I'll go with Purple's solution this time.

"Space Girl Blue, I forgive you."

Then she walked around the room and gave her rainbow mate a hug. That made them both cry, and ended with all the badass Space Girls in a group hug and tears all around.

The important stuff settled, the rainbow got down to the immediate. Taking a seat next to Blue, Red asked, "What exactly is the 'shit we have to do'?"

"We need to end God King Bruno's reign," said Yellow.

Purple slipped a plate of food in front of Red. As she set it down she said, "Which as you know isn't easy. He'd be hard to kill even if assassination was our goal."

"And it isn't," said Yellow. "Apparently."

Obviously this discussion had already been had and some still thought getting a raygun to Bruno's head was a good idea.

"It is a common theme today," said Red. Then she told them about Queen Natalie's plan. She also told them what the Ambassador had explained.

"So there is at least a chance," said Blue "that if we can contain Bruno, his mother can take the throne, without a war between Kitch and Xerces."

"A war could destroy the planet, and possibly its inhabitants," Green said.

"Yes, and probably not the God King. He's hard to kill.

Blowing up my ray guns didn't do it." said Red. "And he might just create a new army of robots like the Zoran to reign over."

"The Zoran aren't really fighters," said Yellow, "After examining them, I'd say they were toys when created. But I don't doubt he could build an actual army if he wanted to."

"What were you two arguing about when I came in?" Red asked Purple and Yellow.

"Whether sending someone to the Dark Dimension is killing them," said Blue before the other two could start. "Yellow says it isn't because you can bring them back. Purple isn't sure you can and if you do they won't be sane."

"Which, in King Bruno's case," said Green, "was how you put him in."

Purple scowled at her. "We don't know what the dark zone is really like. Other than dark. At the least it seems to be equal to sensory depravation. Which does drive people crazy."

"Can you send someone there?" Red asked.

Yellow pulled something out of her pouch and put it on the table. It was a clear capsule about 15cm long and 5cm in diameter. Inside of it was a black crystal. "You can with that. Touch it to skin and it activates. Creates a field all around the person that owns that skin. Everything inside the field is in the Dark Dimension."

Red's eyes could easily discern the edges and lines of the square crystal with pointed ends, but her brain kept trying to resolve it as a hole in space.

"How do you get them back?"

Yellow shrugged, "You touch the field with the crystal. It drops out of the field once it is generated."

"So," Red proposed, "you could trap Bruno in it, then move him off his planet and set him free of it. You can move the field, right?"

Yellow got an unfocused look, "I hadn't thought about that.

Yes, I believe you can. The field itself seems solid." She looked down at the crystal sitting on the table. "Come to think of it, that may just be a field. It just expands when activated."

"Well, in that case we could trap King Bruno in it, get him away from Xerces where his powers are, and then decide what to do with him," Red said. "Or let someone else decide. He's just a man off Xerces Prime."

There was general agreement to this around the table. Then Blue brought up the obvious. "The trick, of course, is getting to God King Bruno. Shooting him might be easier. We could do that at a distance."

"Maybe you could shoot that thing at him," suggested Green. "Build a launcher of some kind."

"I could do that," said Yellow. "But he's pretty fast to react to things like that. I mean Red drew on him and he had time to disable her weapons before she could fire. Aim something at him and his nanites will probably react before it even gets close."

"Or he'll shield himself," said Red. "He'd wrapped himself in something that protected him from the raygun explosion almost as soon as he realized it was going to happen."

They all sat thinking for a minute.

"If his power only works on Xerces, could we lure him away from it?" Purple asked. "Is there something he wants that badly?"

"Maybe me," said Red. "But I don't think he wants me bad enough to leave the planet. Otherwise he would have done it when I escaped."

"But didn't you bury him under his tower on the way out?" asked Green.

"Astroboy did, but we were in system for a long time after that and he could have come after us, but he didn't."

"Is there anywhere on planet that his nanos don't work?"

"I don't think so. I didn't do a lot of research before I got captured, but everyone seems to think he's all powerful."

"Blue, you had to be with him awhile, working your con," said Purple. "What did you learn?"

Blue thought for a second and then said, "It was a lot more boring than you think. A party at the palace. A number of long talks in his office. Some time at the spaceport where Red landed later. He used his powers in all those places."

"You talk to anyone else on planet?"

"No, not really. A few servants to get me to him," Blue said. "Come to think of it, he's probably just as mad at me as you Red. Might want me enough to try and come get me."

"Could we ask the Fairy Queen?" said Yellow. "She might know some weakness we could exploit."

"Don't think we have time. We need to do what we are going to do before the Kitchians invade. We don't have a time for a trip to Keblr," said Green.

"Wait, I do know somewhere his powers didn't seem to work as well," said Red.

"Where?"

"The dungeon."

"But he tortured you there," said Green. "Made those marks. Those were with nanos. And your skin trauma all over. That was nanos."

"The skin damage was after I escaped before Astroboy got to me. He couldn't just make these marks in the dungeon. He had to bring nanos in. I remember because they were swarming around his hand like a flame. He held it just so, right before," she cut off at the memory.

"Great," said Yellow. "All we have to do is get him in the dungeon along with us and the crystal."

"One of us has to get captured," Blue said flatly. Everyone

looked at her. "If he gets me, he'll take me to the dungeon. Then I can put the crystal on him."

"You!" said Red, but she was interrupted.

"Won't work, because he'll disarm and strip you first. You'll never get the crystal in."

"I could hide it," Blue said with a look that the others understood. There were only a couple of places the Space Girl could hide that tube while naked.

"And once you are there, you'll be tied up," said Red. "Not to mention it won't be you."

"Or worse than tied up," said Purple. "And your hiding place would be discovered." She looked at Red, "Is that a possibility?"

The whole rainbow waited for her answer. "If you are asking if he raped me, no. But he implied he might. Or have his men." Then she put the subject back on track. "Plus that thing goes off on skin contact. Do you really want to be pushing it in and out of your vagina under stress? What if the container breaks?"

"And it's kind of big," added Green.

"I assure you the container won't break under pressure," said Yellow. "But it would still be risky."

"Too bad we can't get him to capture two of us," started Purple, "and leave one of us untied."

"And know which that would be in advance so they can shove the death stick up their hoo hoo," said Yellow.

"You said it wasn't death," Purple said with a smile to show she wasn't serious.

"Wait a minute," said Red holding up a hand. "What we need is one of us to get caught and be in the dungeon with Bruno. Then any of the rest of us could sneak in and zap him. Blue's sneaky. I could get caught and she could sneak in while he's working on me."

"No, the other way around, Red," said Blue.

"He hates me more. He'll take me right to the dungeon," said Red.

"Or he'll order you shredded the moment he sees you," Blue countered. "He's already tortured you and that didn't turn out so well. Me, I'm new and he will want to make me pay for setting him up."

Then the two of them went back and forth on who was more likely to be tortured. Around the table the other girls communicated via meaningful looks and undercover gestures.

"All right," said Green loudly. "It is settled then."

Blue and Red stopped and looked at her shocked.

"You two can't make this decision. You're too involved. So we made it for you. Just know we're all going. It's time for Rainbow Capricorn to invade Xerces Prime."

CHAPTER 22
THE WAR FOR XERCES

SOMETIMES I HATE *it when a plan comes together,* thought Space Girl Blue as she hung from the X in God King Bruno's dungeon. She was naked and bleeding from various cuts and bruises she'd received resisting God King Bruno's men. Of course she could have gotten away, but that wasn't the point. The man himself hadn't put in an appearance and those of the more sadistic bent were waiting for his arrival rather take advantage of her.

Implanted in the back of her throat was a microphone, carefully put there in Green's med-lab. It would relay everything she said to the rest of the rainbow. They and Buck were hidden in the rings of Prime's moon, waiting.

She looked around the new dungeon. She'd never seen the old one, but Red had described it in enough detail, she could tell things were different. For instance there was a mirror permanently installed across from the X, so she could see herself. She still had her shoulder length blue hair. On landing she'd ordered Buck back into the air. She carried no rayguns and had worn her standard jumpsuit. No one greeted her but she known

Bruno was watching when her clothes dissolved. She considered it a good sign she hadn't dissolved with it.

Then the troops had shown up. Only 5. She was offended, but she'd demanded to see the God King Bruno. They said something about seeing him in the dungeon, then the fighting had started.

There seemed to be two types of people in the dungeon. Cowering slaves in scraps of cloth and fancy pampered nobles. The slaves kept to the sides of the room and avoided looking at her. The nobles taunted her and made stupid jokes about what they were going to do once the God King let them. It was pathetic.

He didn't make much noise coming down the stairs, she thought as the God King appeared in the mirror.

"Space Girl Blue," simpered the God King, "good to have you back. I am quite unhappy with you. Your negotiation of your sister's dowery did not go as you said it would."

"Yeah, sorry about that, God King. Red can't be depended on to do what she ought." She imagined she could feel the flying saucers break out of their hiding place, heading for the surface at top speed. "That's why I came back, your highness. To see how I could fix things."

"Oh, I'm quite capable of fixing things myself," said the God King. He reached out a glowing hand and touched her chest.

———

"SPACE GIRL ORANGE to the *Hattie Murphy*," said the Space Girl of beauty as her flying saucer exited the Xerces portal. "This is Space Girl Orange to the *Hattie Murphy*. Please do not attack what is coming behind me. They are not here to attack you."

On the bridge of the Space Monkey battleship, the comms

officer shouted, "Captain, Your Majesty, you better hear this." Without waiting for permission, he put the transmission on the main screen. Captain Earnest Mitch of the Kitchian battleship *Hattie Murphy* looked at the Prince who had been talking to the ship's engineer.

"I have the flying saucer on tactical," said another bridge officer.

"Put it on the main screen," said the Caption.

A window opened showing the bright orange flying saucer now turning from its exit vector and moving toward the battleship.

"Captain," said the Prince moving back to the flag seat next to the captain and strapping in, "I'd rescind the shoot anything unknown as soon as you see it order if I were you."

The standing order of portal guard weapon crews was to identify a ship and if you couldn't, or it was hostile, start shooting. There wasn't going to be much time if a fleet came through. Of course all Kitchian ships and the Space Girl Flying Saucers were known. That explained why weapons weren't flying already.

Captain Mitch pressed the all-hands and said, "Weapons, switch to protocol B. Fire only if fired upon. I repeat, switch to protocol B. Fire on incoming craft only if fired upon." He released the button and asked Prince Alfred, "What do you think is behind her?"

Before the prince could answer, ships started coming out of the portal. A broad V of dozens of knife shaped, golden ships were first. Behind a larger golden ship, and behind it even more of the smaller knife shaped ships.

"Possible ID of the first ships, sir," said the tactical officer. "They appear to be Xerces Corsairs, though the coloration has been changed."

The Xerces Corsair was the main part of their fleet. It had a crew of four, but could be flown with just the pilot if needed. They were lightly armed with lasers and carried up to four torpedoes. It was the Corsair that had plagued Kitch for the past decade under control of the pirates.

"Comms, can you get me anyone on those ships? Or the Space Girl?" Captain Mitch asked.

"Working on it," he said. "Space Girl Orange has responded to me, but...sir, I think she put me on hold."

The captain of the Kitchans' most powerful ship rolled his eyes. "Put her through when she is free, please."

The first wing of Xerces ships had changed vectors moving toward the *Hattie*, and was passing under them. The rest of the fleet was following.

"The large ship in the middle seems to be based on the Xerces Bruno class destroyer from the last war," Tactical reported as she analyzed the data from her scans. "But it is heavily modified. Weapons appear to be the same. The formation of the ships implies they are protecting that vessel."

The flying saucer came to a stop almost directly in front of the battle ship.

Navigation added, "Incoming fleet's current vector will avoid us and is on a heading for Xerces Prime."

Another window opened on the main screen showing the cockpit of a flying saucer with Space Girl Orange. Her long bright orange hair layered with red and yellow looked like flames when she moved. She had pale, unblemished skin with little contour in the cheeks, but a strong jaw line. Wide eyes and small bright red lips shaped her face into an inverted tear drop. Large eyes with a monolid and accenting winged eyeliner make it impossible to avoid her gaze as the connection was made. She quickly flashed bright teeth and a wide smile filled with warmth.

"Hello, *Hattie Murphy*, sorry for the surprise, but you know how comms are from the Spaceways. Heard you were here and didn't want you to blast the Queen's fleet out of the sky before the party even got started." She noticed the Prince and said, "Ahh, there you are Prince Alfred. I was hoping there was a royal presence here. Figured there would be."

"And why was that, Space Girl Orange?" Prince Alfred replied.

"Because I have a feeling there is going to be a new regime on Xerces Prime very soon. Possibly by morning." She looked at something off to one side. "Ahh, it looks like my rainbow needs me, so I'll make it short. That destroyer you just saw contains Queen Iveta, the previous King's wife and mother of - I'm not going to call him God King - Bruno. She has been hiding out on Keblr for a long time. In the last few years members of the the Xerces navy - a pretty rag tag lot of oppressed people - discovered they could exit in Keblr. Many of them just chose to stay there. When the Queen discovered them hiding out, she took them under her wings so to speak. Very nurturing woman the Fairy Queen.

"Anyway, this is really going on longer than I intended. She has some of Bruno's powers and has used them to pretty up the Xerces space ships. They all love her and want to be part of a kingdom she rules. But there was always the problem of the God King. His powers are just too much on his home world." She frowned sweetly. "Then Space Girl Red came along and just started stirring the pot as we Space Girls are wont to do. Queen Iveta sees a chance, so we're back."

"How does she intend to defeat her son?" asked Captain Mitch.

"I told her he wouldn't be a problem after my rainbow got done with him." Again the Space Girl appeared to be consulting something off screen, "And I'm missing that party, so I've got to go now. Ta Ta." Then the screen went blank.

There was shocked silence in the control room. Finally the Captain turned to the Prince, "Your Majesty?"

"Yeah," he replied and sighed. "Should we stay here guarding the portal or go join the party?" Orange's saucer was already catching up and passing the Xerces fleet.

"While I do hate to miss a battle, your majesty," started Captain Mitch, "Perhaps it would be better if we didn't get into the middle of a civil war."

Prince Alfred nodded, "Very wise counsel, Captain. And we don't know that all of the Xercian are now part of the queen's fleet. But I do feel we should have a presence nearer the planet. If for no other reason than to observe the outcome."

"We could send the fighter wing. They probably can't get back without a refuel, but the *Hattie* can come for them after things are settled."

Prince Alfred nodded, "We should have a tanker joining us fairly soon if things back home are going to plan. It would be good to send the Queen an update about that Xerces fleet in Keblr being here now and friendly."

"If the Space Girl is right, then it will be settled before any message could get there via drone."

"Why don't we do this?" said the Prince as he unbuckled and stood. "I will take the *Queen Natalie* in with a wing of fighters and observe what is going on. When we know what is what, I'll radio a report and you can send the drone."

Captain Mitch was not pleased with this suggestion. Today Prince Alfred was the royal representative, not just another pilot in the Flying Monkeys. This meant Captain Mitch couldn't order him around. "Prince Alfred, I do not think it is good to have a member of the Royal that near a battle zone. Perhaps you could carry a message back to the Queen now. Your war-yacht is probably our fastest ship."

Prince Alfred smiled at the Captain, understanding his position completely. "Captain, I am going to do one of those seemingly foolish things we royals are stereotypically prone to. I'm going where I want, but where I shouldn't. You are free to do whatever you see fit once I leave. Bring the whole flotilla if you want." He smiled again and headed for the door.

Captain Mitch just shook his head. If he were the prince he would have done exactly the same thing, but that didn't mean he liked it. Then he ordered the flotilla's entire fighter complement to escort the *Queen Natalie*.

———

IT WAS ALL they could do to hold Buck back. If Blue hadn't ordered him to follow the other Space Girls' orders, it was likely he'd be tearing the dungeon tower apart right now, rather than waiting in orbit with the others. The biggest unknown was if the nanos would transmit to Bruno the moment they dropped out of orbit. Therefore they were minimizing their presence. Only Astroboy and Red were continuing on to the surface and the dungeon.

Astroboy's shields didn't immediately grey with attacking nanites as they descended. It was eerie for Red to see the same tower Astroboy had dismantled standing in the setting sun.

"He appears to have rebuilt the tower, Ma'am," Astroboy said.

"Yes, are there any changes you can detect? He had to learn something from the last time."

Astroboy scanned the structure and said, "Nothing of significance, Ma'am. Perhaps he was too busy being crushed by debris last time to realize how you got away."

"All right then," Red said turning control over to Astroboy. She sealed her Space Girl armor and climbed down the ladder to the core. On each forearm were modified versions of Green's bracers. She'd worked on them during the trip and they were now part of her armor, projecting out on demand. All of the armored Space Girls had modded their armor to put an electrical current on the surface of the suit. It could be called on demand and had a low charge running all the time. Hopefully it would hold off the nanites for at least awhile.

"Open the gang plank," she said to Astroboy in the entry room. "Once I jump, go back to position."

"I believe I could better serve to stay here on station."

"I know you do, and I'm sure Buck thinks the same thing. But that's the plan. Go set a good example."

"Yes, Ma'am."

The gang plank opened and Red jumped into the twilight.

———

SPACE GIRL BLUE opened one eye, then the other. Her chest burned and she was having trouble focusing. There was lots of laughter in the room now. She looked down at her chest already knowing what would be there. Sure enough, she now had a black lightning scar—the shadow of Red's chest.

"Do you like it?" asked the God King of Xerces. "I do it to all my special girls."

"Yeah, so I've heard," slurred Blue and raised her head. "At least now, Red won't have something I don't." She looked down again. "But this one is uglier."

"Oh, really, maybe it needs to be washed." He gestured to one of the slaves and a bucket of freezing cold water doused her.

She screamed in pain and anger. Pain where the cold water hit her new burned chest, and anger at this idiot.

He was standing there, one hand still glowing, and laughing at her.

Then Blue thought, *Red doesn't make much noise coming down the stair either.*

———

RED REALLY LIKED the tranquilizer darts. She'd landed with barely a thump on the roof of the tower, where she found two guards and knocked them out before she had even thought about it.

The guards were a change as was the new staircase for them instead of the ladder and trap door. She walked slowly down, ready to fire. There was no one on the top balcony. She looked over the edge all the way to the floor two stories below. She could make out a few people on the floor below, but there didn't seem to be anyone on the levels between.

"We've lost contact with Blue's transmitter," came Green's worried voice in her ear.

"On it," Red replied. Then she leaped over the railing and fell the two stories to the main floor.

Before she hit, she'd already knocked out three people in the area. Might have been guards, or visitors. It didn't matter.

Then she saw one of the scruffy slaves cowering against the wall. She walked over, her arm pointing at her, one finger in front of her visor. When she was close enough she said softly, "Where's the entrance to the dungeon?"

The woman pointed a trembling hand at a tapestry a few meters around the room.

"Ok. Now it is time for you to run away. And tell everyone to get away from the tower. You know what happened last time I was here."

The woman nodded her head and ran toward the exit. Red doubted she would tell any guards to run, but she might get other slaves out.

A door behind the tapestry opened to a staircase. As she descended her suit's exterior started to spark and the charge meter crept up. She was on the right track.

There was no door at the bottom and God King Bruno stood in the center of the room. Cronies gathered around him and slaves backed up against the wall. In the mirror behind him she could see Blue hanging from a metal cross.

Bruno was laughing at something, probably the black mark spidering across Blue's chest. He didn't notice Red until the tranquilizer darts from her left arm started dropping his cronies. Then a bullet from her right got his attention. She didn't expect it to work, and she was right. Nanites from his glowing hand turned the bullet to dust before it had travelled a meter. She followed with a splat bullet to the same effect, but this time something did work. The splat was closely followed by an electric dart, they impacted and nanos flamed into non-existence.

"I came to buy my rainbow mate back, God King Bruno," she said as the last crony went down.

Bruno held out his only slightly glowing hand now, confused for just a second. "Buy with what?"

"This," she said, and tossed the dark dimension crystal at him.

Out of reflex he caught it.

As soon as it touched his outstretched hand, an angular ball of blackness formed around his hand. It slowly started up his arm.

The God King screamed, "Save me! Destroy"

And those where his last words as the dark dimension covered his head and began working down his body.

"We're incoming," said Yellow's voice.

Red turned toward Blue, getting ready to shoot off her restraints, when she noticed a flick of movement from Bruno's feet. The gold nano fire was moving down into the ground and spreading. It seemed to be multiplying, turning everything it came into contact with into more nanos.

She fired a cutting star at one of Blue's restraints, but missed as the floor under her collapsed. Her jet pack engaged automatically and lifted her as the floor disappeared. The nanos were destroying everything and getting very close to Blue.

"We've got a problem here," Red said as she flew over to Blue and grabbed the cross she was chained to. Pushing her jet pack, she was just able to hold Blue away from the growing pool of nanos eating a hole in the planet. "Nanos are eating everything. Floor, walls, people, bodies."

"Making an exit," said Yellow, and there was a thunderous boom above her.

Red looked up, and could see stars. The flying saucers had blown through the tower and just pushed it to one side.

She poured power into her jet pack, but with the weight of the cross and Blue, the best she could do is hold their position.

"Can you get me loose, Red?" yelled Blue.

"No, my hands are full. My jet pack is just holding us both up." She looked down and realized the nanos were digging. Already out dozens of meters, and the only solid thing below her was God King Bruno's dark dimension encased form.

"Red, Sparkles is freaking out!" said Green over the comms. "She said they are going to destroy the planet."

Suddenly Red felt lighter and looked up to see a blue tinted flying saucer directly above her. Buck had locked a tractor beam on Blue's cross and took the weight.

"I've got you, babe," said Buck in her ears. "You can let go, Space Girl Red. I'll take it from here."

Over her speakers Red said to Blue, "Buck's got you now. I'm letting go." Red hovered in air above the growing abyss.

Like a slow moving fire, the circle spread out in both directions. As deep as it was wide, like a half circle digging a hole in the surface. The pile of rubble that had been the tower before the saucers knocked it over fell into the pit and was consumed. Red could no longer see the God King's form. The bowl was full of a black boiling dust and he was undoubtedly down there.

"Anyone have any ideas what to do now?" Red asked.

Above her the rainbow's flying saucers formed a circle. To one side, Purple's McGregor fired a barrage of lasers, then disintegration beams, then missiles. All to no avail. They disappeared into the mass of nanos, possibly destroying a few, but nothing worth noting.

"It was worth a try," said Purple.

Halamar's gang plank opened and a golden spark jetted out. Right behind it Green leaped in to the air. In a second Green hovered next to her and Sparkles the pixie was orbiting at a blur. Despite the translator on her chest, Red couldn't make sense of what she was saying, but she got the feeling of utter terror.

"I know, Sparkles," Red said, "I know. But I don't know how to stop it either. Calm down and tell me if you have an idea."

The little golden figure stopped abruptly right in front of her visor. "Can't you hear them? They are screaming in anger and pain because their god disappeared."

"They are the one's that made him disappear," Red said, "He was right here when the Dark Dimension covered him. Then they made the hole and he fell in."

"No, stupid," said the pixie very disturbed, "They don't care about his form. The have lost his presence. It is like you having your brain cut out. Well, maybe not you. But a smart person."

"Ok, smarty pants, why don't you tell them to stop what they are doing and we'll work on getting him back for them?"

"Ok," she said and zipped off into the hole.

Green looked like she was going to go after the pixie but Red put a hand on her shoulder. "Wait."

While the little pixie zipped around barely visible over the black abyss, Blue dropped down next to them in her battle armor. "What did I miss?"

"Hey, are you ok? I know what that burn feels like," asked Red.

"I'm fine. We can fix it after we fix this."

"Are the nanos active?" asked Green.

"Huh?" said Blue.

"What's inside that thing on your chest is what is down there," Green said with a gesture.

"And apparently it is very angry with Space Girls right now," added Red.

"All I have is pain, but it doesn't seem to be changing."

"Ok, try to give us a warning if it starts burrowing into your heart or taking over your brain," said Red.

"It can do that?"

"Flying Saucers, can you light up this place?" Red said, ignoring her rainbow mate.

Then the full spectrum of light shown down from the flying saucers into the still growing hole in the ground. Each saucer's search beams were tuned to its Space Girl's color. Combined they turned night into day with a clean bright white light.

The mass didn't look any better lit up. Still a growing roiling mass of something that made fear rise in her chest.

Then Red realized the light was white.

She looked up and around, "Orange, that you?"

Of course it was, Merlin hung there in the circle of flying saucers, his gang plank open.

Sparkles flew back to the hovering group of Space Girls and said sadly, "They won't listen to me."

"I'm sorry, my dear," said Green as the little pixie landed on her shoulder.

"Perhaps they will listen to me," said a disembodied voice. Then, just like back on Keblr, the Fairy Queen faded into existence. Hovering, with no space suit or jet pack. Floating next to her, using her jet pack, was Orange.

"Hey, girls," Orange said with a big smile and a wave. "Look who I brought."

"Sparkles," the Queen of the Fairies asked, "Did they answer you when you spoke to them?"

"Yes, Your Majesty," said the little pixie quietly, "but it wasn't very nice."

"I'm sure it wasn't. They are hurting and afraid. Like most who are so, they strike out at those who try to help. I will go down to them."

She started to float away, but stopped when Red said, "Are you sure they won't hurt you?"

The queen's fair skin glowed blue in the light of the saucers. "No, but I must try." She smiled again, "Have you asked for your mark to be removed, Space Girl Red?"

"No, Ma'am, been kind of busy since we stopped the God King."

"Of course, but just in case," she waved a hand at Red. Inside her suit she could feel something happening on her chest, but of course couldn't see it.

Before Red could say anything else, the Fairy Queen fell in a swan dive. As she lazily dropped toward the ocean of black nanos, a gold, fiery flame began to stream away from her.

Then she hit the surface and disappeared. The gold nanos were engulfed by blackness.

They all hung there waiting, expecting the gold to reemerge, or to take over and grow as light among the darkness of Bruno's last command.

Nothing.

After what seemed like a very long time, but was probably less than a minute, Sparkles again let out a terrorized scream. "Nooooooo!"

Before anyone could stop her, she was off Green's shoulder and disappeared into the boiling black.

Then it began to rain pixies.

First a few larger than Sparkles, glowing red from orbital reentry, hit the surface. Then dozens. Then more than you could count as the Queen's ship in orbit emptied itself of the entire population of pixies from Keblr.

Before the last of them hit the surface, the black mess was changing. Black balls were forming on its surface and floating upwards. The hole stopped growing and nanites on the edge flowed down to the bottom of the bowl. From the center more and more spheres piled up. Some floated while others settled to the bottom.

As one of the bubbles floated past the Space Girls, Green pointed her scanner at it and was wide-eyed at the result. Blue reached out and touched it.

It popped.

Inside was a pixie, and orbiting it like electrons were other pixies so small they were just motes.

Out of the bursting bubbles in the bowl Queen Iveta rose. She shown like alabaster in the light. Her already ethereal clothing had disappeared and her white skin now appeared veined with gold. Multiple rings of tiny baby pixies orbited her head like a crown.

"Well," said Red, "you don't see that every day."

CHAPTER 23
HAPPY ENDING

THE RAINBOW'S FLYING saucers were now parked
equally spaced around the smooth bowl that had been the Devil
King's tower and dungeon a few hours ago. It was 10 or 12 meters
across and down, sides smooth as glass.

"Where did Bruno go?" asked Red. They were standing near
Astroboy on the side of the bowl nearest the city. All the Space
Girls had gathered there, still in their armor. The Fairy Queen
was the focus of their semi-circle and Red's query. She stood in a
cloud of golden sparks that were baby pixies, with the larger
grown ones off on some errand she had given them. "We
scanned for him, but he isn't in the bowl or anywhere we can
find him."

"Admittedly," said Yellow, "scanning for something in the
Dark Dimension is hard." And by hard she meant impossible.
"But we should be able to see him if he just fell to the bottom."

"He was not there when I was in the ocean of darkness,
before my precious pixies, came for me." She looked directly at
Red, "Did you kill my son, Space Girl Red? You are the Space
Girl of Justice in this group, are you not?"

Red did not flinch from her. "It was not our intention to do so, though in truth we would have if it had been the only way to stop his reign of terror here on Xerces and beyond."

Yellow took up the story, "Instead we trapped him in another dimension. We intended to recover him, still encased in that dimension. Then remove him from this planet and his source of power. After that..."

"We hoped to find some way to bring him to trial and justice," said Red. "Once he was just a man, he could be tried for his crimes."

The Fairy Queen nodded at this, then asked, "What is this Dark Dimension?"

Yellow shrugged, "It is, well another place. On our plane of existence it looks like crystal encasing someone. Feels and acts like a solid. A very hard impenetrable solid as a matter of fact. Inside that? I don't know."

"And how might you get him back from it?" she asked.

"That's a bit of a problem too," said Red. "I gave him a crystal. When it contacts skin the person is encapsulated in the Dark Dimension. Then it drops free. You are supposed to use it to remove the Dark Dimension as well. But it fell into abyss when he did."

The Queen made a whistling noise and a trio of pixies flew into their midsts. The three of them held the black crystal between them, wings humming to keep them in flight. "You mean like this?"

All of the Space Girls flinched back. "Red, you still have the case?" asked Green.

"Yeah," she said and pulled it out of a compartment on her armor. "If you don't mind, could we put that in this?" She squeezed the lounge and it popped open on one end.

The pixies moved away from the compartment, twittering to their queen. "Yes, little ones, put it in there."

They obeyed her and Red sealed the Dark Dimension

holder. She motioned it back toward the compartment she had just taken it from. But in a slight of hand, tossed it to Blue behind her. She made it disappear without the Queen seeing it, as Red said to the Fairy Queen, "So what happens now, Queen Iveta? Do you gain the same powers Bruno had? Is that what happened when you dove into that stuff?"

"No," she answered. "I admit I thought it might be a possibility, but the nanos were much more...crazy... distraught... I'm not sure the right word. They had so long been linked to their God King - and he very much was a god to them - their cohesive person, as it were, was him. When he was gone, all they could do was destroy. His last command I believe."

"That was the last thing he said," Blue said, "But I think he was specifically talking about Red and me in the dungeon. Kind of got cut off by the Dark Dimension covering him."

"Your majesty," interjected Purple, "I have only just met you, but I can understand this may be a sad day for you. Bruno was your son, no matter what he had done. He is gone now."

The Fairy Queen turned her gaze and said, "Ahh, the Space Girl of Love. Orange said you would offer comfort." She smiled, then added, "My son died a long time ago to the disease of power and ego. I came here today expecting I might have to kill him. A queen must have a coldness of heart that is difficult for others to understand. Especially those focused on love."

"I think, your majesty, you would find I understand more than you think," responded Purple. "People often confuse many things with love. Sentiment being one of them. They think it an emotion, when it is an action."

"Ahh, an interesting perspective." Her porcelain head tilted slightly. "I would hear more, but right now I think we shall get an answer to Red's question of what happens next."

Then she turned around and looked toward the city. Xerces Prime's largest city was not actually where the God King had built his palace. That was still a kilometer or so on the other side of what had been his dark tower. He wanted everyone to pass by that dark place of torture and punishment when he summoned them, but even it was some distance from the city itself.

A road wound up the hill the tower had sat on. When the nanos had ceased to be, the power had gone out in the city and with it the lights that marked its location. Below on the road were a mass of flickering lights in orange. As they drew closer it became clear they were torches, carried by the people of Xerces. Both the black skinned, white haired humanoids, and the dark horsemen. They marched up the road following a cloud of encouraging pixies.

Red moved forward, passing into the cloud of baby pixies, to stand next to the queen. "Queen Iveta, you don't know all of the injustice on Prime was Bruno's doing. If you are to take the throne here, I would hope, in the name of justice, you would do something about that."

"Or," Queen Iveta said without turning her head, "Space Girl Red, the Space Girl of Justice, might become an agent of change here again?"

"Don't mistake our individual purposes as monochromatic. Space Girl Orange would not have brought you here if she thought you would be unjust—even if you are quite beautiful." Then she added, "But I do plan to visit you from time to time. If you don't mind."

The people reached them and formed a crowd in front of them.

The Queen's laugh was a tinkling of glass. "Of course," she said then pitched her voice so everyone could hear her. "The woman who freed us from the oppression of King Bruno will always be welcome on Prime."

The crowd looked at her, then at the Space Girls and the

hole where the tower once stood. The Queen stood there in silence for a long time, waiting to see what they would do.

Then an old, slightly shaggy, horsewoman stepped cautiously toward the queen. "Begging your pardon, ma'am," she began cautiously, "you look familiar. But no two-leg from here has such skin."

"Indeed," she had been looking closely at the horsewoman, "it is Lamia, is it not?"

The horsewoman pranced a step back and nodded confused, "Yes, ma'am."

"You served in my husband's house many years ago. A young mount for an impetuous young queen."

The horsewoman stepped closer to look at the Queen, "Queen Iveta? Is that you, ma'am?"

The pale woman nodded slowly then said, "I am Queen Iveta of Xerces, wife of King Max, and mother of the defeated God King Bruno. I have returned to Xerces Prime. These Space Girls have defeated my son and banished him to the Dark Dimension."

A murmur went through the crowd. The Queen continued. "As many of you know, the humanoids of Prime genetically modified their skin to mimic that of the horsepeople to survive under the red sun. When I abdicated and became a Fair Woman, I used the same method to change my skin to the color you see now. But I am still Queen Iveta, and I have returned at this time to attempt to make right all the wrong my son did." With a small glance at Red, she added, "and his fathers before him."

She looked over the crowd to the eastern horizon, then said, "A new day is dawning on Xerces Prime. I look forward to working with you all to make it a better day. But the skin I now wear cannot stand the red sun. Therefore I must get inside before it rises. I would ask those leaders among you, both human and horse, would come to the palace and meet with me."

Realizing how far she was from the palace, Queen Iveta said to the Space Girls, "I may need a ride to get to the Palace before the sun is too high."

Lamia took the statement as a request to her. "Ma'am, I am older than when I was your companion, but I believe we can make it there before you can cast a shadow."

"Oh, dear Lamia, I was not asking for that. I would never order you to my service again."

"You were always kind to me, Your Majesty. And I know you fought for us, both horse and two-leg, with the old king back then. I'd be honored if you'd let me take you to the palace today."

The queen bowed to the old horse woman. "It is I who am honored." Then with her fairy grace, she sprung to the horse-woman's back. They took off at a quick trot around the bowl grave of King Bruno as the new day broke on Xerces Prime.

———

WHEN THE RAINBOW'S flying saucers exited the portal into Kitch space, there was an honor guard of flying monkey space ships to escort them. On final approach to the space port Blue said, "Look who's here."

Parked where the rainbow's saucers had been was a Maiden Class Saucer. It was three times the diameter of a Space Girl flying saucer and could hold many more people. This particular one was pink in color and Red knew who must be on it. Her mother, Diplomat Woman Pink, head of the Home diplomatic corp.

"I guess with all the upheaval here, Home thought they should send some grown-ups," said Orange.

"Or Red's in trouble and her mother is here to instruct her in the proper methods of regime change," said Blue getting a laugh from the others. They knew if Red had been in trouble the flying saucer would have been black.

"Girls, why don't we give the Space Woman's ship a proper perimeter," said Red, and saw Astroboy draw a circle of landing points on the display. Each Space Girl was assigned a landing place, in spectrum order, around the larger craft.

"I'd also say we need to dress for the occasion," Orange put in. "I see the royal cavalcade enroute to the landing field. Since we know the Prince is behind us, that must be the Queen."

"What do you suggest, Orange?" Purple asked.

"Last time we met a queen we were in armor," said Red.

"Yeah, I think that would send the wrong message this time," Yellow said.

"Dress dresses seem appropriate," Orange said, and there was a murmur of acknowledgment over the comms.

———

ASTROBOY AND SPACE Girl Red were the closest to the gangplank of Diplomat Woman Pink's ship. Red took a little extra time to put on her formal dress and fix her hair to give the others a chance to catch up to her.

The Space Girl dress dresses' neckline revealed Red's marks were gone, and Blue's were in process with the trademark gold nanos of the Fairy Queen. The Space Girls with long hair had it pulled back, but Red's was still short enough to look serious without the need to be held back. Lastly she slipped on the bracelet her father had given her, which had started all of this in the first place.

Her ear comm glittered silver in the Kitch sunlight as she walked down the gangplank to join her rainbow mates. The gangplank of the pink saucer lowered and two figures walked down it to meet them. Both were dressed in a deep shade of pink. Her mother, Diplomat Woman Pink, wore a turtleneck maxi dress with sheer cutouts on the sides. A subtle pattern of multi-colored threads moved around the dress signifying all the colors the diplomat represented. Her heels were high enough to put her head just above her mate's.

Cynwrig stood next to her in sturdy flat boots of white with white pants tucked into them. He wore a double breasted coat in pink that v-ed open at the waist and came down to his knees. In a deviation from the normal Home conventions, he wore a medal on a wide ribbon of white. It was black and silver with the crest of the Kitch royal family.

"Hello, Space Girls," the older woman said as they stopped in loose formation before her. "You have been quite busy here. The light shines on you."

They all head bowed formally at the approbation.

"And it is my understanding your change reaches beyond the Kitch systems," said Cynwrig. "We understand you have put a new Queen on the throne of Xerces Prime, and made an alliance with a new race of robots on Zoran."

"Really, it was mostly Red," said Green. "We were just along for the ride."

"Nonsense," Red said, "None of this would have happened with out each of you." Then she smirked and added, "Especially Space Girl Blue, but Green was the one who took me to Keblr where we discovered Queen Iveta."

"It is well you give credit where it is due, daughter," said Pink. "But most who accomplished this much would be considering Application. Are you?"

Red was speechless. When a Girl from Home felt she had accomplished enough to be considered a Woman, she would create a portfolio and make an application to the head of her division. It never occurred to her she had done enough for the Space Woman Application. It was so fast.

"I don't think I'm ready for womanhood," she answered hesitantly. "And like I said, I didn't do it on my own. I could not have accomplished it without much help from my rainbow mates—and the Queen and Prince here, the Flying Monkeys, Queen Iveta, and so many others."

"Being able to lead is a mark of womanhood," said her mother. "I would never have accomplished any diplomatic mission without others. I know you are a Space Girl and they are more independent than the rest of us, but still leadership is a mark of womanhood."

Red took a moment to look at her rainbow mates. They smiled back at her but didn't volunteer opinions.

"I don't think I'm ready yet," she finally said to Pink. "But thank you for the confidence."

There had been a flurry of activity on the field nearby since they had landed. A stage had been set up and there were troops forming up near it.

"I believe there is to be a ceremony in your honor," said Cynwrig. "The Kitchans are quite the fiends for awards and what not."

"Is that why you are wearing that medal?" asked Orange.

Cynwrig smiled and looked down at it. "Yes, it is the Friend of the Royal Family medal. The Queen would be quite upset if I didn't wear it to a formal occasion."

Diplomat Woman Pink added in the tones she used when instructing, "While we of Home are not much for medals and circumstance, as diplomats we must learn to conform to other cultures. If I were awarded such an honor from another culture, I too would wear it. As I would pick appropriate clothing to a culture. It is important for all of you to understand this concept, because I believe often Space Girls are a form of diplomat. You certainly have been in these recent events."

"Where is your medal, Red?" asked her father. "I believe I heard you had been awarded the Friend of the Royal Family as well."

She shrugged in response, "Never got one. We were busy when I was awarded it."

Two Flying Monkeys were approaching as her father said, "Then I expect that is part of today's ceremony."

The two diplomats turned toward the military members. Flying Monkey Major Winchester Powell and Sergeant Major Rudy James stopped in front of them and saluted smartly. "Diplomats and Space Girls," the Major said with a nod, "It is good to see you all again. Let me be the first to thank you for the peaceful resolution to the Xerces conflict."

They bowed acknowledgment to him and he continued. "Her Majesty Queen Natalie will be here soon and wishes to convey honors on you worthy of your deeds." Then, the formal part done, the Major relaxed a bit and added, "The ceremony will take place here as the Queen believes it is in the nature of a Space Girl to run off before she can be properly honored."

This got a chuckle from the assembled Home worlders. Red replied, "Your Queen is indeed wise. I'm surprised we are all still here." She pulled a data coin from a pocket. "Major, I have a message from Queen Iveta of Xerces for your Queen and would have it delivered as quickly as possible. Could I do that before the ceremony?"

"Space Girl Red, the way these things work, you won't have an opportunity to talk with the Queen beforehand. But if you will give it to the Sergeant here, I'm sure he can make sure she gets it as quickly as possible."

"Of course," she handed the coin to the other monkey. "I

trusted Sergeant Major James with my ship; a message to the Queen is nothing."

The Flying Monkey Sergeant Major stepped forward and took the coin from her.

"As this is going to be a formal ceremony, I will let you know one of the things in the message. On my recommendation, Queen Iveta has reappointed First Ambassador Prazak, and has appointed his assistant Ljuba Reznicek as Second Ambassador. I would like it if they could be at the ceremony today. Depending on the Queen's permission and the First Ambassador's health of course."

The Sergeant Major looked grave and said, "I will deliver the request to the Queen, but I regret to inform you the First Ambassador passed beyond while you were away."

Red bowed her head slightly. "I am sad, but unsuprised. In that case Queen Iveta wishes Ljuba to take his place."

"I will convey it to the Queen," said the Sergeant with a salute and ran off.

"I can tell you, Space Girl Red," said the Major, "the Queen will likely approve your request. She had respect for the First Ambassador, and I know he had spoken well of his assistant."

"OK then. What's the protocol for this shindig?"

———

SPACE GIRL RED returned to Astroboy late in the evening. Only three Flying Saucers surrounded the pink diplomatic ship. Standing at the bottom of the large vessel's gangplank two Warrior Girls stood guard. They gave her and Orange a nod as they passed.

The day had started with the awards ceremony. Each member of the rainbow had been made Knights of the Realm and Honorary Flying Monkeys. Red had been awarded a medal to match her father's for being a Friend of the Royal Family.

First Ambassador Ljuba Reznicek had attended the ceremony wearing a long split skirt in blue and silver. Tall silver heels matched the silver tips of her bob, replacing the old King's orange with the new Queen's silver. She wore a sheer black bandeau in concession to Kitchian morals. Ljuba accepted Red's condolences with glistening eyes. In thanks for her new Queen and new position, the Ambassador had pressed the back of Red's hand to her own forehead—a Xercan gesture of the highest gratitude. One that implied not just thanks but obligation.

After the ceremony there were receptions and parties. Her rainbow mates slipped away at each stage. Blue was gone before the first reception at the space port. Yellow had stayed on port, preferring to hang out with her Flying Monkey mechanic friends. After the big public ball at the palace, Green had left. At the private party with the Queen and the newly arrived Prince, her only escort had been Orange and her parents. When the diplomats and royals start discussing trade and the new dynamics of portals, the Space Girls said goodbye.

"You going to stick around, Red?" Orange asked as they reached Astroboy.

"No, places to go, things to see."

Orange nodded and stood for a long moment just looking at her. Red knew this escort hadn't been an accident. "Go ahead; spit it out."

Orange's smile was so pretty Red almost felt jealous. But she knew how Orange had come to that beauty and wouldn't begrudge her.

"The rest of the rainbow was talking," she began.

Red thought, *Here it comes. They think I got too much credit.*

"We all think you should apply."

Shock jolted through her like the God King's touch.

"Huh?"

Orange laughed. "We talked about it during the ceremony while you were schmoozing with the royals. It's clear you've accomplished enough."

"All of you?"

"Yes," Orange replied knowingly. "Even Blue. I believe her exact words were, 'If I'd done all this, I'd apply.'"

"Wow," said Red. These girls knew her better than anyone. They knew everything that happened and what she had done.

"Yes, we all had something to do with the change here, on Xerces, Keblr, and Zoran. Not to mention your work with the plant people on Kenix. We all plan on putting our parts in our own applications when we are ready. But you did it all. For each part we did, you were there making the way. You were the catalyst and the bright light. You are worthy to be a Space Woman and we'll all be happy to add our recommendations."

Red searched for what. She didn't feel like a Space Woman. Not yet. All of this was great, but was it enough to be worthy?

"I tried to get Purple to have this conversation with you. Or Green. But they said it was on me."

"Thank you, Orange," she reached out and hugged the other girl. "I will think on it. You don't know what it means to me. To know you think I'm worthy."

She released her rainbow mate, turned and walked up the gangplank into Astroboy feeling better than she ever had. Space Woman Red. It had a nice ring to it.

SPECIAL THANKS

This is my first novel and it couldn't have happened without lots of support.

Firstly, of course, my wife and copyeditor, Suanna. She always believes in me and my writing.

Special thanks to my friend, podcast co-host, and model Shawna Pietrangelo. Shawna was the first Space Girl Blue and inspiration for badass and beautiful women everywhere.

The model Annalee Belle, who was the first Space Girl Red.

I don't know how many times I've read my book. There have been at least five complete edits. Much of the major structural changes came from my beta readers. Special thanks goes to those who made it through all of the book, David Cranfill and Topher Fangio. Also beta reader Jennifer Roberts who pointed out when I was glossing over trauma. Jo Helen Cox, for going through some chapters line by line to make my writing better.

My critique group, Team Something. They came to the party late for Red, but will be essential to Space Girl Green's story.

General encouragers, Katie Howe-Travino, Aaron Frankel, and Amos VanHorn.

And Scrivener, the greatest writer's IDE ever.

Lastly, none of this would have happened without National Novel Writing Month. Space Girl Red started during NaNoWriMo 2020.

A GIFT FOR YOU

Thank you dear reader for getting this far. If you would like to learn more about the Space Girls, visit their website, https://www.spacegirladventures.com/.

————

R. A. Davis would like to give the first people to read his novel all the way through a special gift. A limited addition Space Girl Challenge coin. There are a limited number, and once they are gone, they are gone. If you would like to claim yours, contact us via the Space Girl Adventures website.

NOTES

15. RED & GREEN GO TO KEBLR

1. If you would like to read the story of Space Girl Green's good day go to https://spacegirladventures.com/green/

www.ingramcontent.com/pod-product-compliance
Lightning Source LLC
Chambersburg PA
CBHW060908210726
48293CB00006B/2013